RILEY'S
GHOST

RILEY'S
GHOST

JOHN DAVID ANDERSON

WALDEN POND PRESS
An Imprint of HarperCollinsPublishers

Walden Pond Press is an imprint of HarperCollins Publishers.

www.harpercollinschildrens.com

Library of Congress Control Number: 2021943545
ISBN 978-0-06-298597-2

Typography by Carla Weise
21 22 23 24 25   PC/LSCH   10 9 8 7 6 5 4 3 2 1
❖
First Edition

To every kid who feels like they'll never get out

To learn what we fear is to learn who we are.

—Shirley Jackson, *The Haunting of Hill House*

1

RILEY FLYNN REFUSED TO MAKE THE CUT.

Sure, it was already dead, but she wasn't about to mutilate it further, impaling its feet with sharp pins, stretching its spindly legs to the corners, exposing its leathery belly to the glinting blade. She knew others around her secretly relished the thought of splaying it, teasing out the organs, slicing its shriveled stomach to see if they could find any leftovers from its last meal. She could see it in their eyes. Sadists. Barbarians. Seventh graders.

They would poke and prod, making faces as they severed its aorta and stabbed it repeatedly in the heart. They would laugh and squeal and fake gag, despite everything they'd been told about self-control and acting their age and "respecting the scientific enterprise."

But not her. Riley had gotten out of it. There was a Northridge Middle School permission slip with *My son/daughter does not want to participate* checked off, and the "Amanda Flynn" scrawled on the line beneath looked close enough to her mother's real signature to pass. It looked like the other signatures the school had on file, at least: on permission slips and missing homework forms, on detention slips and on tardy notices, of which there were . . . some. Riley had learned to perfectly imitate her mother's rushed *A*'s, lolling *N*'s, and flourishing capital *F*. It was a talent of hers. If this whole middle school student thing didn't work out, she figured she could always drop out and find work as a check forger. And some days this middle school student thing *really* felt like it wasn't working out.

"Today we start our dissections," Mr. Bardem said, clearing his throat to get the class's attention. Mr. Boredom, as some kids—not her—had dubbed him, was wearing his lab coat, the one with the too-noticeable mustard stain on the lapel. At least Riley figured it for mustard. Some of the other students had a different theory, except what they were thinking wouldn't be *that* yellow. But around here, anything could inspire whispered ridicule; every little past indiscretion, real or rumored, could be dredged up to haunt you while you were walking through the halls. Even teachers weren't immune.

Honestly, Riley didn't think Mr. Bardem was that bad. He

fell into the category of teachers who no longer liked spending time with kids but had an unkillable passion for their subject that Riley could appreciate. Mr. B could go on for hours about the wonders of evolution and the marvelous machine that is the human body, and don't even get him started on the carbon atom. Each year he found a few devotees, students who cared about science as much as he did, and that alone seemed to motivate him to make it to summer and come back again in the fall. That and being four years from retirement. Rumor had it he wanted to move to Key West so he could save the sea turtles and write his novel about a middle school science teacher who uses his superior intellect to solve crimes.

Riley was not one of Mr. Bardem's devotees. Science was fine. Better than math. Not quite as good as language arts. But it certainly wasn't something she felt passionate about. She was content to just sit quietly in her corner and earn her B without complaint.

At least until the dissection unit came around. Then she decided to stand her ground.

"I'm handing out your kits, which contain your specimen, your tray, and your tools. Do *not* touch the scalpel until I give you further instructions, understood? I see anyone holding a blade before the frogs are properly mounted and they will be immediately excused from the lesson and sent to Principal Warton."

Some of the students *oohed*. Others laughed as they repeated the phrase *properly mounted*. Riley kept her mouth shut. She wouldn't mind being excused from the lesson, but she certainly didn't want to see Theresa again.

Being on a first-name basis with the principal wasn't something to be proud of.

Okay, they weren't really that close, but she *could* describe the interior decor of Theresa Warton's office in detail, down to the tarnished eight-year-old Administrator of the Year award and color of the thumbtacks holding up the cheesy motivational posters on her wall. The one showing the kitten with its head stuck in the glass was her favorite: the poster said PERSEVER-ANCE, presumably because the kitty was angling for those last drops of milk at the bottom of the glass. To Riley, though, it looked like the poor thing regretted its decision and just wanted to get out.

"When you remove your specimen, you may notice a rather pungent odor."

"That's what she said," Chris Winters quipped, low enough so that Mr. Bardem couldn't hear but everyone within the surrounding tables could, including Riley.

"Could you *be* any more disgusting?" Grace Turner said, slapping him lightly on the arm.

Riley's thoughts exactly, except if Riley had said it, she

wouldn't have smiled coyly, and she certainly wouldn't have added the playful little slap. Grace's flirting was as subtle as an atomic bomb. Of course, if Riley had said it, Chris would have given her a dirty look and told her exactly what he thought of her opinion—which was that she wasn't entitled to one. That's how it had been all year. Grace and her friends had made it clear what they thought of her, and Riley had returned the favor, mostly through cutting side-eyes and behind-the-back gestures of the single-finger variety.

Of course part of the problem was that Grace *had* friends. More than some. And Riley . . . Riley had a history.

Chris whispered something in Grace's ear, earning him another arm slap. If the smell of preserved frog didn't make Riley sick, watching these two stumble through each other's hormonal fogs would. All around the room, students were prying open their Ziploc bags containing their corpses and dumping them in their wax-lined trays. Riley started breathing through her mouth.

"It smells like the fish sandwich they serve in the cafeteria."

"Smells like the boys' bathroom."

Grace pinched her nose and spoke in a nasally whine. "This is *actually* the grossest thing I've ever seen in my life." *Actually* was Grace's favorite word. She used it in place of *literally* because she said she was tired of people using that word wrong, even though she used *actually* the same way. It drove Riley nuts. Not *actually* nuts, but almost.

Mr. Bardem told everyone to stop complaining—the smell really wasn't that bad and they would get used to it, which seemed to Riley to be a much better caption for the stuck kitten poster in the principal's office: LIFE STINKS. GET USED TO IT.

"The diagram on the board shows how the specimen should be pinned in the tray. Remember to put your gloves on first, and please, please, *please*, do not stick each other or yourselves with the pins. They *will* draw blood. Take five minutes to get set up. And Mr. Standler, do not let me see you trimming your bangs with the dissecting scissors again. This is not preschool and you are not four."

Jarret Standler put down his scissors. The girl next to him rolled her eyes. At the next table over, Chris was pretending to be the psychopath in a slasher movie, making screechy violin sounds as he mock murdered his already-dead frog. Riley looked at the empty space on the marble desk in front of her—the only one without a tray and a dead amphibian. Mr. Bardem grabbed a bag from his desk and then circled around the room, checking to make sure that everyone was more or less following directions, making grotesque X's out of their shriveled frog bodies, ready to slice and dice.

Finally he got to Riley, sitting by herself at the back of the room. "I have something for you," he said. He reached into the bag and removed a pair of VR goggles, the black chunky kind that look like something out of a bad 1970s science fiction movie. "I was going to just let you do the walkthrough on your laptop again, but this will be a much more immersive experience." As he talked, Mr. Bardem took his phone out of his back pocket and attached it to the goggles, clicking it into place. "It's an app called VR Dissection," he continued. "They have all kinds of specimens. Pigs. Cats. Even human cadavers. But I think we will just stick with frogs for today."

He handed Riley the headgear. Suddenly she was acutely aware of the many sets of eyes on her.

"Hey, how come she gets to use the cool tech while the rest of us have to futz around with Croakers McCorpsey here?" Marcus Colson whined.

"You worry about your own performance, Mr. Colson. It should be a full-time job by this point."

That was one reason Riley tolerated this class: Mr. Bardem was at least quick with a burn. Of course Riley was prepared to tell Marcus Colson and anyone who would listen why she refused to do the dissection. How it was unnecessary and wasteful, in the age of modern technology, for seventh graders to chop up dead frogs just to figure out where the liver was located. This VR app she was about to use was proof. If Riley had plans to grow up and become a herpetologist, then *maybe* an actual dissection would be useful, but how many budding frog scientists were there in this room? Half of these kids probably wouldn't even make it into college.

Riley fully intended to go to college. Provided she survived middle school. And the four years after that.

"Just press play and put the goggles on," Mr. Bardem informed her. "Pause it if you need a break. It's a little slow, but the narrator's pretty good. He reminds me of James Earl Jones."

"Who?" Riley asked.

"Mufasa? Darth Vader?"

Riley nodded. She was going to watch Darth Vader dissect a frog instead of doing it herself. Well worth forging her mom's signature. Maybe he would use a lightsaber. She put the earbuds in, hoping they'd been sanitized since the last kid had used them, and settled the goggles on her head, pulling her wavy auburn hair through the back. At least she wouldn't have to watch her fellow classmates make fools of themselves, though she'd hate to miss it if Marcus or Chris or even Grace screwed up and accidentally scalpeled off a finger.

Riley tried to block out reality—she'd had some practice at this—and concentrated on the virtual one before her eyes. Sure enough, after five seconds of elevator music, a nasally version of King Mufasa started narrating: *"You are about to take a journey into the inner workings of nature, exploring the biological wonders that make life of all kinds possible . . ."*

She sat back in her chair and watched the virtual dissection. It was just as good as the real thing. Probably better. She had close-ups and diagrams and animations and the voice of a Sith lord walking her through it as she panned across her three-dimensional model. Plus she didn't have to watch Chris and Grace ogle each other. She could just tune them out. Tune them all out.

The center of the cardiovascular system is the heart.

As she watched the digital frog's heart pump, Riley thought she felt something touch her lips, fleetingly, just a tickle. She swiped them with the back of her hand. There was nothing there, though now she thought she could hear someone laughing just beyond the edge of her earbuds. It was hard to tell over the narrator describing the intricate network of blood vessels coursing through the frog's body.

Because frogs, of course, are ectothermic, meaning cold-blooded. Unlike humans.

She felt it again, less fleetingly this time. Something cold and clammy pressed to her upper lip. She was sure of it.

Riley pulled the goggles up with one hand to see a dead frog hovering right in front of her face, the silvery membrane clouding its black marble eyes, its thin mouth set in a disapproving frown.

And Chris Winters holding it there, barely containing his laughter.

"Oops," he said, making his voice unnaturally throaty and guttural, Kermit the Frog if the Muppet was a heavy smoker. "Thought you were a beautiful princess. My bad." He made the frog's face bounce up and down like it was talking, only an inch from Riley's own. Laughter rang in Riley's ears, coming from all directions, at least a dozen people watching.

Riley's blood boiled. She took a step back, ripping the VR goggles off her head, snagging them in her hair, which only caused her to pull harder. They slipped out of her hands and hit the cement floor with a sickening smack.

Mr. Bardem, who was looking over the shoulders of two students at the front, spun at the sound. The dead frog retreated from in front of Riley's face, as did Chris, quickly turning back to his table and tossing his specimen into his tray. Riley glared at him, her laser eyes set to disintegrate.

"What is going on back there?" Mr. Bardem said, clearly annoyed.

Riley looked down at the goggles on the floor with Mr. Bardem's phone inside, then over at Chris, who was desperately trying to keep a straight face. Heat rose to her cheeks. She was *not* ectothermic, obviously, though she *was* tempted to go thermonuclear. She wanted to take that dead frog and shove it straight down Chris's throat until he choked on it.

She was about to say something to that effect when Mr.

Bardem hustled to the back of the room, mustard-stained coat flapping behind him. He wasn't looking at Chris, though; he was looking back and forth from Riley to the goggles on the floor. The room was silent, all eyes pulled in her direction again. The center of attention. Just never in a good way.

"I'm sorry, Mr. Bardem," Riley began. "It wasn't my fault. Chris made his dead freaking frog kiss me and I kind of panicked."

"She's lying," Chris protested. "My stupid frog's lying right there." He pointed.

Mr. Bardem looked at Chris's dissection tray. His frog sprawled in a heap, belly down. Everyone else already had theirs pinned and was working on the first cut. Riley wasn't sure what Mr. Bardem had seen, but it must have been enough; he pointed to Chris. "You. Out in the hall. Now. And take your backpack. You aren't returning."

"What?"

"You heard me. Out!" Mr. Bardem commanded. He bent down to retrieve the goggles but kept his eyes on Chris, making sure he followed orders. For his part, Chris made sure to kick an empty stool on his way, just in case anyone was unclear how he felt about this clear injustice.

Mr. Bardem removed the phone from the headset and inspected it, sighing in relief. Not even scratched. Riley sighed as well—this would have been the second phone she'd broken this year—though her sigh was tinged with disappointment. If she had to put a wager on it, Riley would say that Mr. Bardem was more worried about his phone's screen than why she had dropped it in the first place.

"Maybe it *would* be better for you to stick to the video tutorial," he said, putting the phone back in his pocket.

"I didn't mean to," Riley protested. "Seriously, he had that frog right up in my face—"

"I understand, Ms. Flynn," Mr. Bardem interrupted. "And I promise I will deal with Mr. Winters. But you need to be more careful with the school's equipment. A little dead frog's not going to kill you."

Riley got the message: Chris was wrong and would be punished for acting like a jerk. But this was middle school: mean and stupid came with the territory. You had to learn to deal. To control yourself. Even when someone did something to tick you off. It was a lesson she should have learned long ago. It just hadn't stuck yet.

Riley looked at the trays full of specimens pinned in place, waiting to be cut up, pulled apart, to literally spill their guts. She sort of envied them.

At least they couldn't feel it.

2

SHE HID HER FACE BEHIND HER COMPUTER FOR THE REST OF FIFTH period, the only one with a table to herself. Anyone walking by would have seen she had the dissection video pulled up, but Riley was staring right through it, thinking only about what an apoc-alyptic a-hole Chris Winters had been, was, and would always be. Every now and then she would wipe her lips on the sleeve of her sweatshirt, hoping nobody would see. She was afraid to lick them, certain she would taste the formaldehyde. She could still feel the frog's cold dead mouth on hers. It was almost as nasty as the looks Grace Turner continued to sling at her from the next table over.

Just ignore it. She's not worth it. Be better than that.

That last part was her mom talking. Be better. Be bigger.

Just float above it all.

Hard to float when people keep dragging you down.

She closed her eyes and waited for the bell to ring, then quickly made her escape, the first to leave, as everyone else still had to bag up their half-dissected corpses, depositing them in the supply room that Mr. Bardem kept locked because he was afraid some half-wit student would sneak in and try to make magic potions out of the chemicals there and end up drinking hydrochloric acid and needing a stomach pump. It was little more than a walk-in closet lined with metal shelving, now a temporary tomb for a few dozen dead frogs.

Riley ducked out of the room and down the hall and straight into the bathroom, where she quickly washed her face, scrubbing her lips with acrid-tasting soap. Then she slipped into the last stall, still shaking from frustration as the door banged shut. She perched on the back of the toilet, feet on the lid, backpack between them. It was a familiar spot. She'd spent an unhealthy amount of middle school in these stalls, so much so that she had some of the graffiti memorized. Sometimes this was the only place you could go where nobody could see you.

She blotted her eyes with a wad of tissue. It wasn't even that big a deal. A dead frog can't kill you. Laughter can't either. And it's not as if this was the first time Chris Winters or someone like him had picked on her. Riley had been a target from her first day at Northridge. Sideways glances. Little snickers. Rumors that eventually got back to her. That she was depressed. That she was on medication. That she said nasty things about other people behind their backs, which was ludicrous, really. If she had something to say, she would probably just tell you to your face—one of the reasons she'd spent so much time in Theresa's office, with its rickety leather chairs and its word-a-day calendar and that poor stuck kitten.

It wasn't supposed to be like this. Her mother had insisted that middle school would be different. Bigger. More diverse. More opportunities. Sports. Social events. Clubs. Classes. Dances. Leave it to her mother to see school dances as a selling point: a herd of sweaty teenagers in a stuffy gym with stale cookies and Ed Sheeran on repeat. Riley would rather have her eyeballs pecked out of their sockets by a murder of crows.

Then again, nobody had asked her to go to any of the school dances yet, so it wasn't really an issue.

Oops. Thought you were a beautiful princess. My bad.

She should have punched him. That's what she *wanted* to do. Smack the frog right out of his hand and then wipe the stupid grin off his face with a follow-up right hook. Her dad had taught her how to throw a good punch. Hips and shoulders, get your body behind it, use your weight. She could have bloodied his nose. Except knocking Chris Winters unconscious would undoubtedly have led to a suspension, which would have led to her parents flipping out again. It would have gone on her record. Right below the other things she'd said and done.

Suck it up, she told herself. *Stop hiding in the bathroom stall like a coward and get to class before you get into any more trouble.*

Riley wiped her nose, then gathered herself together and unlocked the stall. She didn't realize anyone else was in the bathroom until she saw Naomi Watters, a fellow sevie, standing at the sink inspecting a zit on her chin. Naomi wasn't a friend by any stretch, but Riley didn't have anything against her either. Most people in Riley's life fit neatly into that category.

"Um, you okay?"

Riley sniffed. "I'm fine." She went to the sink and splashed cold water on her face.

"Really? 'Cause you look like you've been crying."

Cryly Flynn. Cryly Flynn. Say her name she cries again.

"I'm fine. Really."

"Whatever." Naomi finished fiddling with her chimple, grabbed her bag, and left just as the bell for the next period rang.

Terrific. On top of everything else, Riley would be late for social studies. This would make the third time, which meant Mrs. Kingsly would either send a note home or make a phone call. The note she could handle. The phone call was a different story. Luckily Riley knew the chances of reaching her mother at home today were slim. She was working a ten-hour shift at the hospital and wouldn't be back until midnight.

Riley could probably leave the voice mail herself anyway; she knew how they went. *Hi, Mrs. Flynn. This is Sandra Kingsly, your daughter's social studies teacher. I'm calling with some concerns about Riley, particularly her habit of being tardy.*

And turning in her homework late.

And not participating in class.

And sometimes nodding off.

And not always working well with others.

And. And. And.

Granted, none of these things was terrible in its own right— lord knew she'd done worse—but they were starting to add up.

Riley took a deep breath, reminding herself that at least the day was almost over. Only two more periods to go. And neither of them did she have to share with Chris Winters, Grace Turner, or dead frogs.

Though of the three, she'd pick the frogs in a heartbeat.

3

ALREADY THERE WERE WHISPERS AND LOOKS.

It seemed like there were always whispers and looks.

That feeling like somebody's following you—that's what it was like—but of course every time you turn around to catch them, there's nothing there.

When Mrs. Kingsley gave them time at the end of class to get started on their homework, and phones wiggled furtively from backpacks and sweatshirt pockets and secretly swiped underneath desks, Riley could just tell that some of the messages were about her. She could easily imagine the kinds of things that were being texted all across the school.

Did you hear what happened in Boredom's class?

Winters was kicked out of science.

Flynn totally flipped.

Thought she was going to stab Chris with his own scalpel.

Wouldn't put it past her. That girl is cray cray.

Riley sat with her history book open on her desk—some sidebar about bhoots, Indian spirits that could possess human bodies and could be identified by their backward feet—only getting half the words because every minute or so one of her classmates would look down at their phone and then steal a quick glance at Riley in the back corner. At least she thought they were looking at her.

You're just imagining it, she told herself. *They don't care about what you did in science class. You're not even a blip on their radar.* Still, she couldn't shake the feeling that someone's eyes were on her every time she looked back at her book.

Of course she couldn't check her own phone to see what people were posting because it was still resting in peace on top of her dresser, its screen busted, an ornate spiderweb of cracks that rendered it inoperable. She hadn't *meant* to break it. Not really. She'd been aiming for the open closet full of clothes, but her arc had been off and the phone caught the corner of her dresser instead, the crack of the glass instantly causing Riley's stomach to clench. It was an impulse. A surge of bitter energy that overrode all the controls and caused her to lash out, her body reacting, funneling her anger into a concentrated outburst that sent her phone—and the Instagram picture of five girls posing—straight into the solid oak dresser.

Flynn totally flipped.

She'd lied to her parents, of course, said she dropped it on the sidewalk on the way home from school. She begged for a new one. But the Flynns were less than two months away from the upgrade on their contract with the phone company and insisted she could wait. It would teach her to be more responsible with her things. Maybe next time she'd hold on a little tighter.

Sometimes things slip out no matter how tightly you hold them.

She couldn't argue, though. She knew she only had herself to blame. She could have closed her eyes, sucked down a deep breath, and counted to ten like she was supposed to. She could have gone outside and screamed. She could have done what her father did when he got mad and punched the refrigerator— Conner Flynn wasn't a small man by any measure and could easily put his fist through a wall, but the refrigerator door was solid and took the punch with indifference. Or better yet, she could have followed her mother's lead and quietly stewed. But instead she'd reacted in typical Riley Flynn fashion, doing something that only ended up hurting herself.

And for what? The picture wasn't even that big of a deal—just five girls Riley knew sitting at a table, huddled around a cheesecake with thirteen flickering candles. *Celebrating b-day with my besties*, the post read.

Her besties.

Riley knew all five girls in the photo, but only one had she ever been friends with. Good friends. Besties even. Once upon a time.

Still, it was just a picture. Not worth busting your phone over. It's not as if she would have gone to the *b-day* anyway, even if she *had* been invited; Riley couldn't stand cheesecake. Yet staring at the photo, at all those girls with their glossy pouting lips and thrown peace signs, something inside her had snapped. The same feeling she got glaring into Chris Winters's smug little face, fantasizing about how that formaldehyde-soaked frog would taste when she made him choke on it. The same feeling that hit her walking through the doors of this building every morning: that with every step she took, she was getting smaller and smaller, shrinking down to nothing, to nobody.

On the other side of the room, a boy named Sean snorted a laugh, cleared his throat, and pretended to go back to his book. To the haunting bhoots and their backward feet.

Next to him, Emily Sauders glanced up from her own phone and looked around the room.

The girl who'd been sitting in the center of that photo that caused Riley's phone to fly, who blew out all those candles with her new best friends, caught Riley's eye and then quickly looked away.

4

THEY'D MET A LITTLE OVER A YEAR AGO. EMILY HAD NEEDED saving and Riley had come to her rescue. Her knight in well-worn flannel.

She'd considered looking away. Just passing by. Doing nothing like all the other students. But she didn't. She couldn't. Because she'd seen this trick before.

She'd been on her way to first period—early for once—when she overheard Caleb Crossley, a seventh grader who was way too proud of his feathery hair and his starting spot on the middle school football team, trying to mess with some girl Riley didn't recognize. They were standing in the center of the vestibule, Caleb and one of his friends and this girl, all of them staring at the Northridge emblem, its panther mascot growling

23

up at them from the floor, claws extended. The girl looked wide-eyed and more than a little lost. Riley could see she had a sheet of paper—a copy of her schedule, perhaps—clutched in her hands. New student, first day. Fresh meat.

The front of the school had mostly emptied at this point, everyone either at their lockers or headed to class. Which was exactly where Riley was supposed to be going. She only stopped when she overheard Crossley's voice and the truckload of bull he was dumping.

"So it's tradition that on the first day you show your respects to the panther."

The girl shook her head, confused. She was pretty, Riley thought. More importantly for Caleb, though, she was alone.

Nervous laughter followed by a "What?"

"Everybody does it. It's kind of like this ritual thing. You just get on your hands and knees and bow down to it. You know. Like this." Caleb made the motions with his arms, though he didn't bother to get on his knees.

The girl's cat-yellow eyes squinted. "You're joking, right? I mean, nobody does that."

"No joke. I did it my first day as a sixth grader. Everybody does. Like I said, it's tradition. It, like, brings you good luck for the next three years."

That's when the girl glanced over at Riley standing at the

periphery, a nervous look. And Riley decided she had heard enough.

"Don't do it," she said.

"Nobody asked you, noob," Caleb said, dismissing Riley with rolled eyes. He turned back to the new girl. "Don't listen to her. She's a lunatic."

Riley bristled. Ground her teeth. In her head she perfectly pictured herself swinging out with her backpack, catching Caleb Crossley in the gut, but she managed to keep her cool. She looked at the girl instead. "Trust me. It's a prank. He just wants you to get on your hands and knees in the middle of the school and take a picture of you."

Caleb turned a bright shade of pink. He opened his mouth to say something, but Riley cut him off. "Seriously, let it go, Crossley. Or one of us *will* be doubled over on the ground." Riley backed up the threat with a pointed—some might even say dangerous—look.

The pink in Caleb's cheeks shifted to red, and for a moment Riley wondered if she'd stepped over that line again, the one she didn't always see, or sometimes saw and just ignored. The principal's office was less than fifty feet away. She'd only been a Northridge Panther for five weeks. It would suck to be sent to the office already. But there was no backing down now. *Hold your ground, Riley. Stand up straight.*

She waited for Caleb to flex on her or fire back, but the warning bell telling them they had three minutes left to get to class seemed to take some of the fire out of his cheeks.

"Man, whatever. It's not worth it." He dismissed both girls with a wave of his arms, retreating down the hall with his friend.

Riley and the new girl stared at each other awkwardly until the latter spoke up. "Thanks for that. I wasn't sure what to do."

"He's a prick," Riley said matter-of-factly. "The school's full of them. The idea is while you're on the ground he stands in front of you so it looks like you're actually bowing down to him instead. Then his buddy gets a pic and they post it online with some caption about him being worshipped by all the girls in school. It's perverted."

"And people fall for that?"

"Not me. And now not you either. I'm Riley, by the way."

"Emily."

"First day?"

The girl nodded. "Just moved here."

"And you hate it already?"

Emily shrugged. "Too early to tell, I guess."

"Trust me. It won't take long to form an opinion," Riley said. She turned to go, figuring it wouldn't pay to be tardy again, when the new girl held up the piece of paper.

"Any chance you can tell me how to get to D-hall?"

D-hall. The armpit of the school, situated at the very back of the building. If Riley walked this girl all the way there, she would most definitely be late to class.

But there were worse things.

"Come on. I'll show you."

That was the day Riley Flynn saved Emily Sauders from school-wide humiliation.

It was also the day she found someone to sit with at lunch.

5

WHEN THE FINAL BELL RANG, SIGNALING ANOTHER DAY OF torture had ended, Riley was the last to leave the room. It wasn't that she particularly liked algebra or her teacher, Mr. Schweiz, who smelled of cigarette smoke and never trimmed his piratical beard. It was just that she was in no hurry to get home, where all that waited her was a Lean Cuisine, a pile of homework, and the next episode of *Cobra Kai*. That's how it was whenever Dad was gone and Mom worked late: every Riley for herself.

He would be back soon. She had the date circled on her wall calendar in blue marker. November thirteenth. Two more days. Until then, and with Mom working late at the hospital, Riley would either have to learn to cook something more than mac and cheese or be satisfied with microwaved dinners. It wasn't the food she minded—though microwave dinners were nothing if not forgettable. It was the quiet. There was something momentarily heart-stopping about walking into an empty house: standing in the doorway, staring into the shadowy living room, flipping the switch to find that there was nobody there to ask you how your day was or if you were hungry and wanted a snack, hardly any sound at all save for the creak of the floorboard on your first step. That's why Riley always turned on the television when she first walked in, to whatever channel she or Mom had been watching last, just for the comforting background noise. Just to hear another voice.

It was the thought of that dark and empty house that kept Riley loitering in the halls that afternoon instead of rushing to the school's front exit. She took the long way, cutting through D-hall with its posters of Paris and Nice, Madrid and Cádiz, all places she'd like to visit someday, mostly because they were far from the town of Northridge. The hall housed the foreign language classes, as well as all the unused lockers. Enrollment in the district had been going down steadily over the years and there were always more lockers than students now, so the ones lining D-hall were perennially unoccupied, making it something of a ghost town after hours. It made for a more peaceful walk, at least, with less chance for bumped shoulders or dirty looks. Honestly, Riley wouldn't mind moving her locker here, even though some of these probably hadn't been opened for decades. She imagined at least one of them probably contained some disgusting artifact from the last student to use it. A dirty sock. A shriveled orange furry with mold. A notebook full of inappropriate drawings. Something discarded and long ago forgotten.

The school was emptying in front of her, vomiting kids out of every exit. Most of the time students weren't allowed to hang around the school unless they were part of a team or a club that had practice, but Riley had an out, a way to put off the empty house that awaited her. She turned and headed toward the glass doors, waving hello to the poster of Garfield in the window, the fat orange cat contently sleeping on top of a stack of books.

"Riley Flynn. Just the girl I figured I'd see."

"Hi, Mrs. Grissolm," Riley said, closing the library door behind her. "Did you miss me?"

Mrs. Grissolm winked, the smile that followed blunting the edge of a hard day. The librarian reminded Riley a little of her mother: she had kind crow's-feet-cornered eyes and a mess of dark hair at the junction of curl and frizz, plus a dimple-dotted smile. Except whereas Riley's mom was an imposing five ten, Mrs. Grissolm stood shorter than half of her students. She had to lift onto her tippy-toes to get books from the top shelf. Some kids made fun of her, called her Short Stack or Lil G, but those kids never bothered to come to the library. Riley doubted they even knew how to read.

Riley took a deep, calming breath, feeling more at ease already. She liked this place. The smell of so many books. She liked the patterns the spines made aligned on the shelves, the lumpy beanbag chairs propped in the corners, the hand-me-down sofa against the back wall with the stuffing spewing out of one arm. There was a juxtaposition here that Riley relished. The orderliness of the titles marching in a line cast against the ragtag thrift-shop nature of the furniture. The librarian's desk was much the same—perfect blocks of sticky notes and a tidy wire cup of sharp pencils punctuated by an odd assortment of tchotchkes accumulated from Mrs. Grissolm's summer vacations: a conch from Costa Rica, a surfing Santa Claus from Hawaii, a miniature Big Ben that chimed out on the hour. Order and chaos. Just like life.

Along the back shelf behind the desk sat Mrs. Grissolm's menagerie of literary stuffies—plush animals that she'd gathered from trips to bookstores and library conferences. Curious George had one arm draped around Raggedy Ann—the monkey feeling flirtatious like always. Riley thought of Chris and Grace fawning over each other through science and resisted the urge to punch Curious George in the face.

"Want to help me process the new arrivals?" Mrs. Grissolm asked.

Riley smiled for the first time all day. She didn't mind cataloging books. The process itself was dull—affixing labels to spines and writing down reading levels that Mrs. Grissolm hardly paid attention to anyway; *read what excites you or satisfies your curiosity* was more her motto—but it gave Riley first crack at new material.

"Did you get anything good?"

"They're books. They're all good," Mrs. Grissolm replied, though Riley knew that wasn't true.

"Did you get anything I would like?"

"Let's see." The librarian started sorting a stack of shiny new hardbounds. "Three copies of the latest dystopian supernatural romance. Some pretty good historical fiction. Two books on UFOs. And this book about the world's ugliest animals that looks pretty interesting. This blobfish reminds me a bit of my grandfather." Mrs. Grissolm held up the book in question so Riley could get a good look.

"Your grandmother's a lucky lady," Riley said. "Got any new manga?"

Manga was her latest thing. Okay, it wasn't a thing *yet*. To be honest, she was having a little trouble getting into it. But there was a group of girls that she sometimes sat with/by/in-the-vicinity-of at lunch, and it was definitely *their* thing. They talked about it constantly. And you can't sit for twenty-five minutes every day listening to other kids go on and on about *Tokyo Ghoul* and *Death Note* and not take a little interest.

"I've got this?" Mrs. Grissolm held up the newest volume of *My Hero Academia*. Riley kind of wanted it, but she knew that Aisha, one of the girls at the lunch table, would want it more, so she decided to check it out for her instead and give it to her in second period tomorrow. It was the kind of gesture her mother was always urging Riley to make. *If you're nice to them, they'll be nice to you.* Past experience hadn't always borne this out, but she figured it was still worth a shot.

She grabbed the stack of new additions along with the labels and the tape and sat down at the checkout desk to work. It was strictly volunteer labor, though Ms. Lang, the part-time media assistant, sometimes paid her in M&M's she kept stashed in her bottom desk drawer. Unfortunately, Ms. Lang was nowhere to be seen.

"Your mom working late tonight?" Mrs. Grissolm knew Riley's mother outside of school. Her husband was a lab tech who worked at the same hospital. Plus sometimes Riley would complain to the librarian about her mother's demanding schedule, especially when it was raining outside and she didn't feel like walking home. Her house was only five blocks away: an easy distance on a sunny day, but a miserable hike in a downpour.

"She's got the evening shift all week," Riley said.

"Well, she's a saint. I thought teachers had it rough, but nurses? At least around here you don't have to deal with people peeing into plastic bottles. Not most days, anyways."

Riley smiled and went back to her labels. Mrs. Grissolm had started to stack books on a cart when Ms. Lang came bustling in, shaking her head.

"Boys," she said with a huff. "Can't even walk straight."

Ms. Lang was at least a decade older than Mrs. Grissolm, her gray hair several inches shorter, and her opinions sharper, or at least more readily offered. She wore a ring on every finger, every day, and not always the same set. Legend had it she had once followed the Grateful Dead on tour for three years straight, and she firmly believed that books were better company than people. Riley liked her for just that reason.

"That boy, Winters," Ms. Lang continued. "He was running down the hall like a barbarian and tripped over his own feet. Banged his chin and bloodied his lip. You'd think being on the basketball team he'd be a little more coordinated."

"You would think," Mrs. Grissolm agreed.

Riley smiled coyly, imagining Chris Winters face-planting in front of everyone, tripped by some unseen force of karma and justice. See? She didn't need to rearrange his face with her fist;

fate had stepped in to do it for her. Here, at the end, her day was finally looking up.

Then it got even better.

Ms. Lang opened her bottom drawer and pulled out the bag of M&M's.

6

MRS. GRISSOLM LET HER STICK AROUND UNTIL FIVE THIRTY, shelving books and shoveling down chocolate until the carts were empty, at which point the librarian insisted it was time to close shop. Ms. Lang had already clocked out for the day, as had nearly everyone else in the school. Riley checked out her books, including the one for Aisha, and stuffed them into her bag.

Time to head home. To an empty living room, an unsettling silence, and a nuked alfredo pasta with chicken and broccoli and apple cobbler for dessert. They all came with apple cobbler, and all the apple cobblers tasted the exact same.

Riley took her time, meandering through the empty halls, stopping to admire some of the new sketches from Mr. Foote's art class and wondering if she might appreciate manga a little more if she knew how to draw. She wasn't a terrible artist—her stick figures had fleshed out years ago—but she wouldn't exactly call it a *talent*.

She hadn't discovered much that she was particularly good at, in fact. There were things she cared strongly for: her parents, animal rights, helping the environment. There were things she enjoyed: baking cupcakes, writing song lyrics that were never put to music, taking walks in the woods behind her house. But there wasn't anything that really got her heart beating fast.

Except maybe being noticed by the group of girls who suddenly turned the corner, heading her way.

There were four of them. All members of the volleyball team.

Grace Turner.

Danielle Moffey.

Michelle Something-or-Other.

And, of course, Emily.

They were all in their workout clothes, fresh from practice, hair pulled back, faces sheened. They moved as a flock, Emily hanging noticeably back a bit, Grace slightly ahead, her strawberry-blond ponytail in full bounce.

She spotted Riley and her eyes narrowed.

"Crap buckets," Riley whispered.

She looked around. She was halfway down the hall already, right next to the science lab. She could turn and go the other way, but she knew she shouldn't have to. She could put her head down and hope they let her pass without saying or doing anything, but she knew she shouldn't have to do that either. So instead she kept walking, chin up, only stopping when Grace purposely sidestepped in front of her. Riley tried to catch Emily's eye, but the girl she'd once held hands with while leaping off the highest jump at the Pine Lake Water Park suddenly took a deep interest in the tops of her Skechers.

"Look who's still here. If it isn't the princess."

Grace's thick-lipped smirk looked even smirkier than usual. Riley was pleased to see that she stood at least a full inch taller than the girl facing her, though both Danielle and Michelle— the two Elles—were the middle school equivalent of giants. Unlike Emily, whom she knew, and Grace, whom she couldn't stand, these other two were question marks. But it was clear this was a team effort with Grace as the captain, and Riley had no doubt that they would do whatever their leader said.

The two stood less than three feet apart. Riley stared Grace down, hoping she'd flinch and step aside. It worked sometimes. Not this one. Grace was clearly ticked. Riley could almost see the steam snaking from the girl's nostrils.

"Do you know what happened because of your little tantrum in science today?"

Riley cocked her head. "Excuse me?" She would hardly call

that a tantrum. A tantrum would have been Riley taking the dissecting tray and smashing it over Chris Winters's head.

"Because of your freak-out, Chris has in-school suspension tomorrow. Which means he's not allowed to play in Friday's game, which means his parents are probably going to ground him for the whole weekend. Which means he and I won't see each other. And all because you can't take a stupid joke."

She spewed all of this without taking a breath. The Elles had their arms crossed like a couple of thugs in a gangster movie. So cliché.

Emily still wouldn't look at her. So expected.

Riley felt herself coiling, an all-too-familiar feeling. She really thought she'd put this day behind her. The exit was less than fifty feet away. So close. She could still make it, she thought. Just apologize and hope Grace dropped it and let her slide by.

Be better, Riley. Float above.

"Sorry," she muttered, sucking it up, choking it down.

"You should be," Grace snapped back.

Should be? Riley tensed, cheeks burning, jaw clenched. Everything grew heavy inside her. No chance of floating now.

"You didn't let me finish," she said, offering up her biggest, fakest smile. "What I meant was, I'm sorry I didn't want to kiss your boyfriend's dead frog today. It's just that, unlike *some* people, *I* don't make out with things that are brain-dead."

Grace Turner's mouth twitched; the Elles gave her sideways glances, and it looked as if a hint of a smile might have flashed across Emily's lips. There was a pause, long enough that Riley could tell she had the other girl pinned, but Grace quickly recovered, snorting dismissively.

"Who the hell would actually want to kiss *you*?" She took a step toward Riley, one finger aimed at Riley's chest, inching closer and closer. "In fact, if *I* were you, I would have made out with the frog, because that's probably the only action you'll ever get."

With the last word, Grace poked Riley just below the collar of her sweatshirt, breaking the imaginary force field she had put around herself, the one designed to keep Riley in more than other people out. Her chest burned above her heart where Grace's finger had just been.

Riley thought of that frog hovering an inch from her face. It was there, a permanent image in her brain, right next to the sketch of a maze with no exit, a jagged line scratched across its center; the handful of animal crackers buried in a bed of brown mulch; the snowstorm of confetti falling outside her window.

She felt herself cracking. She tried to count to ten, like her counselor taught her.

She didn't even get to two.

It happened that fast, a spike of adrenaline that bypassed her mother's cautioning voice, the one Riley had long ago internalized, concentrating all the frustration in Riley's right arm, which uncoiled unconsciously, swinging fast, the open hand connecting with Grace's left cheek with such force it made the other girl's head whip around. Riley felt the sting of contact in her fingers, tingling its way clear back up her arm to her shoulder.

The slap sounded like the Fourth of July.

It felt a little like Christmas.

Riley could already see the outline of her fingers on Grace's cheek: a festive white imprint with a red aura. Grace reached up tentatively, exploring the tender edge of the mark, her mouth wide with shock. The surprise faded quickly, replaced by cold, avalanching anger.

"You are *so* going to pay for that," she seethed.

The Elles moved like one, like wolves. Before Riley knew it, both of her arms were pinned against the lockers, back pressed against the metal, helpless.

Waiting for Grace and her friends to tear her apart.

7

MR. BARDEM ALWAYS LOCKED THE DOOR TO THE LABORATORY equipment closet, but he also always kept the key in the top drawer of his desk. Riley had seen him sneak it back in today after he put away the dissection kits.

She wasn't the only one who'd noticed.

"What are you doing? Get off of me!"

"I told you." Grace's voice was unnervingly normal, almost cheerful. "You went too far. So now you have to pay."

Riley floundered and flapped, kicked and thrashed, her once-burning anger turning to cold fear. The Elles dragged her by both arms, her feet barely touching the floor. She quickly switched tactics. "Seriously, Grace. I'm sorry I slapped you. Just let go of me." She wasn't *actually* sorry, but she was regretting it, if only because the two Elles were now pushing her through the science lab toward the supply closet while Grace retrieved the key from Bardem's desk. The girls on each arm had twenty pounds on her apiece. She tried wrenching out of their grips, but like those woven finger traps you sometimes get as party favors, that only made them squeeze harder.

Grace ordered the other girls about, asserting her status as both entitled victim and alpha wolf. "Em, stay by the door. Keep a lookout."

Riley saw Emily's eyebrows cinch, her hazel eyes narrow; it looked like she might say something—but she kept her mouth shut and stood fidgeting by the doorway, stealing alternating glances at the hall and the wrestling match happening inside. Riley tried to dig in her heels, to skid to a stop, but her sneakers couldn't find purchase on the smooth cement as the girls muscled her closer to the unlocked supply closet door where Grace stood waiting, key dangling from her hand.

"Let me go or I swear I'll scream," Riley warned. "And then somebody'll come down here and see what's going on and all of you will be suspended."

"Right. And you think when I tell them about how you hit me first that they're just going to let *you* go? I have three witnesses. You've got nobody. Plus, only *one* of us has a reputation for being a troublemaker."

You've got nobody.

Riley looked toward Emily, straddling the entryway, one foot in, one foot out. They'd been friends once, not even that long ago. Ice-cream buddies, going to the Dairy Queen and sitting on the bench outside, hovering over one large mint Oreo Blizzard with their foreheads almost touching. For most of a year they'd shared flip-flops and lip balm. They'd drawn rainbows on each other's knees in permanent marker. They'd locked elbows while ice skating, each of them dragging the other down. They had slept overnight in Emily's queen bed, knees bent and bodies curved so that their combined shape approached infinity. Riley knew Emily Sauders's favorite color—gray—because it was the same as hers. It had probably changed, though. Everything had changed.

Still, she also knew that Emily's mother worked here as one of the secretaries in the front office. She could be there now. Emily could go get her. She could go get *someone*.

Riley called out her name.

Emily's head swiveled, eyes finally locking onto Riley's. There was something there—concern? Pity? Confusion? The girl's jaw worked back and forth. She tugged at the end of one pigtail before turning back to the door.

Grace was right. Riley was on her own.

Which meant it was time to scream. Maybe somebody

would hear. A janitor. Another student. A coach. Riley didn't care if she got in trouble. Anything Principal Warton would dish out would be better than whatever Grace Turner had in mind.

"Help!" Riley shouted. "Somebody help mwrf—"

Grace's hand clamped forcefully over her mouth.

"Hush, princess," she said, close to Riley's ear. "Your princes are all waiting for you."

Riley felt Grace's hands on her shoulders, shoving. She lost her balance and went down backward, slamming elbows and tailbone but managing to keep her head up. Her arms finally free, she scrambled to her feet, but it was too late. The supply closet door slammed shut.

Riley reached for the knob to turn it but heard the click just as her hand touched the metal. She twisted once. Twice. Pulled and jiggled. No use. She pounded on the door with both fists.

"What the hell!" she yelled through the door. "Let me out of here! This isn't a joke!" Riley pressed her face to the narrow pane of glass in the door, but just as she did, Grace's face appeared opposite, her voice muffled.

"Shout all you want, nobody's going to hear you. The janitors have already been through here, judging by the stools on the tables, so I'm thinking you could be stuck in there for a hot minute." She smirked again. "While you're in there, I want you to think about what you did. Think about the choices you've made." She said this last part like a mother scolding her three-year-old.

Riley wasn't thinking about what she did. She was thinking about what she was *going* to do the second she got out. In her mind she already had both hands around that bouncy blond ponytail, ripping the whole thing out by the roots. "Grace, you open this freaking door. RIGHT. NOW." Riley pounded with both fists.

Grace continued calmly. "I actually want you to think about what I'm going to have to tell my parents when they notice this mark on my face. Think about what Chris will have to tell his dad when he finds out Chris is suspended just for making a stupid joke. And think about what you can do to improve your attitude, because, frankly, it sucks."

"*You* suck," Riley spat.

"Really? That's the best you can do?"

"Let me out and I'll show you."

Grace smiled and tapped the key against the glass gently. "See you tomorrow."

Riley watched helpless as Grace and her friends walked away, dropping the key back in Mr. Bardem's drawer. As they left the science lab, Emily hesitated, glancing over her shoulder at Riley's face framed in the supply closet door.

Please, Riley thought, hoping she'd see the desperation in her eyes.

But if she did, it didn't matter. Grace tugged Emily's elbow, pulling her along.

Riley screamed as the classroom door swung shut. "Get back here! This isn't funny! Let me out!" But even if they could hear her, Riley knew none of them—not even the girl who used to be her best friend—would listen.

8

SHE SCREAMED UNTIL HER THROAT WAS RAW.

She pounded until her hands were bruised, the soft meat of her palms red.

She kicked until she split the nail on her big toe, and then kicked with the other foot.

The heavy wooden door responded with indifference. The knob didn't give no matter how hard she twisted it. The lock held fast. Eventually she was the one who gave in, leaning her head against the door. She pictured Grace and her friends, probably at some fast-food place, trading conspiratorial looks over French fries and milkshakes, proud of themselves for having taught Riley a lesson, prouder still for having gotten away with it.

She hoped they choked. All of them.

Riley peered through the window into the classroom. She didn't know how long she'd been locked in. The clock in Mr. Bardem's room was situated on the same wall as the supply closet door and was impossible to see, even if the room lights had been on. What little bit of light was slipping through the slim windows along the back wall made eerie shadows out of the stools sitting on top of the tables, like four-legged monsters waiting to pounce. Riley didn't own a watch, and her phone . . . of course she knew where *it* was.

Celebrating b-day with my besties.

Grace Turner had been in that picture too, standing right next to Emily, their heads nearly touching. Just one more reason to despise that girl. Like she needed it now.

It was stupid. She shouldn't have gotten into it with Grace. She could have been home already if she'd just kept her head down or turned and walked the other way. She could have been curled up on the couch, flipping through Pinterest posts and putting off her homework. There was a chance her mother had already called home to check in on her, though it depended on how busy her floor was. And even if she had, there was an equally good chance that her mom had taken Riley's not answering as nothing out of the ordinary. And her father wouldn't be able to call until late tonight.

In other words, it might be a while before anyone even

noticed Riley Flynn hadn't come home.

There was a phone sitting on Mr. Bardem's desk less than ten feet away; he mostly used it to call the office, but Riley knew it could get an outside line. But between her and it stood the locked door. Of course, if she could get out of this freaking closet, then she could just leave the freaking school.

Riley resumed her pounding, certain that there had to be someone still left in the halls. Even if the janitors had already swept this room, they might do another walk-through. Or some teacher working late to plan tomorrow's lesson would hear her, even through two closed doors. They would peek into Mr. Bardem's room and see the supply closet light on, Riley's panic-stricken face framed in the window. But after another dozen screams backed by the rhythm of her incessant drumming, Riley felt everything inside her deflate.

There was nobody out there. Which meant if she wanted to be saved, Riley would have to do it herself.

That, at least, she was used to. She was nothing if not an independent spirit. Her parents had always said so. Sometimes with a proud smile. Sometimes with a look of concern.

It was their fault, honestly. She'd been raised to take a DIY approach to life, the natural side effect of having two parents with demanding jobs. Her father's work schedule had always been especially tough, for her and her mother both, the hours, days, and weeks long, the timetables unwavering. As a kinder-gartner it had been okay, exciting even, to show-and-tell about her father the engineer. *He's the guy who drives the train*, she said. It was a job depicted in a dozen different picture books, a man in blue-and-white-striped overalls and a jaunty cap and maybe a little soot on his cheeks, even though the last coal-burning trains went all but extinct sixty years ago. The man in the books—it was always a man, for some reason—smiled as he pulled the whistle. *Toot toot.*

What a load.

What the books don't show is how long that lonely, gray-at-forty engineer is away from home. The routes that take him halfway across the country. The phone calls from small towns that you've never heard of and never care to visit. They don't show his wife sitting up late at night watching *Friends* reruns because she mistakes the TV for company. They don't show his daughter huddled in her sheets, staring out the window, wishing her dad would come tuck her in and tell her a story like he does every night he's not out on the rails.

But even in Riley's version of the story, the engineer always comes back, often with a gift for the little girl, in exchange for a hug and a sloppy kiss. Taffy and stuffed animals. Rock candy and T-shirts with silly sayings on them. And lots of little metal model trains. Riley had a shelf full of them. They weren't just gifts, she knew. They were apologies. And she always forgave him for being gone so long the very second he walked through the door.

At least when her father wasn't there, her mother had been, changing her schedule to fit his. But kids are expensive and bills can multiply, which meant more routes and more hours. More phone calls from farther away. Ultimately that meant more shifts for Mom at the hospital and less time that Riley spent eating home-cooked meals at the dinner table bracketed by both parents.

More soggy microwave dinners, garnished with artificial bacon bits to give them some crunch, eaten while sitting cross-legged on the couch.

More hours spent googling the answers to homework questions that either parent might have been able to help her with had they been home.

More nights falling asleep in the living room, curled up on that same sofa, math homework sitting unfinished on the coffee table next to the black plastic tray now crusted with cold, uneaten cobbler.

But if the loneliness that comes from having two hardworking parents with punishing schedules taught Riley anything, it was how to take care of herself. Which explains why she finally stopped shouting for someone to come save her and started looking for some way to pick the lock on the door.

Riley had zero experience in lock-picking. She had experience in sneaking out of the house, skipping class, dodging teachers in the hall, cheating on tests, and spinning lies, but breaking and entering—or, in this case, breaking and exiting—wasn't part of her skill set. She *had* seen at least a dozen spy movies, however, where the hero easily manages to escape from prison using a paper clip or the parts of a dismantled ink pen. Usually it was just a jiggle and a click and the door cracked open.

She was in a school supply closet; surely there had to be a paper clip or an ink pen here somewhere. She looked around, thankful for the bright bulb buzzing overhead. The room was tiny, barely six feet across and maybe twice as deep, one side stacked with plastic bins labeled in Mr. Bardem's sloppy cursive, the other side lined with shelves floor to ceiling. Riley's eyes immediately fell upon the shelf full of large, clear zippered bags, each containing a plastic tray with an anatomized frog pinned to it, plus a handful of dissecting tools. A pair of scissors, a scalpel . . .

And a needle. About six inches long. Used to poke and prod and tease, as if the students at Northridge needed any additional tools for *that*.

Riley looked at the brass doorknob with its tiny hole in the center. The needle would fit inside; she was sure of it. She pulled the first bin from the shelf and held her breath as she broke the seal on the bag, flinching at the stench that wafted up to greet her. She reached inside, careful not to disturb the gutted frog looking shriveled and decrepit in its tray—poor dismantled thing—and removed the probing tool before sealing the bag back up and taking a breath.

She left the bag on the floor behind her and knelt by the door, carefully inserting the needle into the knob, feeling the resistance through the wooden handle of the probe, hoping that if she angled it just right, it would tap something into place and the lock would give way. Just like in the movies.

Riley had already decided on the first thing she would do when she got the door unlocked. She was going to find the Ziploc bag with Grace's name and table number on it. She was going to take what was inside of it, a Post-it note, and the roll of duct tape she kept in her backpack, and she was going to find Grace's locker—she was pretty sure she knew the number. The vents in the top were barely big enough to slip a sheet of paper through, but that was all right. Riley wasn't interested in hiding something inside for Grace to find. She wanted this out in the open. For public consumption. When Grace Turner showed up tomorrow morning, she'd find Riley's nasty message and the equally nasty trophy waiting for her.

Riley knew that using a frog's corpse to exact revenge wasn't much better than cutting it up in the name of science, but she wasn't the one who started this whole mess. Grace could have just let her pass by. She could have kept her poky little finger stuck up her conceited little butt where it belonged.

And as for Emily . . . Riley wasn't sure what to do about Emily yet.

"C'mon," Riley hissed, twisting the dissecting needle around and around. Forcing it. Bending it.

Breaking it.

She took a step back, the wooden handle of the dissecting tool in her hand, the metal tip completely snapped off, now jammed into the doorknob, impossible to dislodge. She kicked the door with her right foot, forgetting her already sore toe. "God, I swear, as soon as I get out of here—"

But she didn't finish the threat. Because something behind her had moved.

Riley froze. She was certain she heard it, even over her own cursing. A scraping sound, like a chair being dragged across the floor. She twisted slowly at the waist, looking back over her shoulder.

Nothing. Just the same row of shelves with microscopes and dissection kits and bottles of ammonia and vinegar. Plus the one bag she'd opened, still sitting on the floor. Right where she'd left it.

Pull it together, Riley. You're all alone, remember. There's nothing there.

She gave it a five count, then looked back at the lock with the needle jammed into it, thinking about how she got stuck in here to begin with, thinking about her choices, just like Grace suggested. She'd screwed up. She realized that now. She shouldn't have slapped that girl in her face and just stood there defiantly.

She should have hit her and run.

Riley rested her head by the window, looking toward the other door that led to the hallway, to the exit, and then to home. Down Fifty-Fourth Street. Right on Rolling Hills. Left on Hawthorne. The house with the blue shutters and the one rosebush growing out of control. How could something seem so close and so far away at the same time? It was just one of dozens of questions she'd been asking since she'd been locked in here. Along with *What the hell is Mom going to say if I have to explain where I've been?* And *Why didn't I just scream at the start when I had the chance?*

And *How could Emily just walk away like that? Like we were never even friends?*

Scrrritch.

Riley turned all the way around now, her back to the door,

scanning the narrow room inch by inch. She'd definitely heard something this time. Maybe there was a mouse in here, hiding. It wouldn't surprise her. They'd caught one in the cafeteria last year and had to eat packed lunches in the classroom for three days while the exterminators looked for more. A building this old was bound to have a few unsavory creatures lurking within its walls.

Riley slowly lowered down to her hands and knees, her cheek close to the cold floor so she could peer under the shelves. Cobwebs and bits of paper. A solid layer of dust. But no monsters and no mice. Yet she swore she could still hear something, a faint thumping, barely louder than her own heartbeat but more erratic.

You're being ridiculous, she told herself. It could be anything. The hiss of steam coming from the pipes in the ceiling. The clunk of the radiator. Some muffled sound from the parking lot. She sat on her knees, the wooden handle of the broken needle still clutched in one hand. She looked at the tray on the floor next to her, sealed in plastic. At the frog lying there, its belly split longways, its insides exposed, its webbed feet . . .

Its webbed feet no longer pinned to the waxy bottom of the tray like they had been when Riley first took it down. All four pins had come loose, in fact.

Strange. Maybe she had done it when she'd opened the bag.

Riley bent over, looking closer, peering through the plastic.

She took a sharp breath as one of the frog's legs twitched.

One of the very dead frog's very dead legs.

Not possible, she thought. Not without some kind of external stimulus. That was even supposed to be part of the dissection unit: zapping the muscle with a low current to watch it contract. Mr. Bardem had promised they would get to it tomorrow.

And yet she was sure she saw the frog's right leg jerk.

There it was again! A quiver in its foot. Riley leaned forward. Looked into the animal's obsidian eye. The one that had been closed before.

Now wide open. Looking right back at her. And then . . .

The frog jumped.

The dead frog.

Jumped.

Somehow, even on its back and with its guts spilling out of it, it twisted and sprang from the tray, hitting the wall of the Ziploc bag that encased it.

"Jesus!"

Riley jumped just as awkwardly, twisting and fumbling, scrabbling to her feet, reaching behind her for the locked door, the bag convulsing as the creature inside continued to spastically leap against the sides of its plastic prison, as if desperate to get free. She grabbed the knob with the needle protruding from its tiny eye, forgetting in her panic that it was still locked, taking hold of it with both hands.

And pushing it open with ease.

7

IN A MOMENT, MAYBE, SHE WOULD STOP TO THINK ABOUT THE HOWS.
She would ask them, one right after the other: How was the
door suddenly unlocked? How did the knob turn with the needle lodged inside it?

And how did that frog, which had obviously been dead for
weeks, packaged and shipped by some science supply company
to Northridge Middle School, a frog whose veins had been
injected with blue latex to make them easier to find, a frog that
had been *sliced almost in half*—how did that dead-freaking-frog
freaking *move*?

But Riley was too scared to think, bursting through the door,
turning and slamming it shut, keeping her hand on the knob, her
shoulder pressed up tight out of some irrational fear—because

it *was* completely irrational—that a half-dissected zombie frog could escape from a sealed Ziploc bag, burst through the door, and come chasing after her.

She closed her eyes and took a deep breath, then peered back through the window into the closet, watching the lone dissecting tray on the floor, waiting for any sign of movement. The slightest quiver. Something to tell her she wasn't crazy.

Whatever was in the bag lay still. Ten seconds. Twenty.

"Yeah. Okay. Screw this."

She'd just imagined it. The stress of being locked in a supply closet had caused her to see things. Or maybe it was the fumes—could you get high off formaldehyde? Or maybe there was some freakish biological explanation for the frog's corpse to twitch. Residual muscular energy. Some latent chemical reaction. Mr. Bardem would know. He could tell her, if she ever decided to fess up and tell him what she was doing in the supply closet to begin with. She had no idea how she was going to explain any of this—not without also getting herself into trouble.

But at least she was out. Riley maneuvered between the tables, using them to steady herself, everything only half in focus like she'd just woken up. It didn't help that the room was getting darker. She squinted up at the clock above Mr. Bardem's desk: 6:25. She'd been locked in that closet for close to an hour. An hour spent with dead amphibians, bruising her hands and yelling her throat sore.

The hallway lights were still on, at least. Maybe that meant there was still someone here. Or maybe they just stayed on 24-7; she didn't know—she'd never spent the night in her *godforsaken middle school*. And she wasn't about to start. This place was even creepier when it was empty. Ironic, she thought, given that all the creeps who normally hung out here had already gone home.

Riley found her backpack right where she'd left it—where the Elles had left it, tearing it from her shoulders as they wrestled her into the room. The hallway was deserted, which was fine. Preferable, in fact. Now that she was out, the last thing she wanted was for someone to spot her, for her to have to explain what she was still doing here. She just wanted to go straight home, take some Advil, inspect her arms for marks, triage her broken toenail, maybe find some ice cream to coat her throat. Then she could spend the rest of the evening deciding if she should tell her mother what had happened—what she'd done. What the other girls had done. Or better yet, planning how to get back at Grace Turner, because clearly the frog-pinned-to-the-locker thing wasn't happening anymore.

The dead frog.

The definitely, undeniably dead frog.

She swallowed, hard. She could have sworn that thing had jumped, flipping itself in the bag like an amphibian acrobat.

And that door had definitely been locked. She'd tried opening it a hundred times, her fingers sore from squeezing the knob so hard. But then it just turned, easy as a lie, setting her free. It all made her brain hurt. None of it made any sense.

I don't know, Horatio. Maybe not. Maybe so.

Her dad's voice sounded in her head. It was a favorite phrase of his, repeated whenever she pestered him with questions he didn't have the answer to or requests he wasn't sure he could meet, which was often. "I don't know, Horatio. Maybe not. Maybe so," he'd say. He claimed he'd mostly borrowed it from Shakespeare. More specifically *Hamlet*. Something about there being too many things in heaven and earth that can't be explained.

Her father would know a thing or two about the inexplicable. Conner Flynn had been conducting trains for twenty-plus years, and in that time, he'd seen too many things that defied rational explanation, he said. A coyote on the track that disappears into a puff of smoke the moment the train hits it. Mysterious green lights pulsing in the night sky. Trees that seem to howl at you as your engine thunders by, sounding like human screams. Even once a person—a woman in a white wedding dress (*with a long train—get it?*), standing on the tracks, arms spread wide as if waiting to embrace the locomotive barreling down on her at fifty miles an hour. Riley's father already had his hand on the air brakes when he blinked and she was gone. Disappeared.

I don't know, Horatio.

Of course Conner Flynn had his own theory on the lady in white, whispered to Riley while she was cocooned in her covers. She was a bride-to-be from long ago, left standing on the altar by a cold-footed man who bailed on her on the happiest day of her life, buying a one-way ticket out of town, hoping she wouldn't come after him. But she did—not in life, but in death, haunting the tracks, searching for the train that would bring her spineless betrothed back to her so she could make him fulfill his promise to love her forever and ever.

Riley's mother, however, had her own explanation. "Your father sees things," she said. Hallucinations. Too many hours in that cab, staring out the window, wishing he was somewhere else. Pilots see things too. Surgeons. Longshore fishermen. Work too long, too hard, and your brain plays tricks on you. It just means you need some time off. It means you just need some sleep. None of this stuff is real. Like mirages in the desert.

Maybe not. Maybe so.

But Riley wasn't a train conductor. She wasn't a pilot or a surgeon.

And she hadn't imagined that frog moving.

Forget it, Riley. Just get out of here. Go home. Advil. Chunky Monkey. Sleep. Revenge.

She shouldered her backpack and went straight for the first exit at the end of the empty hall, passing rows of lockers and noting how loud her own footfalls were when they were the only sound. The green exit sign beamed down at her, always welcome, but never so much as now.

She hit the push bar with her hip, eager to face the blast of fresh air.

The door didn't budge.

She tried again.

And again.

And again.

And again.

"What. The *actual*. Hell," she whispered, momentarily forgetting her annoyance at people who misused that word. She pressed into the bar once more with both hands, but even though she could hear metal scraping against metal, the door didn't budge.

Impossible.

These doors didn't lock from the outside the way Mr. Bardem's supply closet did. You couldn't always get in—not without a key—but you could always get out. It was required. Imagine if there was a fire and a hundred students were herded up against the exit, trampling each other to flee the smoky halls, burning to death because of a locked door.

And yet the door she had her whole weight against didn't move. Neither did the one next to it. Or the two next to that. Each door she tried, the push bar compressed, but the door didn't open, not even a millimeter, as if they'd been welded shut. Riley shook her head and tried all four doors again, rebounding off each one with a frustrated grunt.

Okay. Stay calm, Riley. You can figure this out.

Maybe there was some lever or latch somewhere that allowed them to be locked from both sides. She felt along the bar, looked along the hinges, inspected where the door met the floor and the walls. Nothing.

No way. No nut-sucking way. She could *not* be locked in this stupid school.

I don't know, Horatio.

Riley stared through the door's skinny window at the playground used by the neighboring elementary school. Empty, of course. It was probably close to thirty degrees out. The swings hung still. Part of her—the part that remembered all her father's scary stories—expected them to be slowly arcing back and forth, propelled by some unseen force, the screech of their rusted hinges carrying all the way across the parking lot.

Ghost swings.

Funny.

But they weren't; they were just plain old swings. And these

66

were plain old doors that should *absolutely freaking work!*

Riley gave the last door one last kick, not so much to open it as to let it know what she thought of it, then she turned and looked back down the hall, scanning for open classrooms. She wasn't the kind of girl who would normally ask a teacher for help, always preferring to either figure it out on her own or just give up and take the zero if she thought something was a waste of her time. But this was different.

"Hello? Is anyone still here?" Her voice sounded weak and whispery, lacking the strength to carry the length of the hallway. She cleared her throat and tried again. "Hello?"

Riley walked slowly, glancing through the thin rectangular windows of classroom doors, looking for one with the lights still on. It wasn't even seven yet. Weren't her teachers always complaining about their long hours? Slaving away into the night? Stuck at the photocopier when they were supposed to be at home with their own kids? Yet this place was already a graveyard.

Actually, Riley joked to herself, *graveyards are full of people.* Another gift from her father: a morbid sense of humor.

"Is anyone here?" she shouted again. "I think there's something wrong with these doors. . . . Either that or there's something wrong with me," she added, much softer. She wondered what her teachers would have to say to that. She already knew what some of the other kids would say.

She waited a moment for a response but was answered only by her own grunt of disappointment. There was no one here. Riley's skin started to itch. A prickling that spread up and down her body, the unease shifting to full-out queasiness as she steadied herself against one of the lockers. Something weird was going on. Something clearly beyond her understanding.

She decided it was time to call for backup.

Riley was only supposed to call her mother at work if it was important, an emergency or some serious drama. But being locked inside the school with only a few dozen dead frogs as company—*because they were all dead, every single one of them*—would have to count as one or the other. And if her mother didn't answer, Riley knew exactly who she would call next:

The Warren County Sheriff's Office. To report a kidnapping of a thirteen-year-old girl.

By her own cursed middle school.

10

EVERY CLASSROOM HAD A PHONE, SO IT WAS ONLY A MATTER OF ducking into the first one she came across.

Find the phone, call her mother, and request immediate evac from the premises. Riley wouldn't freak out, she wouldn't scream or cuss or cry—that would only make her mother panic. She wouldn't tell her the whole story, either, even though Riley knew she would ask. She would only say she was stuck at school, that she needed to be picked up, and that she would explain the rest as soon as her mother got here. Amanda Flynn would assume her daughter had gotten in trouble again—smarting back to a teacher, perhaps, or cursing in the hallways—but at this point, Riley didn't care. She could deal with her mom's irritation, as long as she was dealing with it in the car on the way home.

She and her mom didn't always get along—one of them could be stubborn and insistent and irritating and the other was only thirteen—but she knew her mother would ditch her mask and gloves in a heartbeat and come and get her if she thought Riley needed her.

The first classroom was up on the right, just past the bathroom. Make the call. Get the hell out of here.

Except Riley was stopped by another sound before she got there. Not the scritch-scratch of a frog-filled bag shifting on the floor. No. This sound was distinctly human. It sounded like sniffling. She backtracked two steps and paused outside the bathroom entrance, head tilted.

She'd heard right. From somewhere inside came a muffled sob. It was a sound Riley was familiar with: someone sniffle-snotting in a bathroom stall.

Maybe somebody who could help Riley get the door open.

"Hello? Is somebody in here? Are you okay?" Riley stuck her head in the entry. *Please let it be an adult*, Riley thought, though she immediately questioned why an adult would be sobbing in the student bathroom at seven o'clock on a Wednesday night. Not that her teachers didn't have drama too; Mr. Vardo was going through a rocky divorce, she knew, and Ms. Whitten had a kid in rehab. And rumor had it that Mrs. Brendaker, the choir teacher, was madly in love with Ms. Child, which was bound to be hard on Mr. Brendaker, if and when he found out. And then there was Mr. Sharma, the math teacher, who was supposedly seen vaping in his classroom last week. A definite no-no.

Please let it be a responsible *adult*, Riley amended. But it definitely sounded like a kid.

"Hello? Who's in there? Are you okay?"

Riley hated that question, and she was instantly irritated with herself for even asking it. The kid was hiding in the bathroom crying; of course they weren't okay. Maybe it was someone else from the volleyball squad, a girl who had a bad practice and got chastised by the coach or even the other players—because, let's face it, some of them were proven jerks. Or maybe just some girl whose parents called to say they would be late for pickup and to wait inside because it was cold out, so she came in here to hide and be miserable about any number of things.

Riley turned the corner past the entrance and the noise stopped.

"Hello? Is there somebody in here?"

The sinks were all empty, as were three of the four stalls. Only the last one had its green door shut. No surprise. Riley always picked the last one too if it was an option.

"It's Riley. Riley Flynn. I'm a sevie." It seemed like an important detail to add for some reason. At Northridge Middle, you were a sevie, a short-timer, or a noob, depending on your grade. She hoped the girl in the stall recognized her. Maybe they had a class together. Even though Riley wasn't on a first-name basis with most of the kids in her grade, she at least *knew* most of their names. She just never used them because that would require starting a conversation. Not really her thing.

No more sobs came from the stall. In fact, Riley couldn't hear anything but her own shuffling steps. Whoever was in there was suddenly silent, frozen in place, embarrassed probably, waiting for Riley to leave. That's what Riley would be doing. That's what she *had* done. And any other time, Riley would leave the girl alone to whimper, but this wasn't any other time.

"I heard you crying . . ." Riley knelt down, angling to look for a pair of feet resting on the floor. But even that wouldn't mean anything. Six hours ago, Riley had sat on the back of the toilet with her feet on the lid because she, too, had wanted to vanish, afraid someone might recognize her by her discount faux-leather boots. "I'm having some issues with the door out there. I was wondering if you could give me a hand. Maybe together . . ."

A single, shuddering sob escaped from behind the closed stall at the end of the row. There was definitely somebody in there.

"Hey. It's okay. Really. Whatever it is, maybe I can help . . ."

I mean, it's not likely. Let's face it: I'm kind of a mess. I can't even seem to get out of the school by myself.

She placed one hand on the door, assuming it was locked, but it swung inward with a slow creak. Riley squinted.

The stall was empty.

Recently cleaned, in fact. The porcelain shining, the bowl smelling faintly of disinfectant. A new roll of scratchy toilet paper sat in the dispenser, but there was no body to pair with the voice she'd heard.

Riley shook her head. *No. I definitely heard sobbing. Someone was crying in here.*

And yet here she was, staring at an empty toilet.

Riley took three steps back, bumping into one of the sinks on the opposite wall. She turned abruptly and caught her face in the mirror, her skin even more blanched than normal, her sea-green eyes startled wide. She shut them so tight her vision exploded with colored spots, then opened them again, taking in the same haggard-looking face and no other. She was alone.

You've got nobody.

"I must be hearing things," she whispered. After all, what other explanation was possible? The door to the empty stall behind her hung wide open now so that Riley could see the graffiti scratched, penciled, and Sharpied into the back of it, most of it too small to read in the mirror. She shook her head and turned on the water, cupping her hands beneath the stream, welcoming its coolness. Her throat hurt. Her tongue felt thick, swollen. She took a long, slow drink, letting half of it dribble down her chin, and then went back for another. She wiped her mouth with her sleeve and looked at herself in the mirror again. Her auburn hair curtained her eyes, draping down on both sides, darkened crescents arcing underneath. She couldn't remember the last time she'd looked this tired.

Okay. That was a lie. She often looked like this. Her mom was constantly urging her, sometimes commanding her, to shut off her light, close her computer, get more sleep. So she would shut off her light, close her computer, wait for the door to close, and then go back to whatever she'd been doing.

Of course, right now she would kill to be cuddled up in her comforter with the lights off and her baggy eyes shut. Instead she was leaning over this sink in her stupid middle school, staring at her splotchy face.

And the open stall door behind her.

The door.

Riley leaned in and looked closer. There was something off about that door. Something about the graffiti. She shook her head again. Was that . . . had that *been* there before? She

74

squinted past her own reflection in the mirror, taking in the backward lettering. Black marker, all caps, scrawled right in the middle of the stall door.

NoTHING T

She twisted around and looked dead-on at the door itself, keeping one hand on the sink for balance. There were no big black letters at all. Just the usual scrawls etched into the chipped lime-green paint, sketches of students and teachers with exaggerated features, declarations of who sucked (Riley did not make the list—at least not on this door) and who hated who and random quotes from Einstein and RBG.

Riley turned back to the mirror. She froze, a cry caught in her throat. The large black letters were there on the door again, except there were more of them this time.

NoTHING To SE

Riley screwed her eyes shut, jamming the knuckles of her thumbs into them.

It's not there. It's not. It's like the noises you heard. Your mind is playing tricks on you. She was letting her anxiety get the better of her. That's what her mom would say. *Calm down. Count to ten. Get control of yourself.*

Riley went all the way to twenty, just for good measure, before opening her eyes again.

It worked. The writing in the mirror was gone. The reflection showed a door with its usual display of scratches and crude drawings. No big Sharpie letters marching across the center.

See. I told you. Just chill. You're fine.

Riley shook her head. She turned.

The thick black marker stretched across the door. All capital letters. Screaming at her.

NOTHING TO SEE HERE

Riley screamed right back.

11

SHE REENTERED THE HALLWAY AT A STUMBLING RUN, BOOK BAG thumping off her back, feet sliding on the slick hall floor. She dove into the nearest classroom, thankful that the door opened without issue. She didn't recognize whose classroom it was. A math teacher, judging by the laminated formulas posted all over the walls and the banner showing one thousand digits of pi that circled the room—maybe Mr. Sharma's, the vape master. Riley didn't stop to turn on the light, crashing past student desks, cracking her knee hard on one, and wincing as she made her way to the back of the room and the phone that hung on the wall.

It wasn't real, she told herself.

It sure seemed real.

But it wasn't. If you go back in the bathroom, there'll be no writing. No crying. Nothing at all.

But even Riley's more rational self didn't sound convinced. And there was no way she was going back into that bathroom. That was some serious Stephen King, REDRUM, *Paranormal Activity* nonsense, and she was done. Over it. Definitely time to go.

She picked up the phone and started keying in her mother's cell number, one of the few she had memorized.

Boo-dee-bee, the phone beeped. *"We're sorry. You must first dial nine before placing an outside call."*

Riley hissed and slammed the phone back in its cradle and then picked it up again, pressing the nine first this time and then punching in the rest. She held the phone with both hands, pressed close to her ear.

It was there. The writing was there. She'd seen it. And the sobbing. She'd heard it.

Just your imagination.

Not her imagination.

Just the stress.

Name a time in the last year or so when she *wasn't* stressed. She couldn't. But nothing like this had ever happened. Sure, you *think* you hear things sometimes. When you're at home by yourself. A thump in the walls. A stair's plaintive groan. The house settling—whatever that means. But this wasn't that. It's not as if

Riley woke up this morning, wandered across the hall to brush her teeth, and was greeted by angry markings on her bathroom wall. This was something else entirely.

The phone rang once. Twice.

"Come on. Pick up, pick up, pick up."

Four times. Five.

Her mother wasn't answering.

Six times. Seven.

Riley waited for the sound of her mother's voice. *Hi. You've reached Amanda Flynn. Sorry I'm not available, please leave me a message.* But the voice mail never kicked in. Riley lost count of the number of times she let it ring before she hung up. More than ten. Closer to twenty.

She put the phone back gentler this time, taking a deep breath before picking it up to try again. She didn't forget to dial the nine this time. She pressed the numbers carefully, listening for the accompanying tone.

One ring. Two. Three. Four.

Riley danced, tapping her feet, spinning in place, glancing over at the door that led to the hall, the hall that led to the bathroom, with the stall that said there was nothing to see here.

Because there was nothing to see there.

But there had been someone in there. Riley *heard* her.

Eight. Nine. Ten.

"Answer the frigging phone!"

After fifteen rings, Riley slammed the phone back into its cradle with a crash that carried through the dark room.

Okay. It was okay. There were a hundred reasons why her mother wouldn't answer. She was with a patient. She was filling an IV. She was up to her elbows in either paperwork or piss, to use one of her mom's favorite phrases. But it should have gone to voice mail. Unless there was something wrong with her mother's phone. The phone here seemed to be working just fine.

Wasn't it?

There was an easy way to test that theory: she could try calling her dad. But the truth—the shameful truth—was that she didn't know his number. Dad was the one you went to when you wanted to play a card game or build with Lego. The one you conned into taking you to the mall to buy bubble tea. He was the one Riley invited to her own tea parties when she was little because he had the more pretentious British accent and held his plastic cup all snooty-like with his pinkie finger up. But he wasn't the one you called in an emergency. That's what your hardheaded, no-nonsense ICU nurse of a mom was for.

Truth was, Riley only had three numbers committed to memory: hers and her mother's were two of them. She couldn't even remember Emily's phone number—it had been so long since she'd needed it. Not that she would have called her. Even now. Not after what she did.

Riley picked up the phone one more time and keyed in the third number she knew by heart: Mario's, the pizza place three blocks from her house. The one she called whenever her parents worked late and she got tired of microwave dinners. *Brilliant, Riley; you can't get in touch with your own father, but you can order deep-dish and a side of cheesy bread. What are you going to do? Have them deliver to the school?*

It wasn't an awful idea. But even as the phone started to ring, Riley began to get that feeling. The one that starts on the surface as a thousand tiny stings, a prickling that somehow brings the heat to your cheeks *and* sends a rush of cold to the core of you, squeezing you from the inside out. That certain dread that the test you're handing in is an F, that the text you sent to someone you think might like you will be laughed at, the audible frown of the dentist who pokes too long at the same tooth, the one that you lied and said didn't really hurt.

The feeling that nobody is going to answer the phone, no matter what number you dial.

Maybe she didn't know how to use these phones. Maybe the lines were down, the system not working. Maybe. Maybe. Maybe.

Maybe I'm dreaming. But the throbbing in her knee from where she'd banged into the desk suggested otherwise.

After twenty rings, Riley hung up again. There was one more number she could try, though she'd never dialed it before. Not even when she broke her big toe doing a solo gymnastics routine in the living room on one of her afternoons alone, jamming it hard into the coffee table on a misjudged roundoff—she'd just iced it and kept watching the Olympics until her mom came home to take her to the ER. Not even when she thought some sketchy-looking thug might be casing the house, looking for a way in so he could kidnap her—though he turned out, ironically, to be a security alarm salesman hanging a brochure on their doorknob. Neither of those had been emergencies.

Was this an emergency? Like *that* kind of emergency?

Riley considered what she would say. *My name is Riley Flynn. I was locked in a supply closet by a band of vindictive volleyballers and now I can't even seem to open the freaking door of my school to go home. Please send help?*

Yeah. That should do it.

She picked up the receiver, unsure if you had to dial a nine before dialing 9-1-1.

"We're sorry. You must first dial a—"

"Ugh!" Riley said, slamming the phone again. Right back up, finger pressing hard on the 9. Then 9-1-1.

One ring. Two. Three . . .

Seven.

Ten.

Riley shouted something that no doubt would have gotten her sent to the principal's office had there been a soul around to hear her, letting the receiver slip from her hands, dangling by its coiled cord and swinging back and forth like a body from the gallows. So either the police department was unreachable, or the phone really wasn't working. Like the doors that refused to open.

Almost as if the school was working against her. Trying to keep her here.

Now that's *crazy*, she thought.

It was completely crazy. Terrifyingly crazy. Impossibly crazy.

Riley stood by the desk and stared out the bank of windows to the parking lot. No cars. No late after-school buses. No parents idling in the pickup lane, waiting to interrogate their kids about their day. Empty. And across the barren parking lot was a sidewalk that would lead to a street that could take her straight to her neighborhood. Just on the other side of this stupid window.

Window.

Riley shook her head, berating herself for not thinking of it. Screw it. Who needs a freakin' door? She was staring at her way out.

She recalled the time last year when the building's air-conditioning quit. It was late August—the school year was barely under way; Emily Sauders hadn't even moved to town yet. By the end of the day the whole building reeked, and every teacher had their windows pushed as far as they would go. Only the bottom sections slid open, so it did little to dispel the heat, but at least the teachers could say they tried.

Riley appraised the rectangle of space she would have to fit out of. Sixteen by twenty-four inches. It was possible. Riley wasn't skinny exactly—not like the Pixy Stix who ate only salad and seaweed straws for lunch—but she was flexible. She thought of those YouTube videos of cats and dogs squeezing themselves through fence slats. If she could get her head and shoulders through, the rest would surely follow.

Leaning over the sill littered with crumpled paper and candy wrappers, Riley released the sliding lock with a click. So far so good. She braced her palms against the upper lip and pushed. The lower section of the window moved slowly, protesting her efforts with a squeal that made her spine shudder, but unlike the door, at least the window moved.

Up one inch, two inches, three, before suddenly stopping. She could feel the rush of cold air pricking her already prickly flesh. Riley strained, planting her feet and pushing as hard as possible, but the window wouldn't nudge any higher.

For every action there is a reaction of equal or greater force. Her sixth-grade science teacher, Ms. Millford, taught her that. But what force kept the window from opening more? Was it jammed? Had she busted it? Riley stood back and inspected the gap she'd made. Three inches. Enough for that breath of fresh air. Enough to summon the sound of a tree branch rustling, shaking its fist of dry, dead leaves at her. It was enough to get one arm through. Maybe.

Riley braced herself and tried again, this time clamping her fingers along the bottom of the window, which was thin and sharp against her skin. She pulled up, teeth grinding, muscles trembling. She could feel the edge of the window biting into her palms. The cold air continued to roll over her.

Then she felt something else. Something strange, like a shift in the pressure of the room. She sensed it on the fine hairs that ran up and down her arms, which still strained against the window. She heard a creak and looked up.

She barely had time to pull her hands away as the window came crashing back down, dropping like a guillotine, slamming hard into its sill. *Smash.*

Riley stumbled backward, staring at her fingers and then back at the window. "What the hell?" she shouted, not even sure who or what she was shouting at.

Shaking with frustration, she tried again, straining, pushing, but this time the window held fast, not even giving her an inch. She tried the one next to it. Nothing. Just like the door. No matter how much force she applied, the windows did not move.

This was *really* not good. When something happens once, it is an oddity. An outlier. Maybe not easily explained, but at least it could be dismissed or forgotten. But when it happens over and over?

I don't know, Horatio.

Riley let herself fall into the swivel chair behind the desk. This time the sniffling she heard was her own. She could taste the hot mucus in the back of her throat. Doors stuck. Phones not operational. Windows shut tight. And on top of it all she was seeing things, hearing things, *feeling* things. Because she did feel them. She sensed something. Perhaps it was just the burst of cold air, but something hung heavy in the space around her, almost palpable but not quite. Riley could tell when things just weren't right. She could sense when her parents were about to get into an argument, for example, picking up on the strain in their voices, the shortness in their sentences, every word clipped, her mother's jaw tight, her father's hands stuffed into his pockets so Riley couldn't see him making fists. She had that same feeling now.

No. There had to be a rational explanation. Maybe the cold weather had frozen the doors shut. Maybe the phones were on the fritz. Maybe she'd really unlocked the supply closet with her amateur picking attempt and just hadn't turned the knob hard enough.

"Or maybe I'm just going crazy," Riley whispered.

"You're not crazy," said a voice.

It seemed to come from beneath the desk, from right by Riley's feet. And yet not.

"But you are in trouble," the voice added.

Riley put her palms, still creased red from the window's edge, against the side of the desk and slowly pushed herself backward, looking down past her knees.

To the frog staring up at her with its dead black eyes.

12

WHEN SOMETHING HAPPENS ONCE, IT CAN SOMETIMES BE DISMISSED or forgotten. You let it slide. You attribute it to circumstances beyond your control. It was a rando event, a one-time-only thing; it won't happen again.

You tell yourself it had nothing to do with you.

Like the first time Emily turned on her.

It was hardly anything. A moment. Harmless. Silly. Stupid. They'd been sitting at lunch. Just the two of them like always. Five days a week for the last five months. Hamburger day—though Emily hardly ate much of it, the once-frozen meat-Frisbee sitting between a smooshed flat bun. Riley got a grilled cheese instead, pointing to Emily's uneaten lunch as one more reason to go vegetarian. Burger day meant steak fries, though, the long wedges that were way too much potato and not near enough fried but were still worth it as a ketchup delivery system.

Emily had been acting somewhat off all morning—nothing specific, just a little distant, distracted—but at lunch she seemed to warm back up, laughing at Riley's impression of the drama teacher, Mrs. Shenkins.

"Seriously, have you seen her clap? I'm telling you: total seal." Riley slapped her hands together in near-perfect imitation. "Plus she has whiskers. Just a little bit of a 'stache; you can tell if you look real close."

Not nice to make fun of your teachers, Riley knew, or anyone really, but if mocking Mrs. Shenkins would cheer her best friend up, then it was a worthwhile sacrifice—especially when your best friend was, in fact, your only friend. Riley treated Emily's happiness as if it was her own.

Emily rolled her eyes, but she was smiling at least. "She does wear that gray jumpsuit a lot," she said. "But she's more walrus than seal, I think."

"I think you're right." Riley glanced down at her plate, fished up the two biggest steak fries, and bit off the ends. Then she jammed them between her teeth and upper lip, contorting her mouth to make them stay there—her two new walrus tusks dangling down past her chin. She began to clap and make what she thought were walrus barks—"hurf, hurf, hurf, hurf"—those

French fries like oversized vampire fangs threatening to fall.

Emily laughed. At least she started to. But then her eyes caught something over Riley's shoulder and she stopped and looked down at her tray.

Riley turned, her potato tusks still wedged into her mouth, half expecting to see the lunchroom monitor or a teacher hovering over her—*please don't be Mrs. Shenkins*—ready to admonish her for playing with her food. Instead she saw Grace Turner glaring at her from the next table over, her face contorted in a look of pure disgust.

Normally Riley would have smiled real big for her, or shoved both fries into her mouth, overstuffing it, making a big production of biting off way more than she could chew. But it was Emily that stopped her. The way her friend curled up, looked away, her smile vanished. The message was clear.

Riley was embarrassing her. Right in front of these other girls.

She slowly dislodged her tusks, setting them gingerly back into their little cardboard boat. She didn't feel like eating them anymore anyway.

She let it go. It was nothing. It *meant* nothing. Hardly worth remembering. Riley *had* been acting like a fool.

Except it was only the beginning. The first letter scrawled backward on a bathroom door. Eventually Riley would get the whole message: that things had started to change between them. That Emily had changed.

Riley did her best to ignore all the signs. The curt text responses. The excuses for suddenly being busy on a Saturday night. The once-casual conversations that became stilted, conversations that began to feel more and more like Riley talking to herself. She ignored them because it was easier than facing the truth: that her best and only friend was starting to pull away. Even with all the evidence, Riley shut her eyes and told herself it would work out somehow.

Because she wasn't ready to let go.

13

THE FROG HOPPED ONCE BEFORE IT FLEW.

It flew because Riley kicked it.

It was all reflex, the way you swat at a mosquito that buzzes past your ear. Of course she'd said the same about slapping Grace, but this time it was true. She didn't think; she just kicked out with her right foot, sending the creature with its bisected belly and its flopping innards soaring ten feet, straight into a wall, where it hit with a sickening slap.

She didn't see what happened to it after that. She was already halfway across the classroom, headed for the hallway.

And then to the front door. The main entrance. The only doors in the building with an automatic opener. In her moment of panic, her intense desire to get away from whatever that thing was that had just talked to her—it *had* talked to her, hadn't it?—the thought struck her. Just slam that button with the wheelchair on it and get the hell out.

Riley ran down the hallway and turned the corner. The lights were off in all the rooms she passed, the doors all shut. The building was completely empty.

*No. Not completely. There is somebody—some*thing—*here with you.*

Riley tried to force the thought out of her head, the image of it, sitting in the shadows by her feet, looking up at her. Telling her she wasn't crazy. Proof that she *was* crazy—or at least headed in that direction.

You know what you saw.

How could she see what she saw? How could a partially dissected frog get out of a shut supply closet and follow her through the school like that? It was *dead*.

No. Not dead. It moved. It blinked. It *talked*.

You are in trouble.

As if she needed a dead frog to tell her *that*.

Riley turned a second corner, finding herself in the vestibule, the painted profile of the Northridge panther growling up at her from the marble floor, the collages from Mr. Foote's art class lining the walls, and the huge sign saying *Welcome* in twenty different languages stretched from wall to wall. *Welcome*.

Beinvenue. Nayak. Yokoso. Salaam.

Nope. Try again. Try *goodbye*, Riley thought. *Au Revoir. Sayonara. Adios.*

Without slowing, Riley surveyed the administrative offices with a sliver of hope, but all the lights were off there as well, nobody home. The one day she *wanted* to see Principal Warton's frowning face. Or Emily's mother—she could tell her what a terrible kiss-ass, crowd-following, spineless bystander her daughter had turned into.

Save it for later, Riley. Let's just get out of here.

She slowed to a walk at the entrance and practically punched the metal square with the blue wheelchair engraved in it, waiting for the whine of the motor that would open the doors. "C'mon." She hit it again. And again. And again. "C'mon c'mon c'mon."

Nothing. No mechanical buzz. No grinding gears. The front doors didn't move. Riley reared back and kicked the button as hard as she could, hard enough that she was sure she'd break it. Then she kicked it again before throwing her whole body against the door, leading with her hip and shoulder but rebounding off like a Ping-Pong ball.

It wasn't just the doors in C-hall that were shut tight. The front doors were closed to her as well.

To her specifically. That's what Riley was thinking, because that's what it felt like. Like she'd been locked in the school on purpose. The irrational idea popped into her head that somehow Grace and her friends were still the ones behind this—that they had somehow shut her in here. It was a reach, she knew, a long one, but it was as good as any other explanation. Which meant it was really no explanation at all.

The outside beckoned to her through the thin sheet of glass in the doorway. Only a few feet away. So close and yet a seemingly impossible distance. Riley glanced behind her, across the lobby to where the hallways split, looking for the lump of a dead frog come to life, chasing after her, its shriveled entrails smearing the floor.

Instead her eyes fell on something else: the small red box situated next to the office.

The fire alarm.

Pull down, it commanded in bright white letters.

It didn't need to ask her twice.

14

IT WASN'T THE FIRST TIME RILEY HAD PULLED THE FIRE ALARM. OR even the second.

The first time had been on a dare. In the fourth grade at Brightwood Elementary, Missy Reynolds and Sharonda Parker conned her into it. They were unanimously, if not officially, declared the two most popular girls in the class and flaunted their pricy puffer jackets and their glittery gel pens, which they used to make cootie catchers when they were supposed to be writing in their composition notebooks. Riley was beguiled by their whispered conversations and their flaunted friendship-bracelet-making abilities. So when they promised to sit with her at lunch the next day, *if* she did something for them, she knew it was her ticket to rising up the fourth-grade ranks. After all, it wasn't that hard of an ask—just pull the handle.

She didn't realize there were cameras in the hallways. She didn't know how easily she would be caught.

When her mother found out what she'd done, and more specifically why, she sat Riley down and showed her an ancient-looking video of lemmings—adorable, fuzzy little gerbil-like creatures—following each other blindly off a cliff. One by one the furballs would take the leap, plummeting hundreds of feet down, a hollow look in their tiny eyes as they jumped to their possible deaths.

"That's you," her mom said, pointing to a random lemming somersaulting toward the icy water below. "Or at least it was you today pulling that alarm. Don't do something just because somebody tells you to. Don't follow other kids over the edge. Learn to think for yourself." In the video a platoon of drowned lemmings washed slowly up onshore, their bloated bodies knocking against each other. It was a massacre. Riley could hardly stand to watch. But she did. Because her mother made her.

"And don't ever pull another stunt like this again," her mother added.

Riley nodded. But later that night, haunted by the image of the lemmings catapulting themselves to their doom, she snuck down to the computer in the living room and looked it up. Turned out her mom didn't give her the whole story. Lemmings don't blindly follow each other off cliffs to die; they are actually migrating, looking for a better place to live. Though many of them don't survive the journey, it's worth it for those who do. It's how the species survives.

Which was what Riley thought all along: following the crowd can be worth it if it leads you somewhere worthwhile.

Her mother didn't know how hard it was for her to make friends. To fit in. She just wanted to sit with Missy and Sharonda at lunch. Instead she had to eat in the principal's office for the rest of the week. When she told the two girls everything that had happened and asked if she could eat with them the next week instead, they laughed. "Sorry. No rain checks," Missy told her.

Riley got nothing out of the deal. Save for one lesson about lemmings and another about hallway monitoring systems.

At least the next time she pulled the fire alarm, she was prepared.

Beginning of sixth grade. A math quiz she was destined to fail because she hadn't bothered to study. So instead she fished a baseball cap out of her backpack, tucked her hair underneath, and put on a jacket swiped from the lost and found. She snuck out of the bathroom, pulled the alarm, and then merged with the herd, all of them crowding and pushing their way through the doors. Perfect crime.

Unfortunately, a description of the prankster went out over email that afternoon, and students were asked to open their backpacks so that teachers could check them. Riley's Reds cap sold her out.

She tanked her quiz the very next day.

Riley's mother was furious this time. She made her call her father and tell him, even though he was out on the tracks, five hundred miles from home. The disappointment in his voice devastated her. "You can't shirk your responsibilities, Riley. There are no easy outs in life. Some things are just hard and you have to suck it up and face them head-on. Do you understand?"

She understood. Problem was it felt like everything was hard, all the freaking time.

He made her promise, right there on the phone: when she faced a challenge, she wouldn't back down. She would deal with it. She would be strong. And she would do the right thing, because that's the kind of girl she was. Strong. Capable. Determined. The kind of girl who didn't shrink from a fight.

But there were challenges, and then there was *this*. And this—whatever was happening to Riley right in this moment—was beyond the scope of anything she had ever experienced.

Which was why she didn't hesitate to pull a fire alarm for the third time in her life.

It gave with a satisfying, reassuring click.

And everything, inexplicably, went dark.

15

RILEY WONDERED WHAT SHE HAD DONE.

There was no screeching siren. No flashing blue or red lights. No lights at all, in fact. The moment she pulled the lever, all the hallway bulbs immediately blinked out. It was as if the alarm had been wired to the wrong switch, and, in pulling it, she'd managed to somehow shut off all the power to the entire school. That or . . .

Riley didn't want to think about the *or*. She floundered there, drowning in the darkness. Her eyes adjusted as much as possible, seeking out the edges where black shifted to gray, taking in what light there was. It was still evening outside, but evening in November meant the sun had set. The streetlamps studded around the parking lot cast their halos like giant fireflies, illuminating the empty spaces below. The little bit of light seeped through the windows, just enough for Riley to see a few feet around her. Everything else was shadow, caught at the edge of reality and imagination.

She shivered and crossed her arms, giving herself a hug. There was something innately troubling about the dark. Riley's father thought so too. It came with the job, he said. Driving a car was one thing, on the road, where lamps often stood guard against the black backdrop. But out on the tracks, chugging through the countryside, the darkness was almost total in places, save for the swath cut by the engine's headlights. The space directly in front of you was fine, but that tunnel quickly collapsed on both sides, and there was always the possibility of something—a deer, a fallen tree, an oncoming car—lurking at that edge, at the bend, right at the corner where light fell into the void.

"So you're really afraid of the dark?" she'd asked him once.

"I'm not afraid of the dark," he told her. "I'm afraid of what's *in* the dark."

That thought made her shiver even harder now.

Riley tried to push the alarm lever back into position, thinking to undo what she'd done, but it was stuck, perhaps waiting for the key that would slide into the slot above it. A key that was held by the principal or the secretary—somebody who was already at home, turning on *Wheel of Fortune* or taking their chicken pot pie out of the oven.

Not that there was anything *to* shut off. She supposed it was possible the alarm had still sent its signal to the fire station down the road. It had taken them less than five minutes to get to school the last time the alarm was pulled. Riley had timed them. Except even as she hoped for it, *wished* for it, part of her knew they weren't coming, that the alarm didn't work at all. That she had somehow only made things worse. Every attempt she made to leave was met with added resistance.

For every action, a reaction.

Riley's skin dimpled as a chill worked through her like an electric current. Was it just her imagination or was it already colder in here? Riley moved back to the front doors and tried to open them again, first with the button, then with her hands. The definition of insanity: doing the same thing, expecting different results.

And yet . . . there was the supply closet. The one with half of a dissecting needle still shoved into its knob. The one that refused to open no matter how hard she twisted or kicked . . . until it did. She could get out of there, but no farther? Why? None of this made any sense.

Riley pressed her forehead against the door. "Please. Please just let me out of here." She wasn't even sure whom she was asking, but she sensed there was someone or something out there. Listening.

Go ahead. Say it. You know what it is.

She didn't know what it was. Not for certain. Because what she was thinking—what she had been thinking ever since she burst through that supply closet door—was impossible.

In truth, Riley always liked a good ghost story. Her father did too. Her mother took responsibility for the read-alouds—sitting on the edge of the bed, her free hand resting on Riley's knee or gently rubbing her feet, ripping through Junie B. and the A to Z Mysteries. But when it was her father's turn to tuck her in, he waved off How to Train Your Dragon. Nothing against those stories—he was sure they were fantastic—but he would rather make up his own.

Her father only told two kinds of stories: funny and scary. Riley never picked the funny ones.

They weren't always about ghosts. Some were about witches with knives for fingers or monsters with mouths full of serrated teeth that sank deep into your flesh to suck out the juices. Some were about shadows that stayed pressed against the wall until you looked away or fell asleep and then crept up over your blankets, across your chin, seeping into your nostrils, your ears, slinking down your throat as you snored, worming their way into your soul and turning it black so that you woke up the next day cursed. Some were about a nest of nasty bugs—roaches and earwigs and millipedes—that formed in the attic above Riley's room, getting bigger and bigger, and heavier and heavier, until, at some point, while she was sleeping, the nest would get too large and crash through her ceiling, blanketing her in a million skittering legs.

Many of her father's stories ended in a bloodbath. He was notorious for not skimping on the gory details: leaking entrails and eaten brains were common motifs. But Riley's favorites were the ghost stories, and her favorites of those—naturally—were the ones about trains.

One told of a train that only came out on the anniversary of President Abraham Lincoln's death, traveling from Washington, DC, to Lincoln's home in Springfield, Illinois, supposedly stopping the watches and clocks in every town it passed. That one wasn't scary so much as eerie.

Another told of a passenger train that passed through a miles-long tunnel cut through a haunted mountain. The conductor had to increase the speed through the tunnel because every second spent in the darkness took a day off your life. Until one fateful night, the train broke down in the middle of the mountain and the passengers felt their future days slipping away, tick by tick, ultimately running for the end of the tunnel until their old legs gave out and turned to dust beneath them.

And, of course, there was the train of souls, which stopped in each and every town each and every night to collect the spirits of the dead. Some were taken to the junction where they would catch a transfer to their final destination (depending, Riley's father told her with a wink, on how virtuous they were in life, especially when it came to obeying their parents), but others— those whose eternities were still undecided—were forced to ride the phantom rails. A sort of limbo train. A purgatory on tracks.

Some people who pass away aren't allowed to move on, he said. Something keeps them here. Usually something they did while they were alive. Or something they failed to do.

Of course, the worst thing about the train of souls was that you knew when your time was up. The night before your last day on Earth, just as you closed your eyes to go to sleep, you would hear the whistle, faint and far away but unmistakable, letting you know that it was coming for you. That death was on its way. *It's time*, that whistle said.

Finishing this particular story, her father would kiss her good night and shut off her light, and as he walked down the hall *he* would whistle, just loud enough for her to hear him through the walls. It always gave her goose bumps.

But then Riley would roll her eyes. Because she knew the shadows always stayed stuck to the wall. She knew that witches with knives for fingers didn't exist. She knew it was always her father making those somber notes in the hallway and that the train wasn't really coming for her. That there was no train at all.

Riley knew in her heart there was no such thing as ghosts.

16

SHE THOUGHT ABOUT HER FATHER, WISHED HE WAS STANDING NEXT to her now. He would tell her she had nothing to be afraid of. And if he was here, she would believe him.

But she didn't know where he was. Maybe Iowa. Maybe Idaho. Could be anywhere.

Riley's teeth rattled; she clenched her jaw to keep them still. It really couldn't be that cold in here already. Maybe outside, where Riley could see the wind wrestling with the trees, but not here, even if the heat had gone off. She stepped back and studied the long narrow pane of glass to the right of the door in front of her, the one she'd been looking out of. It was one solid sheet about eight feet high and two feet wide, a gap she could easily squeeze through, except there was no way to open this one. No latch. No lever. No sliding lock. Just glass permanently set into the frame.

Shatterable glass.

Not a good idea.

Maybe not. But standing there, in the dark, with who-knows-what lurking somewhere in this school, it was the best one she had. There would be consequences. Principal Warton would frown when she discovered someone had put a hole in her school. But a little property damage was a small price to pay if it meant getting the holy hell out of here, and Riley was past the point of not breaking things. It was a line she'd crossed before.

She would need something heavy, preferably with a point or a sharp corner. And solid; nothing that would easily bend or break. She mentally ran through the contents of the backpack still slung over her shoulders: A binder. An empty lunch box with a plastic water bottle. A handful of ink pens. Three new books checked out from the library. And a roll of duct tape, which her father claimed could fix anything but a broken heart and was handy to always have around. Maybe she could use it to tape up the window when she was done.

She did have a flashlight—one of those expensive fits-in-your-front-pocket tactical types with lots of lumens and a handy wrist strap. Her mother made her carry it for her walks home, even though the three streets she had to take were all well lit and through friendly and familiar neighborhoods. Riley fished it out of her pack and flipped it on, relieved at how well it pushed back against the darkness. The flashlight was metal and felt solid, but it was too small to do any real damage. She needed something bigger. She needed a brick. Or a sledgehammer.

She looked around the hallway, following the spotlight of her flashlight's beam as it slid along the walls, coming to rest on the welcome sign—*velkommen, bem-vindo, selamat datang*—and then on the sculpture sitting beneath it. A small tree made of twisted copper wire and tinfoil leaves, meant, Riley supposed, to symbolize the potential growth of every Northridge Middle School student. The title on the little gold placard on the wall called it *Branching Out* and said the artist was Sandra Mirano, a former Northridge eighth grader. The first time Riley saw the sculpture and the sign above it, she wanted to barf—too cringy for words.

This time she looked beneath the wire tree to the base that held it, a solid, serious chunk of stone at least a foot all around.

Riley set her backpack by the door and propped her flashlight against it, angling it to provide the most light possible; she was going to need both hands for this. Her teeth had stopped chattering, at least, though the hairs still stood on her neck as she crossed the hall.

She paused above the emblem of the Northridge panther, remembering a time—it felt like forever ago—that she'd stopped the new girl from doing something embarrassing, something she would regret. Maybe Riley should have let her.

Forget Emily. Stay focused. Hulk smash.

She bent down and grabbed hold of the tree by its wiry metal trunk with one hand, lifting it just enough to get her other hand underneath it. It was even heavier than she'd expected. Heavier than the paving stones she'd helped her father carry to the backyard last summer so they could build a patio. Her back strained as she wrestled the sculpture across the hall to the front door, walking hunchbacked, the tree already starting to bend at the base where it had been welded to the stone. The tinfoil leaves and sharp wire branches scratched at Riley's arms with every step, drawing tiny red lines.

One good hit, she thought. *One good swing. That's all it will take. Break the glass, squeeze through, run home. And then . . .*

She would worry about *and then* when she got there.

She lifted the sculpture as high as she could, arms shaking, holding the stone square base like a shot putter, shoulder level, aiming for the center of the glass. *Branching out,* she thought.

Riley heaved, aiming for the middle of the window. She felt a sharp sting as one of the wire leaves tore through the skin on the back of her hand, but she was too fixated on the glass to notice, anticipating the sound of it shattering, splintering into a thousand pieces by the force of her throw.

Instead, all she heard was a dull thunk as the corner of the stone struck, hitting the glass just a little off-center, making a small divot, barely noticeable.

Riley made a sound, something close to a growl, and then looked down at the slash that zigzagged its way from the base of her thumb clear to her wrist. Bright blood bubbled like lava all along the crack, and it suddenly hurt with a razor-sharp pain. She stuck the back of her hand in her mouth, pressing her tongue against her skin and licking away the blood, then shaking her arm as if she could somehow whisk the hurt away. The blood quickly returned, smearing along her hand and down her wrist. It was deeper than she'd thought.

In the faint light from outside, Riley examined the mark the stone pedestal had made in the glass. Then she remembered. Two years ago, after yet another horrific school shooting three states away, they had taken steps to make Northridge safer, including installing bulletproof glass in all the doors and windows.

Sculpture-proof too, apparently.

She could try again, except it had nearly broken her back to lift and throw the thing the first time, and all she had to show for it was a bloody gash in her hand and a chip in the glass smaller than one of Mrs. Grissolm's dimples. And with it the possibility, too hard to ignore, that no matter what she tried, Riley wasn't going to find a way out of here. Exits locked. Phones not working. Fire alarm busted. Glass impenetrable. Power and lights all out. Two tries. Twenty tries. What if it didn't make a difference?

I don't know, Horatio.

Maybe she should just wait right here. Camp out in the front lobby right by the office. Curl up with her backpack and flashlight and bloody hand next to the mangled metal tree and under the watchful eye of the Northridge panther and wait for rescue. Some teacher coming in early to finish grading would find a thirteen-year-old girl balled up and shivering in the corner. Or maybe her mother, finally slogging home after a ten-hour shift, would find an empty house and call the police. Eventually someone would retrace Riley's steps, track her down to her last known location; she only had to wait it out.

Except there was still the matter of the dead frog. And the graffiti on the bathroom door. The window crashing down, nearly severing her fingers.

And the cut on her hand, bleeding freely, dripping down to

her wrist into the cuff of her sweatshirt.

There's no easy out, Riley. Some things you just have to face head-on.

That's what her father would say.

Her mother would tell her to take care of this nasty cut first.

Riley decided she would listen to them both for once.

17

SOME DAYS IT FELT LIKE SHE WOULD NEVER GET OUT OF THIS PLACE. Like the bright green exit sign mocked her with empty promises. *You can leave, sure, but you'll be back the very next day. And the day after that, and over and over for what feels like eternity.*

The end of last year had been rough, that last month especially. By April, Emily was already sitting with the volleyball squad at lunch, spending her weekends playing pickup games with them at the park while Riley spent her weekends bingeing on Netflix and Nutella, ignoring her mother's pleas to get up off the couch and go outside. At school she'd already checked out for the summer, failing to turn in assignments and barely scraping by on tests, counting the minutes and then the seconds until the next bell rang and she could start counting down again. The first week of May she was sent to Warton's office for telling Randal Willis—a little too loudly, perhaps—to stop kicking the back of her mother-blanking chair. Of course it was suggested that next time Riley could simply scoot her chair up a little rather than drop the f-bomb in the middle of math class during a quiz, especially since Randal claimed he wasn't doing it on purpose. It was a bald-faced lie, of course; he'd done it to just get a rise out of her and it worked. He could barely hide his laughter as Mrs. Richards wrote out the pink pass.

Then, finally—mercifully—summer arrived. Riley spent a few weeks at the Y making clay pots and temporary acquaintances. She tried, and failed, to learn how to play tennis. She badly burned her shoulders falling asleep on the patio and spent hours picking at the dead white skin, removing layer after layer, as if hoping to reveal a different version of herself. Her parents managed to coordinate enough days off to take her to Michigan to spend a week on the lake, where she drank bottled root beer and furtively took pictures of older boys on her phone to look at later, all the while pretending that summer was infinite and that seventh grade would never come.

But June too quickly gave way to July, which too easily melted into August. The first day of school looming, her mother promised—again—that it would be better this year, "but only if you set out to *make* it better." Riley thought of kittens with their heads stuck in glasses, but she promised herself she'd at least try.

So the night before that first day, Riley sat down at her little wooden desk, took out a sheet of paper, and scrawled the words *The Plan* at the top. It wasn't really a plan. Plans have steps. A natural progression, one thing leading to the next. This was more of a to-do list. A short one.

- *Make new friends.*
- *Get nothing lower than a B in any of my classes.*
- *Try out for a sport (not tennis).*
- *Don't lose my temper.*
- *Don't get in trouble.*

When the first day of school started, Riley arrived with her list tucked into the front pocket of her backpack, folded into a neat little square. Any part of the plan-that-wasn't-really-a-plan that she pulled off would get a check mark. Failures would get crossed out. She wanted all check marks, of course, but she'd be happy just to get a majority.

The first item on the list proved difficult. Riley was never great at making friends. She wasn't like her mother, bursting with energy and easy conversation, chatting up patients she'd just met like they'd known each other for years. Instead she took after her father, who was content to spend whole days with nothing but his thoughts and the endless stretches of track laid out before him. And it wasn't as if there were lines of kids forming in the hallways waiting for Riley to bless them with her quick wit and spot-on walrus impressions. The closest she could come to claiming victory here were the girls who let her sit with them at lunch and one boy named Sam who sometimes waved to her in social studies. Not exactly friends. Amiable acquaintances. Barely worth half a check mark.

Item two should have been easier, except Mr. Schweiz bored her to tears and caused her to space out about halfway through every class, all amounting to a very low C for her first quarter in math.

Item three was kind of a long shot anyway. The moment she walked onto the field during soccer tryouts and saw how good the other girls were already, she turned around and came home. She didn't need the added embarrassment or the whispers that would come with being the worst player on the team.

But even those were all still better than the last two items on the list. The ones that had been crossed out since the second week of school. The day some girl named Amber Forsythe started saying mean things about Riley behind her back. That she was kind of a freak. A weirdo who lost it in class, which was probably why she didn't have any friends. Not anymore, anyway.

Riley waited until lunch to let Amber know how she felt. Calmly retrieving her plate full of spaghetti with an extra ladle's worth of meatless sauce, she hunted down Amber sitting with her friends, and accidentally dropped the entire thing of pasta in the girl's lap, the watery red sauce seeping into the girl's expensive-looking jeans. The scream was deafening.

Item five was crossed out approximately thirty seconds after item four, with another pink slip to the principal's office.

By November, the plan had changed. The folded square of paper no longer took up space in Riley's backpack, having been replaced with a roll of duct tape and a flashlight, both of which proved infinitely more practical than a list of personal goals. The new plan consisted of one word, one that Riley didn't even bother to write down because she didn't need to. It was the word she whispered to herself every day when she walked through those double doors into Northridge Middle School. When it came right down to it, it was the only word that mattered.

Survive.

18

SHE HAD A PLAN.

It wasn't a good plan, she knew, but it was better than curling up in a corner, waiting for rescue. That wasn't the girl her parents raised. Her father tamed a twenty-thousand-ton behemoth raging along a set of skinny rails at forty miles an hour. He had a fifty-item checklist memorized, everything he had to inspect and verify before one of his trains moved so much as an inch. Her mother could reach a diagnosis faster than half of the doctors she worked under. They taught Riley how to attack the problem, to study the angles, to eliminate options of lesser worth, and then, when the best course of action revealed itself, to commit.

The plan was simple: she would walk through the entire

school, starting with A-hall and working her way around to D-hall and then back. She would try every exit she came across; there were at least eleven, she knew, and she'd only tried two so far. It was important to rule out every possibility—that's what Mr. Bardem would say. She would also look into every open classroom, flip on every light switch, try every window, try dialing out on every phone. She would be systematic. She would exhaust all her options.

But first she had to address the nasty cut trailing blood down the length of her arm.

The nurse's office neighbored the main office, but of course it was locked. Always. You don't leave a cabinet full of Adderall and Ritalin—not to mention enough shots of epinephrine for all the nut-allergy kids to jump-start a hippo's heart—unattended with middle schoolers roaming around. Nurse Garner also had a drawer full of bandages in every size you could imagine, but since Riley couldn't get to them, she had to improvise.

The Northridge cafeteria was huge—that had been Riley's belly-fluttering impression the first time she saw it. It was at least three times the size of the one at her elementary school. Forty octagonal tables sat in staggered rows, each one sitting up to eight kids . . . or sometimes just three manga-loving girls and one half-interested bystander. For most, lunch was the best period of the day, but not for Riley. It was somehow easier to blend in in the classroom, where half the kids were fixated on the teacher and the other half were in a trance or full-out sleeping. The cafeteria was different. It was like the Wild West; anything could happen. She briefly pictured Amber Forsythe's horrified face, her hands holding clumps of spaghetti like bloody entrails. Not Riley's fault; the girl had it coming.

All the hallway lights were out now, so Riley followed the beacon of her flashlight beam, thanking her mother for insisting that she carry it and wishing that she hadn't pulled the fire alarm. Though she still couldn't fathom how that could have shut off the school's electricity. Didn't they have backup generators in case of a power surge? Weren't there fail-safe mechanisms in place?

Yeah, probably. Under normal circumstances. And under normal circumstances the doors open and the windows stay up and the frogs stay dead. Under normal circumstances Riley would be finished with her dinner by now. But Riley knew she was a long way from normal.

As she moved down the hall, she noticed how different the school appeared in the silent gloom. In the light, with the din of a few hundred students in the background, the building was sort of strangely comforting in its tedious familiarity. Now it seemed alien to her. The darkness was deceiving. Sometimes it seemed to expand the emptiness of the hallways, stretching them out so that the rooms became like branching caverns in some subterranean maze. Other times it closed everything off, the hallways growing thinner, the walls pressing in on her from both sides, the ceiling bearing down so that Riley had to stop and catch her breath, blinking away the illusion that the whole school was caving in.

The pervading silence made her own noises more intense. The sound of her boots slapping the hard floor pounded in her ears. The audible whisper of her breathing, the scritch of the backpack shifting against her sweatshirt. A cough crackled like a gunshot in the darkness when there was no one else around. Riley slowed her pace, taking catlike steps, as if she was sneaking up on someone, or was afraid of someone sneaking up on her. The flashlight beam caught glimpses of things—lockers, posters, doorways—which, when isolated, seemed slightly out of place, like a puzzle where a handful of pieces have been forced into the wrong spots.

The cafeteria was pitch-black, no windows to let in even the slightest seepage of outside light. Riley wondered if the refrigerators and freezers in the kitchen now lacked power as well. What a cluster that would be come morning. She tried to imagine what the cafeteria ladies would say when they showed up to find pre-thawed mystery meat and sweaty cartons of spoiled milk.

What are any of them going to say? Riley wondered. What was

Mr. Bardem going to say when he walked into his supply closet and found the mess she made breaking out? Or Principal Warton discovering the school's beloved copper wire tree sculpture in a mangled heap by the front entrance? What would she tell them? What was she going to tell her parents? No matter what she said, she wasn't sure they would believe her. How could they? She wasn't even sure herself what to believe.

One thing at a time, Riley Flynn. Take care of your hand first.

Riley swept her flashlight across the metal partition that barred access to the counter after hours. No chance of her sneaking into the kitchen, but that was fine; all she needed was some bandaging material and a little hand sanitizer, and the cafeteria had both. She grabbed a handful of brown napkins from the counter by the tray drop-off and took them to the Purell dispenser, which seemed to be the only thing in the school still working. She soaked one of the napkins in sanitizer and then closed her eyes. This was going to sting.

She thought of her mother. Amanda Flynn didn't believe in kiss-and-make-it-better. When Riley fell down and gently scraped a knee or banged an elbow, her mother would inspect it and then give her prognosis, which was almost always "I think you'll live." Riley supposed she couldn't blame her. Her mom had seen ten-year-olds dying from cancer, held their sweaty hands while their own bodies betrayed them. She spent her days in the intensive care unit with patients who were right on the edge, passengers listening for the train whistle, wondering if this was their stop. If Riley wasn't bleeding and/or broken, her mother grabbed a tissue, told her to wipe her nose, and suggested being more careful. If Riley had been crying especially hard, she got a hug.

You pick yourself up. You brush yourself off. You get back to business.

Riley pressed the napkin against the cut, feeling it suddenly catch fire, burning all the way down to her fingertips. *That's how you know it's working*, her mom would say. Riley blew on the wound and wiped it clean, then pressed another folded napkin along the length of the cut, two inches from the web of her thumb down to her wrist. She found the closest table and sat down to fish through her backpack, angling her flashlight so that she could see. The duct tape was at the bottom. She tore off a strip with her teeth and then wrapped it around her hand twice, careful not to make it too tight or to restrict her thumb movement any more than necessary; she wanted to be able to make a fist if she had to—just in case. She secured her bandage with another swatch of tape and flexed her fingers.

Riley took a moment to admire her handiwork in the flashlight's beam. Perfectly serviceable. Her mother would be proud. She stuffed the roll of tape back into her bag. "Bring on the broken hearts," she whispered, then snort-laughed to herself.

The sound echoed in the cafeteria. She listened to it bounce off the ceiling and the walls. The darkness was messing with her senses. The emptiness made everything louder. Riley listened to her absurd little laugh fade away.

And then, inexplicably, it echoed again, except more drawn out this time. Longer and louder.

Riley froze. This wasn't her laugh. It sounded strange. More of a tittering. A mocking sound.

In fact, it didn't sound like just one person laughing at all. It was made up of multiple voices. Several laughs blending together. It started in one corner of the room and carried to the other side, jumping from table to table. There was no joy in it. It was cruel, smug, dismissive. The kind of snickering that hooks into a middle schooler's ears like barbed wire.

Riley spun in her seat, flashlight in hand, light leaping around, finding the corners, dancing across the tables. The cafeteria was empty.

"Hello? Is somebody there?"

A few ticks of silence passed and then the laughter started up again, coming from her left this time, jeering, needling, sharp. She spun the other way as it whipped around and then came at her from the right. Which meant she was in the center.

She was hearing it everywhere now, steadily growing in volume, shifting in pitch, multiple voices overlapping, the laughter of boys and girls both. It danced and gamboled, seeming to hit her from whatever angle she wasn't looking, always, inexplicably, right behind her, sneaking up on her; then she would turn and it would disappear only to circle around again. Everywhere at once.

Riley stood up, grabbing her backpack with her unbandaged hand. The laughter enveloped her, growing louder and louder until her head started to ring. She dropped her bag and put both hands to her ears, pressing them tight. "Stop it!" she yelled. But her voice was lost among the cacophony of a hundred other voices, determined, it seemed, to drown her out. All of them laughing.

All of them laughing at her.

She turned to run, flashlight beam aimed at the floor.

Nearly stepping on the not-so-deadish frog jumping right into her path.

19

THE GOAL WAS ALWAYS TO GET HER TO JUMP. OR TO AT LEAST GIVE her the heebie-jeebies. But Riley wasn't easily frightened, which meant her dad had to work at it.

He sometimes turned off all her lights when he told her his stories, using the flashlight on his phone to illuminate his face, which often took on grotesque shapes when a villain appeared, twisting it into the leering grin of a luring witch or the squint-eyed grimace of a bloodthirsty vampire. With the ghost stories he would keep the phone perched under his chin, giving off just enough light to cast him in an ominous, sickly yellow glow.

There was more than one kind of ghost story, of course. Riley's father could recite a couple dozen off the top of his head, and could make up a new one on the spot when the mood struck him. Some were scarier than others, but, to Riley at least, they all seemed to have one thing in common: underneath the thrills and chills, they carried a hint of sadness. At the start they made her shiver underneath her embroidered bedspread, but by the end the anxiety had faded, leaving a kind of heaviness in her heart.

She said as much one night, as her father pulled her covers to her chin.

"Well, of course they're sad," he told her. "They're ghost stories. Ghost stories are all about loss. About getting left behind. Which is pretty scary if you think about it."

"I'm not afraid," she'd told him, which wasn't entirely true. Some of her father's stories actually did give her nightmares— though she wouldn't dare tell him so, afraid he would stop.

"I'm not talking about you, monster. I know you're not scared. I'm talking about the ghosts."

"What does a ghost have to be afraid of?"

"Same thing as everybody, I suppose," her father said. "They're afraid of being forgotten."

Riley said that was stupid. Why would a ghost even care?

"Nobody wants to be forgotten," her father replied.

There was one story he told about a square wicker basket that wasn't scary at all. A couple had just gotten married; the husband was flighty, scatterbrained, always forgetting where he put things, so the wife bought a basket to keep on the counter by the sink and nagged the husband endlessly to put anything important—anything he would need—inside it for easy finding. "Where is my—" he would start to say, and she would answer with, "Check the basket."

Even when the wife got leukemia and the husband spent much of his time taking care of her, she still reminded him about the basket where he kept his keys and wallet as well as her growing medical bills and medications.

The wife's condition deteriorated, and six years after buying the house and the wicker basket, her body succumbed and was buried in a cemetery miles away.

But her spirit remained.

The husband knew this because whenever he misplaced something—his cell phone, his watch, the television remote—he would ransack the house, stomping around in frustration, looking in all the usual places, including the basket by the sink. The first time he checked it, of course, the thing he was looking for was never in it. Only when he came back to the kitchen later and opened the basket one last time would he find it there, waiting for him. A little reminder of what he'd lost for good.

That's how it worked. Sometimes a ghost's power manifested itself in a particular object. An old pair of reading glasses that allowed a woman to see her long-lost lover. A fireplace that crackled and spat with a constant orange flame even though there were no logs to burn, keeping a family warm after their father passed. A piano that played a young girl's favorite piece in the middle of the night for her bereaved parents. A bathtub that would fill itself in the house of a boy who drowned. These objects were often the source of a ghost's power; they were also the anchors that kept the spirits of the dead from moving on.

A ghost is only as strong as the memories that keep it here.

What that meant for Riley, of course, was that a ghost could be anything. The static on an old television set. The silence on the other end of the phone. A lock of hair that appears in a brush that hasn't been used in years. Footprints in the freshly vacuumed carpet. The window that opens in the middle of the night to let in fitful dreams.

"Ghosts aren't always floating sheets or wisps of smoke," Riley's dad told her. "They take on many forms. You might see them in the shimmer of a puddle or the reflection from a window. You could see them in a bird that perches on your mailbox every morning. Sometimes you don't even see them at all, but you still know they're there. You can feel it in your bones. In the way the hair stands up on the back of your neck. In a tickle that starts all the way down at your feet!"

Then, of course, the hand Riley hadn't been watching—the rough, calloused engineer's hand that was twice the size of her own—would slip under the covers by her feet and tickle her toes.

Riley would scream and jump and tell him to quit it before begging him to tell her another story. A scary one this time. Not another sad one. Something bloody. With cannibals. Better yet, *zombies*. Because, in truth, those kinds of stories never stayed scary for long. They were too ridiculous. Good for a cheap thrill but easily forgotten. Not like the ghost stories. Those were the ones that lingered.

Sort of like the ghosts themselves.

20

IT HAD TO BE THE SAME ONE AS BEFORE.

One half-eviscerated zombie frog looks much the same as another, Riley thought, but she remembered the patterning, the collage of black spots, especially up around the nose and eyes. Eyes that were looking up at her in the pool of the flashlight's beam.

"So . . . um . . . ribbit?"

Riley choked down her scream this time. She had enough self-control not to send the creature soaring through the air with her boot again either. The frog stood in the entryway, as if trying to block her way, though she could easily have stepped right over him.

Except she wasn't sure she could move. Her feet felt like

they'd been welded to the floor. Behind her, the raucous laughter had faded, enough that she'd been able to hear the dead frog speak.

No. Speak wasn't quite the right word for it. Riley wasn't sure it actually made any sound. The frog's voice seemed like it came from inside and outside all at once, almost as if Riley had *thought* it rather than *heard* it. As if the frog had opened up her brain and spilled the words inside, bypassing her ears entirely.

The frog's throat bulged the way bullfrogs' do when they send out a mating call—except Mr. Bardem had said these were grass frog specimens. And the sound that came to her wasn't an animal croak. It sounded like a grown man's voice. It sounded almost like her father.

"Please don't kick me again," the frog pleaded. *"Last time I'm pretty sure something came loose."*

"Huh?" Riley's own voice sounded froggy to her, phlegmy and hoarse.

The shriveled creature adjusted itself on its hind legs and she could see the two peeled flaps of its belly hanging down, the incision that started from just beneath its throat. A reminder that it was long gone—or should be. *"I understand. You're scared. But I promise I'm not here to hurt you, and it makes it hard to have a conversation when one of us is flying across the room."* The voice in her head paused, then added, *"I'm Max, by*

134

the way. Max Trotter. And you are?"

Crazy. That's what she was. *Actually* crazy. Like double back-flip off the high dive into the deep end of Nutsville. Riley dug her knuckles into her temples as if the pressure might release some insanity valve in her brain. At least the laughter in the cafeteria had fully subsided, and even the echo of the empty room seemed to have lessened, though Riley felt like the frog's—Max's—voice still held a resonant quality, like it pinballed around inside her skull.

"You talk," she said, ignoring his question. "You're talking."

"More or less," Max said.

"But you're a freaking frog!" Riley said, louder. *A dead frog,* she thought, *but let's take this one shaky step at a time.*

"Yeah. Sort of. At least in body, if not, you know . . ."

Riley shook her head. If she hadn't been hallucinating before, she definitely was now. Her mother was right. In times of stress you see things that aren't really there. Phantom trains on the tracks. Flashing lights in the sky. Floating sheets and wisps of smoke. Maybe she'd had a nervous breakdown during the hour that she'd been locked in that supply closet and this was the result. She took a step back and fell into a seat at the table, shaking her head but keeping the eye of the flashlight trained on the frog. "This can't be real. You can't be real."

The frog took a couple of labored hops toward her and Riley

recoiled instinctively, muscles tense, boot ready to strike out again, though the creature didn't look dangerous. It looked as if his left hind leg had been hurt; it rested at an awkward angle.

"I already told you, you aren't crazy," he said.

"So says the dead frog," Riley whispered to herself.

Maybe she was just seeing things. And hearing things. But she could *smell* him too—the mix of chemicals and the underlying . . . *ripeness*, the sickening sweet scent of slow decay. Could you hallucinate a smell? And a voice? Could you imagine all these things at once?

The frog reached up with a foreleg and scratched his nose. It was an oddly human gesture.

"No. Impossible. You're just in my head," Riley said. "You're not real."

"You're not imagining me. I wish you were. Trust me when I say I don't want to be here any more than you do."

"I could be imagining you telling me that I'm not imagining you," Riley countered.

"That cut on your hand doesn't look too imaginary," the frog said. *"Probably doesn't feel imaginary either."*

Riley glanced at her bandaged hand; you could already see a little red stripe soaking through the brown napkin. He was right. The pain felt real enough. "But you can't be . . . this isn't . . . I mean . . . just *look* at you."

The frog's eyes moved in all directions as if he was trying to do just that.

"Sorry," he said finally. *"I thought it might be easier for you to handle if you had an actual body to talk to. Something substantial. And this was the best vessel I could get. If you'd like, I can probably go find a cockroach or something? Or a spider. But some people are afraid of spiders."*

Riley shook her head. She thought back to the bag on the floor in Bardem's supply closet, the one she'd taken the probing needle from. The one that had twitched and jumped the moment just before she managed to bust through the door. "So if that's not you . . . I mean, if you're not really, you know, a frog . . ." Riley swallowed hard, determined to finish her question. "Then what the hell *are* you?"

Max blinked up at her. *"You know what I am."*

I don't know, Horatio. Maybe not.

Or maybe so.

Riley put her hands up; she leaned back in her chair; her voice shook. "No. No way." She stood up, but the voice in her head grew more pressing.

"I get it. Believe me, it took me a while to adjust to the fact, too. But let's face it, I'm not the only strange thing you've seen or heard around here." The frog's eyeballs glanced around the room again, taking in the cafeteria that less than a minute ago had been filled

with derisive laughter. Riley thought of the sounds coming from the girls' restroom. All the doors that wouldn't open. The lights suddenly shutting off. The frog was right. He wasn't the only strange thing.

Just the strangest.

You know what I am.

She shook her head. All those bedtime stories. She knew they weren't real, but she'd asked her father anyway. *Wait . . . . You think I'm just making this stuff up?* he'd say, but then he would wink at her, and she would be in on the joke. He'd blow her a kiss and flip off her light. And she would watch his shadow move, pausing in her doorway, back to her, head slightly cocked. *Then again, you can never be too sure*, he'd say.

She was sure.

She had been sure.

She wasn't so sure.

The frog bobbed up and down. *"I know how you feel, and I don't blame you. But I can help. I know what you're going through, and I can help you get out of here. At least I think I can. But you have to promise to help me too."*

Get out of here: the same words she'd been shouting in her own head since the moment she was locked in that closet . . . with this very same frog. Riley cocked her head. "Help you?"

Max rose up, lifting his chin, exposing more of his tattered belly. *"For starters, you could patch me up so I'm not tripping over my own guts anymore. Then afterward we can talk."* The frog glanced left, then right. *"But not here. This place gives me the creeps."*

It gives you *the creeps?* Riley thought to herself. But then she recalled the laughter that had surrounded her only moments ago. She wasn't sure she would ever get it out of her head.

"So how about it? Do you want my help or not?"

I don't know, Horatio. She pictured her father sitting on the edge of her bed. That sly wink. The break in the facade. There's no such thing as ghosts.

Then again, nothing seems real to you until you've had the chance to see it, hear it, touch it.

Until it's staring up at you with its empty eyes, proving you wrong.

21

RILEY HAD HAD LITTLE DIRECT EXPERIENCE WITH DEATH.

She was the kind of girl who gently guided spiders into paper cups to take them outside. The kind who would find a twig to carefully move earthworms that had surfaced from the rain-soaked earth and lay sprawled across the sidewalk back into the grass so they wouldn't be squished under a bicycle's tread. She'd been a vegetarian from the age of eight—minus one McDonald's-fueled relapse brought about by stress, in which she laid waste to a twenty count of nuggets, though they would later get their revenge. When she was little she would try to pet the bumblebees that circled the tiny flower garden she tended with her mother. That, also, was a mistake.

Only one of her grandparents had passed during her lifetime—her father's father—but she was three and had no memory of the funeral. Her one and only solid memory of Grandpa Gage was of him going crazy with a can of spray whipped cream, giving both her and himself delicious, dripping Santa Claus beards and laughing like lunatics. He died suddenly, a brain aneurysm while sitting on his porch doing the daily jumble. It was, Riley thought, a good way to go.

Outside of Grandpa Gage, Riley had never personally known anyone who'd passed. She'd never even lost a pet, because she'd never had one to lose. With her parents' schedules it was difficult to give a dog the attention it deserved, and her father was allergic to cats. But none of that stopped her from trying. She brought home every living thing she could find in the small woods three blocks from her house with the hopes that she could keep it. Garter snakes that she snatched bare-handed. Crickets and caterpillars captured in jars. Buckets of tadpoles that never turned into frogs, or, in turn, princes. In a moment of desperation she adopted a garden slug that she'd found attached to her bedroom window. She was always told to put them back where she found them, and she always did. Except for the slug, which she set on a rock in the shade, assuming it would be happier there.

Then, last summer, her father brought in from the yard a

young rabbit, barely more than a kit. It had burrowed beneath one of the hedges and was fortunate that he hadn't caught it with the trimmer, though it was clear something else had already gotten a piece of it. The neighbor's husky, perhaps. Blood matted its fur and patches of skin had been roughly torn, revealing the muscle twitching underneath. Its right ear was half chewed off, its back leg broken. Riley's heart broke just looking at it.

Her mother the nurse was at work, so it was up to Dad and Riley to care for the frightened damaged thing. They cleaned it off as best they could, disinfecting the wounds with hydrogen peroxide. The rabbit thrashed, but Riley's father had a strong grip and wouldn't let go until the job was done. They wrapped the back leg, splinting it with half a Popsicle stick from Riley's craft supply box, then her father let her hold it.

It was small enough that she could practically cup it in both hands with only its head peeking out. She could feel its tiny heart pulsing rapidly beneath its fur still slicked wet from antiseptic. She could feel its heat. Its small solemn eyes seemed to swallow the whole world at once. Riley stroked the top of its head, careful to avoid the damaged ear. Its whiskers tickled her fingers.

All at once Riley felt something surge inside her—a deep connection to this broken thing that had been chased, attacked, abandoned. This creature who was scared and lonely and lost. And so, when her father returned with a shoebox and opened the lid, Riley shook her head.

"We need to keep it. We need to take care of it ourselves."

"Riley, it's a wild animal. It's not a pet. Its leg is busted and it's got cuts and scrapes all over. It could already have a serious infection. We need to take it to the wildlife rehabilitation center. They will know what to do."

"But *I* want to help it," she said, her breath hitching, holding in her tears because it seemed silly for an almost teenager to cry over something like this.

Her dad wrapped his arm around her as she wrapped hers around the rabbit, layer upon layer squeezing just tight enough.

"You *are* helping it. But you can only do so much, and this is more than we can handle." He covered her small hands with his giant ones, taking the trembling, twitching ball of fur and placing it gently in the box, quickly covering it with the lid. "The wildlife center is a bit of a drive. You hold on tight to the box, okay?"

Riley sniffed and nodded. She would take what she could get.

For the next twenty-five minutes, at least, she had a pet rabbit—albeit one that she couldn't hold or see or hear. But she could feel the weight of it on her lap, the weight of a living thing that is counting on you, and it was almost too much to bear.

And yet, heavy as it was, when the woman at the wildlife center held out her hands for the box, Riley couldn't bear to let go of it.

22

FIRST, SHE HAD TO TAKE CARE OF HIM, LIKE THE POOR RABBIT THAT her father had dragged in last summer. She helped Max and Max helped her. That was the deal.

Riley looked at the frog sitting in the center of the desk, the beam from her flashlight encircling him like a Broadway star. They were in one of the classrooms now, just down the hall from the cafeteria. He'd asked her to carry him because it would be faster that way, but she shook her head. She wasn't about to touch it . . . him. Not with her bare hands.

"Afraid of getting warts?" his voice echoed.

Riley didn't answer. Warts were pretty far down the list of things she was currently scared of. Still, she set her backpack on the ground and unzipped the front pouch, shaking her head in continued disbelief that she was talking to a dead frog. And that he was talking back. "Hop in."

"Funny," he said.

She wasn't trying to be. She saw no humor in *any* of this. Max struggled, the one leg limp and uncooperative, but he managed to get settled in the pocket, turning to poke his nose out. Riley shouldered the backpack slowly, careful not to jostle him too much, and headed for the first room she could find, grateful to be getting away from the cafeteria with its lingering memory of laughter, but wondering what in god's name she'd just agreed to and who in the heavens she was toting around.

Now the frog sat on the desk in front of her, much closer than before. Riley could see the webbing on his front feet, the shifting patterns of the spots marching down his back. From the top down he didn't look so bad; only at eye level could you see his guts hanging out.

"Don't worry. I won't feel much. And this guy definitely isn't going to feel it. I'm guessing his soul hit the road a while ago."

His soul. Did frogs even have souls? Riley thought of her father's phantom train, whistling its warning to oncoming passengers, the ones who wouldn't make it through the next day. One-way ticket to froggy heaven. That's how it worked, right? The body turns to dust and the spirit transcends. Unless you're one of the ones stranded at the station, somewhere in between. Unless you're a . . .

Just say it, Riley. Unless you're a ghost.

Except Riley didn't believe in ghosts.

Of course, belief was a funny thing. At one time she'd been convinced that fairies trafficked in human teeth, and that portly, white-bearded men with rosy cheeks broke into people's houses, leaving them gifts in exchange for carrots and cookies. At one time she'd believed that every person you meet is basically good inside, and that friends always keep other friends' secrets, and that adults would never hurt children. She believed you always apologized for the mistakes you made and that lying was always wrong.

Then she started to grow up.

She'd believed all those things once. So there was no reason she couldn't suddenly believe something that she hadn't before. After all, here was the evidence, this . . .

ghost

. . . thing. Staring right at her. Talking to her.

Haunting me?

A thing with a name, capable of inhabiting the dead, damaged body of a dissected frog. What had he called it? A vessel? It sounded like an old word, full of antiquity and ritual. It reminded Riley of a museum she'd gone to once that had a sarcophagus of some pharaoh on display; scattered around it were jars of lime-stone that supposedly held the dead man's lungs and liver and stomach. Vessels.

Except Max's stomach and liver were on full display thanks to the incision straight down his middle.

No. Not *his* exactly. This body was a loaner; he was borrowing it, animating it like a puppeteer. And if he could control this frog, did that mean he could control other things? Inanimate things?

Like windows? Like doors?

Could he somehow manipulate the phones, the lights?

Could he . . . somehow take control of *her*?

"Does it hurt?" Max asked, breaking Riley's train of thought. It still freaked her out the way that he could talk to her without making any sound, projecting his voice straight into her brain.

"What?"

"Your hand. It looked like a nasty scratch."

Riley shrugged. *Not as bad as yours,* she thought.

"It might leave a scar," Max added. *"The deep ones usually do."*

The comment took her by surprise. From everything she'd ever read or seen, ghosts didn't talk in complete sentences. They moaned or wailed. They screamed like banshees. They rattled chains. They didn't inquire about your well-being. They didn't make jokes about warts. None of the ghosts in her father's stories had a sense of humor.

"It's fine," she said. At least, it was something she could do something about. Something she could fix, though undoubtedly her mother would have done a better job of it. Right now she would have endured a hundred such scratches over being stuck here with this creature, whoever—*what*ever—it was. "You said your name was Max?"

"Was Max. Is Max. I'm not quite sure what tense you'd use in this situation."

"What tense to use," Riley repeated. Not just a ghost, but a ghost concerned with grammar. "And who are . . . I mean, I guess, who *were* you?"

The frog lifted one leg to give Riley a better look at his flopping innards dangling free. *"Patch me up and I'll tell you."*

"Right." Riley scanned the desk, finding a box of tissues hiding in the dark corner. The duct tape in her bag would easily patch up what was left of Max's vessel—but the tissues would keep her from having to touch the frog . . . ghost . . . ghost frog directly. "Flip over," she ordered.

Max blinked at her. "Not sure that's how frogs work."

Riley exhaled slowly, channeling her mother's sense of composure. She grabbed a pencil from the cup on the desk and nestled the eraser underneath the creature's wrinkled body, then quickly jerked upward, turning him on his back, legs splayed out next to him. He looked like he was sleeping. Or dead.

Good one, Riley, she thought. *Freaking hilarious.*

Still using the soft end of the pencil, she gently pushed the frog's deflated bladder back into its body cavity. She'd recognized all the digestive organs instantly from the video. *See, Mr. Bardem—no dissection necessary. I'm an expert.* "This really doesn't hurt?" she asked.

"I can barely feel it," the upside-down frog said. *"Pain works differently now."*

"But you *can* still feel pain?"

"There are different kinds of pain," Max replied. *"And some are so much worse than others."*

Riley scooped the rest of the stray intestines in. She couldn't believe what she was doing. What he . . . it . . . was saying. Her hands trembled; the pencil quivered. One of the frog's back legs—the non-gimpy one—suddenly twitched, causing Riley's knees to jerk, banging against the bottom of the desk, a very real, visceral pain shooting up her leg. A curse shot out of her mouth.

"Sorry," Max said. *"Reflex. You almost done?"*

Am I done? Oh yeah. I am so done. I was done the moment they locked me in that closet. I am absolutely over all of this.

"Yeah, almost" was what she said. Riley nudged both flaps of skin back into place, meeting in the center, revealing a cut as long as the one on her hand. Except hers was still bleeding. Max's veins were pumped full of rubber. Using a second tissue as a bandage, she wrapped one long piece of duct tape around the creature's midsection, securing it to itself, then she flipped him back over, careful to only touch the tape. The dead (possessed? haunted? demonic?) frog took a tentative test hop, then another. The tape held everything in place, though the one back leg still dragged a little.

"Better than the last guy that tried to fix me," he said.

"The last guy?"

"After my heart attack," Max said.

Riley thought of her grandfather sitting on the porch, newspaper in hand. *Did this frog just tell me it had a heart attack?*

"So that's how . . . you know . . . that's how you, um . . ." Riley's voice trailed off. She couldn't quite bring herself to say it. The frog scratched at his nose again.

"Bit the big one? Yep. That's how. At the ripe old age of forty-five. Right in the middle of the produce aisle. I was picking out an avocado—and then bam, down. Sharp pain in the chest. Couldn't breathe. My vision clouded. I caught glimpses of people hovering, shouting. Some guy next to me, pounding away, but it was no use. I felt everything just sort of stop for a moment, the whole world went dark, and when I woke up, I was here. Not in body, of course. But definitely here."

"Wait," Riley said. "Here? Like *here* here?" She shook her head. "You're telling me you died and went to *middle school*?"

It was quite possibly the most absurd thing she'd ever heard.

"Not exactly my idea of heaven, either," Max replied. *"But I wasn't given much of a choice. I just found myself stuck here. Trapped . . . kind of like you."*

Riley took one hard look at the frog, the broken vessel. Her hands had started trembling again. Her head swam. It was just too much.

"Are you okay?"

"Am I okay?" Riley repeated, shaking her head slowly, her volume steadily escalating. "How in the world am I supposed to be okay? I'm stuck in this freaking school, freezing in the freaking dark, talking to a freaking *frog* who is also a freaking *ghost*! Nothing about this is even remotely *okay*! It is seriously messed up!"

She let her head fall into her hands.

"I'm so messed up," she added, softer.

Max took a little hop toward her. *"It's not you. Trust me,"* he said.

Riley forced herself to take a long, shivering breath. The frog settled himself on his haunches, the tape pulled tight around him like a girdle. He looked up at her from the desk.

"We made a deal," he said. *"You help me. I help you. So let's have it. What do you want to know?"*

23

IT WAS A LOADED QUESTION.

But she asked it anyway.

It was the day of middle school orientation. Riley's entire fifth-grade class had piled onto a bus and ridden the fifteen minutes to Northridge to "get a feel for the place." They'd already spent an hour fidgeting and secretly texting through speeches in the auditorium from one Principal Theresa Warton—a buttoned-up, deep-voiced woman with short blond hair and dangly earrings meant to show off her fun, spontaneous side— and a song from an eighth-grade choir that clearly didn't want to be there. There were brochures and handouts and bookmarks and the promise of punch and cookies. Everything had the Northridge panther growling menacingly on it.

But before they could feast, the students were all broken into small groups and given a tour of the school by one of its current inmates. The building itself was huge, sprawling, so many different hallways branching off each other that it felt like a maze. Riley used to like making mazes when she was younger—a hobby of hers until it wasn't—but this place seemed confusing and intimidating and it made her head spin as she tried to keep track of which hall was which.

Thankfully, Riley's tour guide was funny and approachable and surprisingly blunt, doing her best to make her gaggle of fifth graders feel comfortable.

This is the gym. Physical education is an elective here. I didn't take it because who wants to be sweaty and gross for the rest of the day? This is the cafeteria. We have more choices here than the elementary schools, but none of them are that great. The chicken fingers are okay if you drown them in ranch and on Tuesdays we get a taco bar. This is D-hall, sort of the butthole of the building. They stick all the foreign language classes back here. These lockers never get used; I'm not even sure they still work. This is the music room. If you decide to play an instrument, pick something that's easy to carry home, like the flute. I play the oboe. Don't pick the oboe. It's impossible.

The guide was an eighth grader with frizzy black hair and knee-high boots. Her name was Maya and in addition to her honest appraisal of the school, she also mentioned that she had

154

a boyfriend *and* a pet dog and that the dog was cuter. She stood at least a foot taller than most of the fifth graders who followed her. Of course all the middle schoolers looked enormoous to Riley. Maya also looked suspiciously happy. Probably all an act, but even as she talked about the terrible food or the amount of homework, she smiled as if to say that it was all worth it. That life at Northridge Middle School was manageable. That the signs in the front of the school in twelve different languages weren't, in fact, beckoning them to the underworld.

After the tour, they stopped back in the gym and sat around Maya in a circle, crisscross applesauce, staring up in awe at her like she was some kind of preteen idol.

"So," she said. "Time for some tea. What do you want to know?"

Some of the kids in Riley's group shot up hands and Maya called on them in turn. They asked about lockers and passing periods and how easy it was to make the basketball team ("try out and see"). They asked if there were a lot of tests and group projects and if you were allowed to chew gum in class. "You're not supposed to," she answered, "but most teachers don't care, so long as you don't stick it on the walls or in each other's hair. Other questions?"

Riley's hand went up halfway, barely past her chin. Maya noticed.

"Are the other kids, you know . . . nice?"

She expected her classmates to scoff. Of course Riley Flynn would ask that. But none of the other seven kids in her group laughed at her; it seemed they were just as interested in the answer as she was. Some of them, including Riley herself, had actually had gum stuck in their hair at some point.

Maya hesitated—three, maybe four seconds, nearly an eternity—then smiled again.

"Oh yeah. Of course. I mean, there's drama, right? It's middle school. But you're all going through the same stuff. You have to have each other's backs, you feel me?"

That's what she said, but the pause hadn't escaped Riley's attention. It confirmed everything she suspected, the doubt and dread that had hit her the moment she walked through the front doors. In Maya-the-cool-eighth-grader's hesitation, Riley knew what she was in for.

This is middle school, kid, the pause said. *Nobody gets out of here without a few scars.*

"If there are no more questions," she said, "who wants to go crash the cookie booth?"

All the hands went up again except for Riley's. She actually still had one more thing she wanted to ask: *Is there any way to get out of this?* But she knew the answer already. Northridge was her destiny. She was trapped here for the next three years. And more likely than not, she would have to navigate those next three years alone. She tried to tell herself that it would be all right, but the feeling in her gut suggested otherwise, telling her there was no escape.

Riley glanced behind her at the exit sign hanging above the door, then shoved her hands into her pockets and got into the very back of the line.

24

RILEY RAN A FINGER ALONG THE OUTLINE OF THE BANDAGE ON HER other hand. It still hurt, a throbbing made worse any time she moved her thumb, though it looked as if the bleeding had finally been stanched. When she got home she would strip off the bandage and wash the cut for real, then douse it in peroxide and let it air out for a while before rebandaging it with the proper supplies her mother stockpiled in the medicine cabinet.

When she got home.

The frog—Max—blinked up at her. *What do you want to know?*

It was obvious, wasn't it? The only question that really mattered right now: *How do I get out of here?* And yet, if Max really was what he said he was—what Riley was still trying to fully convince herself that he was—there were so many other questions that came to mind. Not so much about the here and now, but about after.

She'd be lying if she said she never thought about it. And if he really was a ghost, if he really had keeled over in the middle of a grocery store, then he must have some answers. He must know how it felt. Did it hurt? How much? Was it peaceful? Did you see your life flashing before your eyes, perhaps, or was that just a cliché? Max had already said it was nothing, darkness, and then this. But there had to be more to it than that. Didn't there?

There were times she wondered what it must be like. Lying in bed at night, staring up at her ceiling or through the window across the room, her parents already asleep, trying to wrap her brain around the certainty of it, and the uncertainty—this thing that would happen to everyone, that would happen to her, but could still be so arbitrary, so random, so unexpected. Sitting on your porch with the newspaper in your lap. Standing in the produce aisle with an avocado in your hand. A clogged artery. A burst blood vessel. And then boom, gone. But gone to where?

Here, apparently. Northridge. Home of the Panthers.

She probably shouldn't be surprised. She always said that middle school was proof that hell exists.

Which brought her back to the most pressing question of

159

all. The most pressing for her, at least, right at this moment. So that's what she asked.

The vessel Max occupied seemed to frown at her. Or maybe that was just his default expression. He was a frog, after all. Sort of.

"I don't know," he said.

Riley raised her voice again. "What do you mean, you don't know? You said I was in trouble and that you could help me!"

"I know, but getting out is not that easy."

"Yeah, tell me about it!" Riley shouted. "The freaking windows are stuck. The phones won't work. The doors won't open. I'm hearing all these crazy sounds and seeing things that can't be real. And then you . . ."

She hesitated, taking in the taped-up frog sitting in the flashlight's glow. A frog that had escaped from its plastic bag and then from Bardem's supply closet all on its own. Even though she'd slammed the door shut.

Frogs can't turn doorknobs. It didn't take a herpetologist to know that.

Ghosts, on the other hand . . .

In so many of her father's stories the ghosts never talked, but they let their presence be known in other ways. Chairs rearranged around the dining room. A drawer open that you swore you'd just closed. A bed lamp that blinks off and on. They could

160

manipulate the physical world, perhaps because they never fully parted from it. That's how they exerted their will over you. That was the haunting.

Riley tensed, pressing her back against the chair.

"Riley," Max began, as if reading her thoughts—who could say what all a ghost could do—but she voiced them anyway.

"It was you, wasn't it?"

"Riley, listen to me."

"You unlocked the supply closet door. You're the one who let me out. And if you can do that . . ." Riley remembered the window, how it suddenly slammed shut, crashing down like a guillotine. As if someone much stronger than her had been standing above, putting all their weight on it. The phones. The lights. There had to be a reason. There had to be a cause.

Riley shook her head, pushing the chair backward but keeping the flashlight steady in her hand, trained on the frog hunched at the edge of the desk. In her father's stories, some ghosts could do more than just scare you. They could manipulate you, possess you, even physically hurt you. They weren't all content to rattle doorknobs and wear white bedsheets; some were much more powerful than that.

And they all had something they wanted.

Riley stood up, took a step away from the desk.

"Riley, please . . ."

"The windows, the doors—"

"It's true. There are some things I can do. Some things I can control. But I'm telling you, it's not what you think."

"How do you even *know* what I'm thinking!" Riley yelled, hands cupped over her ears. "How are you inside my head! What do you want from me?" She closed her eyes, suddenly dizzy. "How do you even know my name?" She had never said it. Not out loud. At least she didn't think so.

"Riley, please, just hear me out . . ."

"No! You tell me why you're doing this," Riley pressed. "Why are you keeping me here?" The flashlight shook in her hands. The floor felt like it was shifting beneath her. Or maybe her legs were about to give out.

The voice inside her head suddenly exploded.

"IT'S NOT ME!"

Riley stumbled backward, forearms to her ears as a sharp pain stabbed behind her eyes, filled her skull, sent her reeling. But then, just as quickly as it hit her, the pain vanished, and she heard Max's voice, so much softer now.

"It's not me," he repeated. *"I'm not the one holding you here."*

Riley knew what question came next, but before she could ask it, a bright flash illuminated the doorway. The hallway light was somehow back on.

And then she heard it, faint but unmistakable.

Footsteps.

Somebody else *was* here.

Riley snatched her backpack, shoving her roll of tape back in.

"Riley. Wait. Where are you going?" Max called, but she didn't answer and she didn't stop. She just circled around the desk and headed for the hallway, following the sound of retreating steps.

"Don't go out there!" Max said, his voice pleading. *"It's not what you think."*

But all Riley could think was that someone else was in the school. Another living, breathing human being.

All that she could think was that this nightmare was over. And she was saved.

25

SHE'D ONLY BEEN SCARED, TRULY SCARED, ONCE IN HER LIFE.

There were hundreds of times when she'd felt uneasy, anxious, belly-sick with worry. Like in the fifth grade, coming home with an F on her report card—her first, mostly from missed work that she couldn't bring herself to finish—knowing her parents had probably already heard about it through an email from Mrs. Hyde, the frowns of disapproval they would wear all night, the lectures and ultimatums they would deliver.

Or the first day of middle school, sixth grade, the clock ticking down to fifth period—lunch period—with no plan in place for where to sit. And for the next five weeks at that same hour. Until she met Emily, and then the only thing turning her stomach was the rank smell of school taco meat.

And then there was the time when she was nine, standing behind the garage at Billy Denson's house with him and Kyle Blackwood, Billy holding the steak knife he'd borrowed from his kitchen, promising she could be in their club if she was willing to perform "the ritual." Riley, tired of spending her summer alone, snatched the knife out of his hand. The cut across her palm hadn't even hurt that much, though it turned out not to be worth even that little bit of blood—just to be let into Billy's basement and watch the two of them belch their way through a two-liter of Faygo and play video games all afternoon. There were worse things than being alone, she decided.

Riley was no stranger to anxiety. But anxiety wasn't the same as fear.

She knew the difference, too, between being afraid and being startled. She jumped at the movies when she was supposed to, when the bogeyman emerged from the closet or appeared from behind the back seat. That wasn't real fear, she knew; it didn't turn your blood cold.

She'd only had *that* feeling once: three years ago, when she'd come out of her bedroom late at night to find her mother standing in front of the television, phone pressed to her ear, her face drained of color.

Riley looked past her mother to see what she'd been watching. At first she couldn't quite make it out, just broken glass and twisted metal. As the camera panned and zoomed, though, she realized what she was looking at: the jagged hunks of metal became the fronts and backs of two freight cars that had smashed into each other. Zoomed out further she could see more cars, some of them turned sideways, many of them scrunched together like an accordion. The flash of sirens and the black-and-yellow dots of firefighters swarming the scene showed just how serious it was.

And then the part she would never forget—the engine, half on and half off the track. And the white SUV, bent into a V from the impact, nearly severed in half. The banner headline along the bottom: *Deadly train crash kills two.*

Riley's mother didn't see her standing there at first; her attention was split between the horrifying images on-screen and whoever had just picked up on the line. "Yes. This is Mandy Flynn. My husband is Conner Flynn. He's one of your engineers. I just saw the news. Can you please . . . can you please just tell me what operator was on board that CSX? Yes. I understand that. I've already tried calling him but he's not answering. I need to know . . ."

Riley moved to get a better look at the television. Her mother stopped talking. Her free hand covered her mouth, then quickly cupped the receiver on the phone. She looked at Riley with warm, wet eyes. "Go back to bed, sweetheart." Her voice sounded soft, but there was an underlying edge to it, letting Riley know this was an order, not a suggestion.

Riley didn't move. "Is that Dad's train?"

"It's not Dad's train, it's—" Her mother removed her hand from the phone. "Yes. Yes. I'm still here. Just one second." She turned back to Riley. "I'm serious, Riley Cooper Flynn. Go back to bed right now. I'll be there in a minute." She pointed toward the hallway with a shaky finger.

Reluctantly, Riley turned to go, but not before taking another glance at the news, which now showed a close-up of the wreckage and a pair of paramedics loading a body into the back of an ambulance.

The next ten minutes were the worst of Riley's life. Lying in bed, staring up at the glow-in-the-dark sticker stars that constellated her ceiling, wondering if the person in the ambulance was the same man who helped her stick up all those stars. The same one who taught her how to fish and tie a knot and blow a bubble. Wondering if that person was going to make it.

Finally her door opened and her mother came in holding her phone.

"Someone wants to say hi to you," she said.

Her mother put the phone on speaker and her father's voice sang out. "Hey there, monster. Do you miss me?" And in that instant Riley's blood thawed and the fear melted away. And her mother curled up in Riley's skinny twin bed beside her as her father wished them both good night, holding her as Riley softly cried herself to sleep.

Only later did she learn just how close it was. That the train involved in the accident was taking the same route that her father had taken just that morning, passing through the same small town, the same intersection with its faulty wooden crossing gate that finally gave up on coming down. That the two people who died were both in the SUV and the engineer had suffered only minor injuries.

It hadn't been her father in the cab. It hadn't been her father who didn't throw the brake in time. It hadn't been her dad lying on that stretcher. She had been so scared, afraid she might never see him again, but she'd had nothing to be afraid of. *Her* father was safe. *Her* father was on his way home.

Only later did she think to feel guilty for feeling so relieved.

26

RILEY STOPPED AND LISTENED FOR THE FOOTFALLS AGAIN, THE sense of relief already starting to give way to uncertainty.

The fluorescent lights along C-hall were blazing, though all the classrooms remained dark. She walked slowly, staying in the middle, glancing through the window of every door she passed.

Okay. So what? The hall lights were the ones on before the power went out. Obviously they would be the ones to come back on.

Except the power wasn't back on everywhere. Riley could see that the lights at the intersection at the *end* of the hall were still off. C-hall made a single illuminated path, like a runway.

"Hello? Anybody there?"

As if in response, the lights in the adjoining hall flickered on.

Oh thank the sweet baby Jesus.

She took off, her backpack slamming against her shin until she hoisted it onto her shoulder, approaching the corner at a sprint until she saw something that made her slow again: the lights in the connecting hall weren't *all* on, just the ones leading off to the left. The path to the right was still dark.

She remembered a poem she'd read in language arts last year, about two paths diverging in the woods. She could only remember the first and last line and then two lines in the middle because they stuck out to her the most: *Yet knowing how way leads on to way, I doubted if I should ever come back.* She'd liked those lines at the time. She didn't anymore.

Riley's heart thumped hard against her ribs. The hallway was empty. No movement. No further sounds. But she'd distinctly heard footsteps.

You've heard a lot of things.

She glanced behind her and then stepped cautiously around the corner, peering down the lit half of the adjoining hall. It led to another block of classrooms, rooms that, during the day, held social studies and language arts classes where poems about choices were read. At the very end sat the gym.

Don't go.

It was her own voice inside her head this time, but Riley glanced back over her shoulder anyway. C-hall, the one she'd left, was empty. Not just empty; it was dark again, even though five seconds ago all the overhead bulbs had been beaming. It was as if the only lights that worked were those near her. As if they were activated by her presence.

Or as if someone was lighting her way.

"Max, are you doing this?" Riley whispered, but there was no response.

Riley looked back toward the gym, the momentary burst of hope she'd felt at the thought of finding a teacher or custodian slowly draining, leaving only that unsettling feeling that she was being watched. The same feeling she got when she threw those goggles on the floor today, everyone in science spinning around, staring at her as if she was some kind of aberration. All those eyes, all on her.

The lights overhead flickered once, as if giving her a nudge.

This is a bad idea.

Right. She should go back. To the room she left behind. Go back to Max and force him to tell her exactly what was going on. What he'd done. What he *was* doing. Or maybe return to the front office. See if the electricity was back on there. Try the automatic door again. Pull another fire alarm. Pull all the freaking fire alarms.

Or maybe just light the whole stupid building on fire. Even if the alarms didn't work, surely somebody would see the smoke.

She could use one of the Bunsen burners from the science room and live out the fantasy of half the student body: Northridge Middle School, up in flames. Except Riley wasn't keen on being trapped inside a burning building, and arson seemed like a measure of last resort.

Plus, as creeped out as she was by the flickering lights, she still preferred them to the darkness.

She stood at the intersection looking back and forth, considering her options and reciting poetry in her head, when she heard the footsteps again.

Except these were different. Not the click of dress shoes on tile that she thought she'd heard earlier. This was the shuffle-squeak of sneakers on a laminate floor, the sound of someone skidding to a stop on the court. It was followed by a sharper, shriller sound that was just as unmistakable.

The sound of a whistle.

27

RILEY LEARNED THE TRUTH WHEN SHE WAS ONLY FOUR—THAT SOME things aren't at all like you imagined them. That was when her father broke the news, and nearly broke her heart, at least for an afternoon. It was the day she stopped wanting to be just like him.

And all because of a whistle.

It was a weekday morning. Riley's mother was at work and Riley and her father were crowding the center of the couch watching *Sesame Street* and eating microwave popcorn as a sort of after-breakfast snack. Elmo was talking to a police officer about his job and the officer was showing Elmo some of the things that he carried with him: his radio and his badge and even his handcuffs (though not his gun, Riley noticed. No firearms on the *Street*). He then showed Elmo his whistle and they both took turns blowing it, which caused Oscar to pop up out of his can and start complaining about all the racket. Riley liked Oscar. He was her favorite. Him, or Cookie Monster. Cookie Monster just *got* it.

"That what you use?" Riley asked, pointing at the whistle in Elmo's furry mouth. She meant the one on the train, of course— the shrieks it made whenever it came to a crossing, the loud, wailing warning that could be heard for miles. Her four-year-old self imagined a whistle like the one Elmo was holding but so much bigger, about the size of a watermelon, and her father pressing it to his lips, blowing so hard his cheeks puffed red and his eyes shot out of their sockets, like an old cartoon.

Her dad laughed. "'Fraid not. Trains don't have whistles anymore. We use air horns now—real loud, obnoxious ones. I just press a button and the train honks like a hundred angry geese. *Honk. Honk.* 'Look out, coming through!'" he bellowed.

He made a funny face. He was trying to make Riley laugh, but she pouted instead. This wasn't right. She thought of the wooden train whistle Santa had put in her stocking only a month ago, a skinny block of wood with her own name burned into it in fancy letters. *RILEY.* She knew it wasn't the same as the ones on real trains—not big enough, for starters—but she'd at least imagined they were related. Her wooden toy whistle sounded nothing like a hundred angry geese, though. Not even one angry goose. It sounded more like the music they played on the carousel at the fair.

Her father took in her grouchy face. "I know. It bums me out too sometimes. Those old steam whistles were cool. They'd make different sounds depending on how you tugged the cord. They had personality. The air horns all sound the same. But they get the job done. Most of the time."

"So all you do is press a button?"

Conner Flynn pretended to be offended. "Okay, little miss. I'll have you know I do a lot more than that. Operating a train is hard work. But I guess when it comes to that part, yeah. I just press a button."

Riley gave it some thought. Frowned again. "I don't think I want to be a train driver anymore," she said, turning back to the television with her arms crossed, not realizing that that was the first time her father had heard anything about her wanting to be an engineer to begin with.

He crossed his arms in imitation of hers. "Well, in that case, neither do I," he said. He pretended to watch for five more seconds, waiting to make sure her guard was down. Then he turned and pounced, teeth bared, hands in the shapes of claws, and gave her the full-out belly attack she deserved. "I'm going to be a professional monster tickler instead!" Riley squirmed and squirmed.

She forgave him for the tickling, but she never forgot about the whistle, or how he said he missed the way they used to be. How when things changed, they didn't always change for the better.

On the television, Oscar demanded that Elmo be arrested for disturbing the peace. Even at age four, Riley knew it was impossible to get arrested on Sesame Street. Almost nothing bad ever happened there, and even when it did, it was all fixed by the time the show was over. She guessed that was probably all a bunch of baloney too.

Few things are ever as good as you hope they will be.

28

RILEY MADE HER WAY DOWN THE HALL, THE TRILL OF THE WHISTLE echoing in her head like the last song played on a radio. She pulled open the gym door.

She wasn't surprised to find that the overhead lights were all on. *Should I be?* she wondered. *And what does it mean that I'm not?*

Riley wasn't sure about the answer to that one, but she knew what she'd heard, that piercing shriek that usually meant that it was time to stop horsing around and pay attention as the PE teacher explained what new physical torture awaited them. Riley had despised gym class in elementary school. Not because she was unathletic. A little uncoordinated maybe, but she was the third-fastest girl in her class and she could do twenty push-ups, which was nineteen more than some of the boys and twenty more than Tristan Wales, who bragged in fourth grade about having a six-pack even though it was just his ribs poking through. No, she hated PE because the other kids always took it too seriously. It was as if the moment they entered the gym they became a pack of Neanderthals, hooting and grunting and baring teeth. Someone usually ended up with a bloody knee or elbow rash, and feelings were always bruised.

Of course Riley might have administered a few of those bruises herself. Like the time she rammed into Caroline Silton so hard in sharbade that she knocked the girl off her scooter and then *accidentally*—because it *was* an accident—rolled over Caroline's hand, sending her to the nurse. Of course Caroline had called her pathetic for not making a shot only moments before, but nobody else in Riley's class heard *that*. They'd only heard Caroline's wailing, shouting that Riley had broken every finger.

They could all see the ice pack that poor Caroline kept on those swollen fingers for the rest of the day as well, and Riley didn't miss any of the dirty looks shot her way, especially from Missy Reynolds, who was suddenly Caroline's new best friend. Thankfully by the end of the week Caroline's mashed digits were fine and the incident was mostly forgotten. Probably because it didn't leave a mark.

Leaving a mark was so much worse.

Riley tucked her flashlight into the front pocket of her jeans and took a few tentative steps into the gym. "Is there somebody in here? Mrs. Robards?" Mrs. Robards was the only athletic coach she knew by name. She'd been Riley's sixth-grade science teacher and was the one who suggested Riley try out for the tennis team instead of the soccer team. That was before summer camp proved what a bad idea *that* would be. "Hello? Someone in here?"

Hours ago the gym had likely been full of sweaty bodies, Grace and her volleyball friends with their short shorts and elbow pads bumping and spiking, pointing and hollering. Now it was empty, save for a couple of wrestling mats stacked against the far wall and a rack full of basketballs that someone had left out by the bleachers. Along that same back wall sat an office, the boys' and girls' locker rooms, and another set of double doors that led to the parking lot and the football field beyond. The lights to the office as well as both locker rooms appeared to be off.

Riley crossed the court, her boots making audible clicks with every step. You weren't supposed to wear boots like hers on the gym floor—might leave scuff marks. Then again, you probably weren't supposed to try and break windows with the school's beloved tree sculpture either. Not to mention locking other students in closets and leaving them alone with a ghost frog.

Not a ghost frog, Riley corrected herself. *A ghost* inside *a frog.*

179

It was an important distinction: the frog had croaked and moved on, but Max was still here, *stuck* here, just like her.

Or so he said.

Riley stopped in front of the gym's exit—another set of doors with push bars that looked like they could only be locked from the inside. "Please open," she whispered, leaning her full weight into one, thinking maybe it was simply a matter of brute force, that a girl who could do twenty push-ups might just be able to muscle her way through solid metal. But the door didn't give. She spat a long string of cuss words, the kind you would find scratched into the yellow paint of a bathroom stall, then leaned her head against the door.

She was never getting out of here.

Why is this happening to me?

She shut her eyes and tried to imagine she was somewhere else. At home on the couch with her mom, flipping through magazines. Sitting in the car with her dad, trying to teach him the words to the latest Rihanna song.

Slouched on the bench next to Em, squinting through the brain freeze and fighting over the last chunk of Oreo.

Floating on a lake in the middle of the night, staring up at the stars with nobody around.

Anywhere but here.

"Give it back."

Riley's head snapped up and whipped around, taking in the empty gym, seeking the source of the voice she'd just heard.

"Max?"

No Max. At least not in the vessel that he'd picked for himself. But the voice was like Max's in that it was at once inside her head yet coming from somewhere else, not so much heard as remembered.

This voice, however, was a young girl's.

"Give it back to me," the voice cried out again. Riley scanned the back wall, past the office with the lights still off and over to the girls' locker room. The voice seemed to be coming from that direction.

She shuffled toward it, pausing between each step, waiting to hear it again, until she stood a few feet from the entrance, thumbs looped through the straps of her backpack, trying to see around the corner. "Is somebody in there?" Riley called. "Hello?" She started to take a step inside.

Thump.

Riley jumped, startled, spinning to see that one of the basketballs had tumbled off the top of the cart and was now dribbling slowly across the hardwood floor, matching her heartbeat. *Thump-thump-thump,* each bounce smaller than the last— *thumpthumpthumpthumpthump*—until it began to roll toward the basket. Riley tracked it, her body stiff. It finally came to a stop directly underneath the net on the north side of the gym.

Gust of wind. Must've been. Kicked up and knocked the ball off the cart.

In a room with no windows.

That did it. Riley didn't want to be in the gym any longer. She managed only one step, however, before more voices— different voices—hit her from opposite directions. Young voices, like hers. Like the ones in the cafeteria that seemed to dance and circle and jab, these voices were filled with laughter, but Riley could make out words this time.

"As if you need it."

"What a joke."

"Check this out."

These new voices all sounded like girls as well, some like girls she knew, hauntingly familiar. Then came the same voice from before, pleading.

"What are you doing? Stop! Give it back!"

The laughter undulated, louder and then softer before rising again, coming first from the direction of the locker room, but then from all around. Riley felt her whole body listing dizzily, rocked one way and then the other. The voices continued to grow. There were boys' voices now, laughing and shouting, and the one girl's voice, louder than the rest, furious. Frantic.

"Here. Toss it."

"I've got this."

"Just give it!"

"Let me try."

"Let go!"

Riley's head erupted with the sound of cheering. She spun around, hands cupping her ears, until her eyes locked onto something on the north backboard, dangling from the peeling orange rim. Something that Riley clearly hadn't noticed before. Because it most definitely hadn't *been* there before.

It was a training bra, not that different from the kind Riley had started to wear over the summer, hanging half in and half out of the hoop. All white, except that someone had written on it, in black marker across the front, the ink soaked in, making the letters dark and puffy. And even though it was hard to make out from so far away, Riley knew what it said, because she'd seen those same words scrawled somewhere else.

NOTHING TO SEE HERE

Riley felt a quick, sharp pain behind her eyes that made them shut, and suddenly she could picture it as clear as any memory of her own, like a movie projected onto the inside of her skull.

One girl sitting by herself at the edge of the wooden bench, away from the rest. Riley could only see her from the back, the dark brown hair, approaching black and longer than Riley's, the angular shoulders, the pale, skinny arms. The bigger group of girls whispering, scheming behind her. The comments, clichéd but cutting. Then it happens in a flash.

Stop. Give it back.

The giggles circulate around the girls' locker room. A game of keep-away. Someone produces a black marker, capital letters, bleeding into the fabric. Then another girl runs out of the locker room with the bra, ruined now, waving it like a flag.

The boys, basketballs already in hand, turn and stare. It takes them a minute to realize what they are looking at. To decide what to do. Whether to join in or stand back. Those are the only options—no one's going to stop it. The thief hands off the bra like a baton and the laughter transfers with it. Infectious, it spreads. It's just a joke. That's what they tell themselves. A harmless joke.

The girl comes out, wearing her T-shirt and jeans, tears already stinging her eyes. She can taste blood from biting the inside of her cheek. She launches herself at the pack of boys, reaches for her stolen bra, but the boys are quicker. They pass it back and forth between them. One boy looks up and sees the hoop. Calls for a pass. Wads up the bra and takes a shot. He misses. The girl tries to grab it from the floor but she's too slow. Someone snatches it out from under her.

Let me try.

And this time the shot goes. Up and in, getting hung up on

the rim. But the basket counts. Everyone cheers. Loud enough to finally pull the teacher out of his office. The whistle causes the boys to scatter so no one takes the blame.

Leaving the girl standing alone underneath the basket. Sick to her stomach. Sobbing, broken.

Nothing to see here.

29

RILEY WAS NO STRANGER TO EMBARRASSMENT. SHE KNEW HOW IT felt to want to be somewhere else. Anywhere else.

Like that day at the Kohl's. Mid-May. The calendar lurching slowly but surely toward the end of the school year, the temperature inching up past eighty. Riley's mother had been blessed in the mail with a 30-percent-off coupon, which meant it was time for the Flynns to augment their summer wardrobes. Amanda Flynn got caught up looking at breezy dresses—a far cry from her scrubs—so Riley got to wander off on her own.

That's how she found herself in the swimsuit section, staring at an expensive stripey two-piece, while also snatching furtive glances across the aisle at the shoe section.

And the boy standing there.

She didn't recognize him. He was clearly older than her. A high school freshman, perhaps. Or even a sophomore. Curly hair. Dark eyes. Wearing a shirt that seemed tight on purpose. He was staring at his phone—no doubt stuck here with his parents like she was and bored out of his mind. He must have been watching something good, because he smiled and laughed. Then he looked up and caught Riley's eye.

The smile held.

And Riley melted just a little around the edges. He was only being polite, she knew, but even as she looked away, she imagined otherwise. That his smile was directed at her. That she had prompted it.

"Bikini, huh?"

Riley startled, turning to see her mother standing right behind her. The woman could be so stealthy sometimes. Like a ninja. A nosy, annoying ninja who constantly gives unasked-for advice and nags you about leaving your wet towel on the floor.

"I was just looking," Riley said, her eyes darting to the boy, who was staring at his phone again and then back to her mother. She thought she was quick enough. She wasn't.

"Do we know him?"

Riley shook her head, then pretended to flip through some more swimsuit tops, the one still hanging off her wrist, her back to that boy that *we* didn't know, hoping, praying the conversation was over. Her mom continued to steal glances at him, though.

"He's a hottie," she said in a knowing, under-the-breath voice. "Do they still say that? Hottie?"

Riley groaned. Continued to flip. Not really even looking, just trying to tune her mother out.

"What is it, then? Heartthrob? Hunk? Stud? Am I close? I'm getting colder, aren't I?"

"Would you please stop?" Riley hissed. "Somebody's going to hear you."

"Nobody is going to hear me."

"*I* have to hear you. That's enough." She glared at her mother now, careful to keep her eyes locked on, not let them stray back to the aisle, afraid the boy might still be standing there, that he might be watching them.

"What? It's perfectly normal for you to be checking guys out," her mother whispered.

"I'm not 'checking anyone out,'" Riley said, changing her voice to imitate her mother's deeper tone. "I don't even know him. He's just some guy."

"I know. Of course." Her mother's voice was softer now, but more serious. "I'm just saying, you're getting older. And things are happening. Like . . . biological things. Changes."

Riley's face, already a warm pink, suddenly blazed a blood-red. She could feel her armpits dampening. She spoke through gritted teeth, her voice a low growl. "Oh my god, will you just stop? We're standing in the middle of the freaking Kohl's!"

Her mother put a hand on her arm. "You're right. Of course. This isn't the time or the place. I just wanted to say that I noticed you noticing . . . and that if there are things that you *wanted* to talk about—"

"None. No things," Riley snipped, brushing the hand off. "Believe me, there's absolutely nothing that I want to talk with you about, okay? Can we just go already?" She shoved the bikini back on the rack with an unsatisfyingly angry click, then turned sharply, her head down, bangs shielding her eyes, but not so much that she didn't notice that the boy who started this whole thing was already gone. She glanced back to see if her mother was following or just letting her storm off to the car and saw her take the striped bikini back off and put it in the cart.

Riley spent the entire drive home not saying a word. Even though part of her wanted to.

Because her mother was right—though she hated to admit it. There were things Riley wanted to talk about. Personal things. Confusing things. Private things. Changes, yes. So many, and all so fast. And not just the kind her mother was thinking about. Across the board it seemed like everything was in flux, the very ground shifting under her. But these were conversations she wanted to have in her room with the door shut, sitting cross-legged on one end of the bed with a pillow in her lap. Across from a friend who was just as curious and confused as she was.

Except the person she had in mind didn't come and sit on Riley's bed anymore. In fact, Emily hadn't been to Riley's house in over three weeks. Their conversations, once so rambling and easy and full of secrets and suppositions, now seemed strained. Riley couldn't bring herself to ask Emily if she thought Adrian Rosales, the new transfer student, was cute. Or if she thought it was time for Riley to start wearing a trainer. She couldn't imagine talking to Emily about hormones or making out or any of the things her mother the nurse was prepared to give her awkward lectures about. Couldn't imagine the uncomfortable looks that her friend—were they still even friends really?—would give her, even though Emily was probably having all these same conversations with her other friends—the ones she sat with, laughed with, whispered with—all the time now.

Doing it all without her.

When they got back to the house, Riley silently got out of the car and her mother wordlessly handed her her new bikini. Riley took it upstairs to her room, shoved it in a drawer of her dresser, still on the hanger, and slammed the drawer shut. Then she sat on her bed, cross-legged, staring out her window as two boys played football in the street.

30

IT WAS COMING. AND THERE WAS NOTHING SHE COULD DO TO STOP IT.

She could feel the surge in her belly, the ripple up her esophagus. She looked around for a wastebasket, a cardboard box sitting out for recycling, a container of any kind. There was another bathroom down the hall, but she knew she wouldn't make it in time, and she wasn't keen on going in there after what she'd seen last time. The sick burned its way out of her, scorching her throat and filling her nose with its rotten tang, which only caused her stomach to lurch again, a second heave, splashing the floor between her feet as she doubled over, head pressed to the walls, the sound of her retching carrying down the hall.

Her head pulsed. Her heart pounded.

What is happening to me?

Riley looked down at the puddle of vomit, some of it smattering her boots. Somewhere, in the pocket of her brain that still registered rational thoughts, she felt a twinge of guilt at the mess she'd made. *Mr. Graham, your assistance is needed for a bazooka-belly-blow outside the gymnasium.* Nobody likes to lose their lunch in school—it's the kind of thing you can be laughed at or whispered about for the rest of the year. Riley the Retcher. Taste-It-Again-Flynn. She knew how these things went.

Riley wiped her chin on her sleeve and stumbled woozily toward the exit at the end of the hall, suppressing another wave of nausea. She knew it wouldn't open, knew deep down in the pit of her now-empty stomach, but she tried it anyway, because she was desperate. Lost. Confused.

Alone.

She didn't kick this time. She didn't shout or curse or slam her palms against the cold metal. Instead she let her book bag slip off her shoulders, slumping to the floor alongside it. She pressed her sweat-soaked back against the door and felt her legs buckle like they were made of tissue, her head back, eyes closed.

She thought of her mother. The phone call she'd surely missed by now. How much longer would it be till someone realized that Riley Flynn wasn't where she was supposed to be?

You've got nobody.

Riley kept her eyes closed as she drew her knees to her chest, wrapping her arms around them and burying her face in the gap they made. She wanted to sink into that hole and vanish, to crawl through it and appear somewhere else, on the other side of these walls.

The noises were out of her head, at least. The footsteps, the shouting, the laughter. Even the images were fading, which was strange because they felt so much like her own memory, so immediate and intense, and yet already they were starting to blur. She could barely even remember what the girl looked like—that poor girl standing all by herself beneath the basketball hoop. Riley could no longer conjure her face, but the anger and shame lingered, almost as tangible as the awful taste on her tongue.

It had happened here, at this school. That Riley was sure of. But not in her time. The glimpse she'd been given, it was of the same gym, but there were fewer banners on the walls, the paint a different shade, the scoreboard smaller and without the advertisement for Stiner's Chevrolet. Was it a memory? And if so, whose? The images had been dreamlike, fleeting, but the voice had sounded so familiar. So real.

Give it back.

She thought back to the writing on the bathroom stall. The laughter in the cafeteria so similar to the mocking giggles emanating from the locker room, the message the same.

"I told you."

Riley jerked her head up. Her eyes, salty with tears, looked over her knees at the frog sitting only ten feet away. She hadn't heard him approach.

"It's only going to get worse."

His voice sounded different than before. Bitter, angry. Riley stared as if she was seeing him for the first time, hunched there, held together by tape, so small, so fragile. But she couldn't stop herself from shaking, because she knew he was so much more. She wasn't sure what he was capable of, but she was certain *what* he was now. There was no point denying it.

The smell of her own sick hit her all over again. "How could it get worse?"

Max's voice cut straight into her. *"You have no idea."*

It sounded like a threat. Riley studied the vessel hunched before her, and though she saw nothing in the frog's vacant milky eyes, she could *feel* him here, so close to her, and it chilled her. "It's you, isn't it? This is all *your* fault." Riley sat up. The rush she had felt in the gym—the surge of some other girl's anger and shame—gave way to Riley's own, her fear transforming, turning

194

from cold to hot, taking control of her as it had too many times before. Without really thinking, she reached for her backpack and pulled it toward her, making sure she had a firm grip on each side, raising it like a soccer ball up over her head and throwing it at the ghost as hard as she could.

The frog moved fast, faster than Riley would have thought possible given his gimpy leg. The backpack skidded harmlessly along the floor, missing its target by inches.

Riley pulled herself to her feet, shaking off another wave of dizziness. She slammed the palm of her hand against the smooth metal behind her, keeping her eyes on Max. "Open this door."

"I can't," Max said evenly.

"You're lying!" Riley spat. "I know what you are. I know what you can do. I know what you've done. Now open this door!"

"I already told you—I'm not the one keeping you here."

Riley twisted violently, slamming her body into the door again, pounding with both fists. "OPEN THE GODDAM DOOR!"

"I'm sorry," Max said after a beat. *"I would. I want to. But it's out of my control."*

Riley turned and looked at Max, all her frustration and fear boiling into a white-hot anger. There was no counting. No deep breaths. The frog sat less than ten feet away, a distance she closed

195

in three forceful strides, raising her right foot high, the thick heel of her boot poised.

"*Riley, wait—*"

Bringing it down quickly, but not quick enough. The dead frog jumped out of the shadow of her bootheel.

"*You don't understand—*"

He was inside her skull. She heard him, but she wasn't listening. Her boot came down again, stomping the empty space where Max had been only a half second before. "Let me out of here!" she screamed.

"*Listen to me.*" Stomp. "*I can't . . .*" Stomp. "*let . . .*" Stomp. "*you . . .*" Stomp. "*. . . go!*"

Riley chased after the frog frantically leaping down the hall, trying to smash him under her bootheel like a toddler squashing bugs on the blacktop, until she cornered him in the entryway of a classroom, backed against the door.

"*Riley, please. I swear to you. It's not me!*"

She swooped down, quickly covering him with both hands the way she'd done with a wounded rabbit two years ago. She could feel what remained of the frog's insides shifting beneath her fingers. She could smell the delayed decay surfacing in its leathery skin. Its bulbous white throat quivered and she squeezed harder, wondering how hard she would have to squeeze before he split right back open, right through the tape, guts spilling out over her hands, squishing between her fingers.

"What are you going to do?" Max's voice echoed in her head. *"Kill me?"*

Riley hesitated.

"Go ahead. Do it. Squeeze until these eyeballs pop. Won't change a thing. I'll still be right here, stuck in the same place. And so will you."

Her fingers tingled. It would be easy to snap his spine, to feel it splinter.

"I don't believe you. I know what you are," she repeated. "I know what you're doing."

"You think you know," Max replied. *"But you're wrong."*

What did she know? That she was trapped. That she was alone. That someone was keeping her here, someone with a power she didn't understand. But if not Max, then who?

"Tell me what's going on! What's happening here? What *did* happen here?"

The frog's lids closed over its hollow black eyes. The voice in Riley's head stilled. She shook him with both hands. "Answer me!"

Outside of her own head, Riley heard the click of metal against metal coming from the far end of the hall by the gym doors. Riley knew that click. She heard it dozens of times each day, enough that she'd learned to tune it out. But here, in the dead silence of the empty school, it was impossible to ignore.

In her hands she felt the frog twitch. Max opened its dead eyes again.

"She's coming," he said.

31

"SHE'LL BE HERE SHORTLY."

Riley lay on the cot in the nurse's station clenching her finger, willing herself to throw up. She felt like she might; she'd nearly convinced herself, but her body wouldn't cooperate, not without sticking a finger down her throat, and she just didn't have the guts to go that far.

The school nurse smiled politely. No doubt she knew Riley was faking it. No fever. No clammy skin. No loss of color. Just a girl with her hands on her stomach complaining of pain, trying to get out of class for some reason. A test? A presentation? Forgotten homework? The nurse applied the usual remedy—took Riley's temperature, a cool washcloth, fifteen minutes on the cot in the dark. But when asked if she was feeling better, Riley mustered a pathetic moan and shook her head as if she couldn't bear to open her mouth. That's when she asked if Riley wanted to call someone to come get her.

There was no way the nurse could have known what was really wrong, what had caused Riley's stomach to ache for real. But she was right about one thing: Riley was avoiding going back to her classroom. Not because of a test or unfinished work, but because of what had happened on the playground. And what Riley had done about it.

She could still smell it somehow.

It started with the animal crackers, smuggled out of her lunch box and brought outside. Lunch wasn't until 12:15, but fourth grade had recess at 10:30, and Riley had had stomach-grumbling visions of snapping the crisp heads off cracker giraffes all morning.

So when it was her turn for one of the playground's six swings, she pulled the Ziploc baggie from her pocket, keeping it mostly concealed in the flap of her jacket, sneaking lions and monkeys one at a time and chewing them slowly, imperceptibly, as she went through the motions of kicking her legs. She kept her back to the teachers and to the shouts of the kickball game in the parking lot. She tuned it all out.

She couldn't see Daniel Delano whispering to his friends. She didn't know he was even there until he shouted, "Time to fly, Flynn," grabbing both chains and pulling her back before pushing as hard as he could. She had no choice but to grab the chains as well, both hands clenched, shrieking as her legs flew out in a desperate attempt to catch the crackers she wasn't supposed to have. The bag catapulted from her lap, landing on the ground, most of its remaining contents scattered in the mulch.

Riley dug in her heels, skidded to a stop, and jumped from the swing, rounding on Daniel, who was laughing with his friends.

"Look what you did!" Riley pointed to the menagerie of crackers half buried in the mulch, like dinosaurs sinking in a tar pit. Riley didn't care for Daniel Delano. He was a prankster and a cutup and was all the more popular for it. His mother sat on the Board of Education and he thought that gave him a longer leash when it came to his teachers. It certainly seemed that way to Riley; the boy could get away with anything.

In that moment, though, she didn't care how long his leash was or where his mother sat. She only cared that her morning snack had been ruined.

"Chill. I was only playing," Daniel said. Some of the other kids from her class had gathered now, including Missy and Sharonda. Pretty soon the little mob would get the attention of the only teacher on patrol. The girl who had been waiting for the next available swing decided she would go slide instead.

"Besides, food's not allowed out here," Daniel added, suddenly defensive.

Butt-faced jerkwads aren't allowed out here either, Riley thought, *yet here* you *are*.

"You owe me a pack of animal crackers" was what she said.

Daniel laughed, then pointed at the ground. "Just eat those." He bent down and rescued a lion from the mulch, flecks of dirt clinging to it, and pressed it up to her face. "C'mon. A little dirt's not gonna kill you." It was almost touching her lips, which were locked tight. The other kids started to giggle. Missy arched an eyebrow in expectation.

Riley snatched the cracker from his hand and threw it back at him. It bounced harmlessly off his chest.

Daniel laughed. "Ouch."

He made it *seem* like a joke. A game. Kids like him got away with stuff like this all the time. *Just messing around.* Like it was her fault for not playing along. Like *she* was the one overreacting. And she struggled with finding something to say that wouldn't just make it worse.

What she *really* wanted was to deck him. Lay him out right there in the mulch. But she knew the penalties for fighting: phone calls, suspensions, meetings with the principal, not to mention the looks on her parents' faces. She didn't need that.

Any of it. So Riley gathered up her baggie with only three crackers left and stalked away, ignoring the sighs of disappointment from the cluster of kids who would have rather seen her at least eat the cracker if not throw a punch.

Riley's whole body hummed. And the farther she walked from the swings the worse it got, the initial anger at Daniel turning to resentment and doubt. Why did she just walk away? Why did she back down? She should have made *him* eat it instead. Put him in a headlock and pinned him to the ground and shoved that lion straight up his nose. She could take him; he wasn't that much bigger than her. She retreated to the fence surrounding the playground where a few other kids were loafing, wrapping their fingers around the metal links and staring through the holes like convicts in a prison yard.

Let it go, Riley. It's no big deal. It's not worth getting worked up about. Her mother's voice. Calm. Collected. Always so reasonable. Riley looked back over her shoulder to see that Daniel and the other boys were picking the crackers off the ground, daring each other to eat them now. But that was different. They were laughing *with* each other.

She turned back to the fence. *Not worth it, not worth it, not worth it*, she repeated.

That's when she noticed it. The pile just on the opposite side of the chain links, well within arm's reach.

Dog poop. Black as tar and shaped sort of like a croissant, still fresh judging by the pungent whiff she got when she bent down to inspect it.

It looked a little bit like fate.

Riley looked at the Ziploc bag clenched tight in her hand.

When the whistle blew five minutes later and the kids gathered by the door, Riley kept a straight face, despite the load weighing down her jacket pocket. She'd been careful not to touch it, inside-outing the bag first and using it as a glove, only smearing a little in the collection process. But the thought of the sealed bag and what was inside it, mashably soft and repugnant, filled her with dread. And a sort of sickly satisfaction.

Daniel's cubby was only two down from hers, with his Avengers backpack dangling from the hook and his jacket balled up underneath. As luck would have it, the main pocket of the backpack was already partially unzipped, providing easy access.

She waited until most of the other kids had put their jackets away and took advantage of the post-recess chaos—the sharpening of pencils, the slamming of desks—to make her deposit, prying open the baggie and squeezing from the bottom, feeling the dog turd tumble free.

She could make it worse, she thought. She could give the backpack a good hug, guaranteeing maximum coverage, but that seemed like a step too far. Instead she calmly disposed of the baggie, tucking it in the trash can, making sure to bury it under some used tissues and Mrs. Landry's Starbucks cup. Then she just as calmly washed her hands at the classroom sink using two healthy squirts of antibacterial soap—citrus scented—and took her seat.

Daniel Delano's desk was in the opposite corner of the room. He had his back to her, but she could see him just fine. She waited for him to look around. She wanted him to catch her eye. To see how composed and collected she was. To see that she was over it, bygones and whatever. It would be her alibi—that cool expression—when she had to deny all wrongdoing.

And yet, as she sat there listening to Mrs. Landry yammer about fractions, Riley felt an itch work its way up the back of her legs and down along her arms. She sniffed once. Twice. She looked around the room. Did Missy Reynolds just wrinkle her nose?

Riley could smell it. She brought her fingers up to her face but only got a whiff of orange zest and glycerin. It wasn't on her, but it was all around her. She glanced back at the cubbies. It was definitely getting stronger, seeping out, permeating the air. How could the other kids not smell that? Ajay Patel sneezed. Riley kept her hands pressed to her cheeks so that she could keep the soapy scent close, but it was no use. The stench of fresh dog feces haunted her, made her stomach tight. The smug smile she'd been wearing since she came in from recess vanished.

This was a mistake. She felt it. But there was no taking it back now, even if she wanted to. There was no way she could fish the turd out of Daniel's backpack without him—or someone, at least—knowing. The only way to undo what she'd done was to own up to it, to raise her hand and confess. Maybe Mrs. Landry would be lenient, especially if she told the teacher what Daniel had done to her on the playground.

Riley considered herself a principled person.

She raised her hand.

"Yes, Riley?" Mrs. Landry leveled her with a slightly suspicious stare.

"I think I'm gonna throw up. Can I go down to the nurse?"

And so there she found herself. Lying on a cot with an uncomfortably moist washcloth on her forehead and something foul gnawing away at her insides, wondering if anyone in her fifth-grade class had discovered the source of the smell yet. Wondering if Mrs. Landry had peered into Daniel's backpack herself, or made him do it. Wondering if her mother would come get her in time to escape before the you-know-what hit the fan.

The problem with principles is that sometimes they contradict each other. One tells you to stand up for yourself. The other tells you to turn the other cheek. One says to inform the teacher. The other says don't be a tattletale. One says to own up to your mistakes. The other says to stay out of trouble. Sometimes the right thing to do isn't always the best.

And Daniel really had asked for it.

Riley heard a familiar voice talking to the nurse on the other side of the curtain. She could see her mother's white Converse sneakers underneath.

She was here.

Riley, for the moment, was saved.

32

"*IT'S TOO LATE. SHE'S HERE.*"

Riley followed the frog's gaze to the end of the hall. She didn't see anything. Then again, it was possible Max could see things that she couldn't. Possible he could do all sorts of things that she couldn't, which was why she'd been about to squeeze the guts back out of him. But now her anger was suddenly sapped, the cold, certain terror taking its place again. What if he was right? What if he *wasn't* the only thing haunting these halls?

"I don't—" Riley began but was cut off by the low rusty moan of the last locker at the end of the hall slowly swinging open.

Crereee.

The sound caused every nerve in Riley's body to light up.

Her words caught in her throat as she stared at the now-open locker, waiting for something to come crawling out of it. Some monster or demon or an army of half-dissected frogs. Waiting to see a gnarled, rotted hand curl around the edge of the door, its jagged fingernails caked brown with dried blood like in one of her father's stories. But the yellow door simply hung there, revealing nothing.

Then she caught movement, not from the already open locker, but from one across the hall, the dial combination spinning on its own, as if twirled by some unseen hand. Quick revolutions. Right. Left. Right. Another metallic click reached her as the handle lifted. Another long creak as the locker opened.

Riley unconsciously let her fingers go lax, and, sensing his chance, the frog squeezed free, leaping to the floor and landing awkwardly, immediately making his way down the hall in the opposite direction from the two open lockers.

"Max! Wait!"

She took a step after him, but then froze as all the dials on *all* the lockers started to spin. Up and down the hall. Every locker, all at once, turning one way and then the other in unison. Riley watched, horrified and mesmerized, as combinations were completed on both sides of her, in front and behind, even past the T where the lights were still off.

There was a pause, long enough for Riley to try and swallow

before realizing her mouth was too dry, before the simultaneous *click* of two hundred metal lockers unlatching then swinging open at once, like a choreographed routine. Two hundred quiet screams of old hinges in an empty hall.

These were followed by a voice. A new one. Definitely not Max's.

"Did you hear what happened?"

And another.

"Well, you saw what she did."

And still more.

"She totally deserves it."

"What a freak."

"What a loser."

Riley spun around. All different voices, seemingly coming from the hollows of the lockers themselves, first on one side of the hall, then the other, moving closer. A hundred metal mouths hung open. The voices sounded conspiratorial—the hushed murmur of people talking with their backs turned.

"You had to see it coming."

"So awkward."

"So weird."

"What's her damage anyway?"

Riley stood in the middle of the hall, paralyzed. The voices built as they approached, like a wave gathering strength, as if each locker held a secret, a revelation. First a few, then a dozen, then so many more, all talking over each other until the murmuring became a roar in her head.

"*Gone.*"

"*Thank god.*"

"*Good riddance.*"

Riley jumped, accidentally biting her tongue as the sound of one of the locker doors suddenly slamming shut again struck her. It sounded like a gunshot, but even the echoing clang of metal against metal didn't stop the whispers from growing louder still.

"*Freak.*"

"*Loser.*"

"*Lamoid.*"

Another slam, as the locker directly opposite the first clanged shut with sudden force. And another. And another, down both hallways now, the locker doors crashing closed as if a tornado was sweeping down the hall. The sound rattled Riley's teeth. Coming closer.

Slam. Slam. Slam.

Loser. Freak. Weirdo.

Riley's paralysis finally broke and she started to run, abandoning her backpack in the middle of the hallway from where she'd launched it at Max, heading for the intersection where half the lights were still off, the smash of lockers closing in behind her. She kept going, plunging into the darkness, not even know-ing who or what she was running from. *Freak. Loser. Pathetic.*

Good riddance.

Riley turned the corner into the adjoining hallway, almost pitch-black, but at least the lockers were closed, as was every door.

Except one.

That was the door Riley ducked through, hoping to escape whatever was chasing her, calling out to her, mocking her—the sound of dozens of slamming lockers filling the halls, like the roar of some metallic monster on the prowl.

Looking for easy prey.

33

IN TRUTH, RILEY KNEW SHE WAS A MONSTER.

Her father always told her so. Starting when she was little. While her mother fretted over her daughter's sudden temper tantrums and penchant for making trouble, Conner Flynn often laughed it off. If the offense was minor—thrown broccoli, a scribbled wall, a dirty look—he would gobble her up in his arms and say, "You little monster" before commencing to zerbert her into submission or swing her upside down by her ankles. It was better than her mother's reaction, which was to stick Riley in the corner with her nose anchored to the wall, a punishment administered so liberally that eventually Riley could identify every corner of her house by smell alone.

She also—eventually—grew out of her terrible toddlerhood,

though her quick-fire temper remained. And so did her father's nickname for her.

"Go get 'em, monster," he'd say the morning before a big test. "How's my little monster today?" "Did my monster miss me while I was gone?" He always said it with adoration and a playful growl, but underneath, Riley could sense something else, an apprehension, a kind of impending sadness for the day when she wouldn't be his little monster anymore.

It wouldn't be a sad day for her, she thought. Riley never liked the nickname, though she never said so. Not to him. She didn't hate it, at least. She knew there were far worse things to be called.

Like the time the kids at school caught her crying. The only time they ever caught her crying.

Kids cried all the time in school. The third graders cried when they got a paper cut. The second graders cried when the book they wanted was checked out by someone else. The first graders cried when they noticed their shoes were untied. The kindergartners cried because it was Tuesday. But once you got to the fourth and fifth grade, it started to change. You learned to suck it up. You could pout and roll your eyes and bang your chair and glare until your eyeballs dried out. You could write nasty notes or scratch mean graffiti into your desk. But you didn't cry.

Even if you got knocked down on the playground, you pulled yourself up and brushed the grass off your knees and the mulch out of your hair and held it in until you could be alone.

And so, when Kaylee Riser caught Riley crying in the bathroom after lunch one day, it followed her all the way back to class. Had it been Janira or Gabby or one of the quieter girls who'd found her, they might have stopped and asked her what was wrong. But not Kaylee. Kaylee was part of Missy's group. She saw Riley with her head hung over the sink, red-cheeked and sobbing, and immediately shared it with everyone else. Before the day was over, Riley had a new nickname.

Cryly Flynn.

Of course nobody knew what Riley had even been crying about or even bothered to ask. Not that she would have told them about the fight with her mother the night before, her mom blowing up about some missing homework, delivering a lecture about how Riley needed to apply herself and stop making excuses. How Riley responded by saying she wished Dad were here and that she—Riley's mother—was the one who was gone all the time. How she'd run up the stairs and slammed her bedroom door hard enough to knock one of the framed family photos off the wall, refusing to open it, even when her mother knocked.

And then the note that she'd found in her lunch bag. Scribbled on a yellow Post-it.

Riley—
I know I can be hard on you sometimes.
I only want what's best for you.
I love you no matter what.
Eat your carrots.
— Mom

It was the carrots that got her. She couldn't say why. Maybe because her father never made her clean her plate. Probably because he knew Mom would. He could be the cooler parent when he was around—because he wasn't always around. He could pick her up and swing her around and call her monster and forgive her for everything instantly, so there was no reason to ever be mad at him.

Her mother, on the other hand, was an easy target. It wasn't fair, Riley knew, but her anger didn't always stop to ask what was fair.

That day at lunch, Riley sat by herself. She ate as many carrots as she could stomach, and then she went to the bathroom and cried, thinking about what she'd said, how she'd wished her mother away. That's when Kaylee caught her.

Cryly Flynn. Cryly Flynn. Say her name she cries again.

Two weeks. That's how long the name stuck. Except nobody ever caught her crying again. Cussing, yes. Kicking. Glaring. Spitting. Pouting. Sneering. And things even worse than those. But never crying. She showed her anger. Her disgust. Her disappointment. But never her sadness. She learned to bottle that one, shelve it, store it—at least until she could make it to the bathroom stall and lock the door and keep her feet up where nobody would know it was her. And even then she would always remember to dry her face before opening the door.

Nothing to see here.

34

RILEY SLAMMED THE DOOR, MUFFLING THE CADENCE OF THE lockers, coming closer at first, and then diminishing, like a train barreling along the tracks before click-clacking off into the distance.

She held tight to the handle, waiting for something else—the door she was leaning against to blow right off its hinges, perhaps, or the handle to twist out of her grip by some unseen force working on it from the other side. But the room stayed quiet, and Riley allowed herself a deep breath. Even in the near-total darkness, even with the poster of a fat orange cat obscured by shadows, Riley recognized the room she'd escaped to. The smell of it welcomed her, told her that she was somewhere safe.

At least, she'd always considered it safe. In the almost year and a half that she'd been at Northridge, this had been one of the few places she'd felt welcome. Part of it was the books—a constant comfort with their promises of escape. Partly the welcoming smiles of Mrs. Grissolm and Ms. Lang, who'd stopped asking why Riley was there on the third or fourth visit. But mostly it seemed safe because it was hardly ever used. Some days the library was nearly deserted—that's when she loved it most.

But not now. Now she would have given anything to see another human being. Even Chris Winters's arrogant, annoying face would have been a welcome sight, split lip and all.

Riley kept her back to the door and took in the empty space around her, eyes readjusting to the darkness. A bank of windows lined the back wall, the same kind as in the classrooms, letting in some little light from the streetlamps in the parking lot. That meager glow was enough for Riley to make out familiar shapes: desks and tables, the center aisle of computers, the slowly expiring sofa hemorrhaging stuffing from its open wounds, the shelves and shelves of books. In the darkness, though, even these familiar sights looked off to her somehow. Things that normally made her smile, like the row of stuffed animals on the shelf behind Mrs. Grissolm's desk, took on a grim countenance. Pete the Cat's comically grumpy face looked almost malevolent, his marble eyes catching a glint of light and reflecting it back at her. The Very Hungry Caterpillar looked like it wanted to eat her.

Maybe there were no safe spaces.

Riley pulled away from the door and became suddenly conscious of her empty shoulders. Her backpack was still in B-hall where she'd thrown it at the frog. *Stupid, impulsive.* She would have to go back for it. Or not. She still had her flashlight, at least, though it struggled somewhat against the gloom. She tried the bank of lights against the wall first, just in case, flipping them up and down to no effect. Like the windows and the doors, the phones and the fire alarm, the lights were operating under someone else's control. Max's perhaps.

Or not.

She's coming.

Riley took the flashlight from her pocket and used it to scan the dark patches of the room, keeping the beam low, sweeping the floor. "Max? Are you in here?"

No reply. Maybe it shouldn't surprise her. Less than five minutes ago she'd tried to mash the ghost's already broken vessel into the polished floor. He'd disappeared, jumping down the hall as fast as his dead legs would carry him.

But not from me. He wasn't running from me. I'm not the one he's afraid of.

Riley knew what real fear sounded like. She'd heard it in her mother's voice on the phone the night of the train wreck. She'd heard a quiver of it in Grace's nasal whine the moment

Riley slapped her. The hesitation. The hard swallow. The stutter. She'd even heard it in Max's echoing voice. The moment when the worst you can imagine suddenly becomes possible. When you can almost see it. Feel it even. When it's right there, just behind you, chasing you through your school, driving you into the library, shivering, alone, with not one but two spirits out there haunting the hallways, filling your head with voices and visions.

Guess there are worse places. After all, didn't Mrs. Grissolm always tell her that libraries were portals to other worlds? And if Riley ever needed a portal in her life . . . She zigzagged her flashlight beam along the shelves, not even sure what she was looking for. Across the walls and windows, over the stacked chairs, back to the checkout station, and up to the round-faced clock, where she paused, the light glinting against the glass.

Riley squinted; the time was 7:03.

She shook her head. That was impossible. How could it only be 7:03? When she'd gotten out of the supply closet, Mr. Bardem's clock said it was 6:25. She knew she'd been trapped here for longer than that. It *had* to be longer than that.

Unless . . .

She looked closer. The second hand on the clock wasn't moving. Stuck in place just past the twelve.

"No," she muttered, taking steps toward the clock fixed to

221

the wall. "No. No. No. Don't you *even* . . ." Was it possible? Ghosts couldn't *stop time*, could they? I mean, *what the actual hell?*

Riley shook her head, fighting another wave of dizziness and nausea. Even with everything else—the stuck doors and the stubborn windows, the phones that wouldn't work, the whispers, the cries, the laughter, the stupid frog that was dead and not dead, the possessed demon lockers crashing down the hallways—even with *all* of that, there had at least been that one assurance: that eventually somebody would find her. That time would pass; evening would turn to night. Her mother's shift would end and she would hunt Riley down, forcing the principal to search the school at two in the morning to find her missing daughter.

But in order for that to happen, there had to *be* a two in the morning. And there couldn't be a two in the morning if it was always 7:03. If *that* was the case, she could be stuck here forever.

For eternity.

The sinkhole that had opened inside Riley sucked her in deeper, the panic seizing her, building to a scream, but then she caught something out of the corner of her eye. There, on Mrs. Grissolm's desk, sat her mini Big Ben, her battery-operated souvenir clock.

Her battery-operated clock that read 7:38.

Riley sighed. Of course the clock on the wall was stuck. The clocks hanging on the walls of every classroom were wired to the school's electricity, which meant they would have stopped working the same time the lights went out. The moment she pulled the alarm.

Though some of the lights still worked just fine, she reminded herself. *When someone wants to show you something.*

Riley stared at Mrs. Grissolm's replica London landmark, refusing to blink until she saw the minute hand move one notch closer to the one. So not forever. That was something. The deep breath that followed brought the faint whiff of sick from the toes of her boots, echoed by the nasty taste that lingered on her tongue. She looked at the desk beside her. Vomit breath was one thing she could do something about, at least.

She moved her flashlight beam over to Ms. Lang's desk, the spot of light landing on the picture of the assistant librarian and her ex-husband on their Alaskan cruise, and then down to Ms. Lang's bottom drawer. Snatching a glance over her shoulder at the door and the hallway that lay behind, Riley circled around and let herself collapse into the library assistant's chair, pulling the drawer to her knees. There it was, snuggled between packs of labels and a replacement toner cartridge: the three-pound bag, still half full.

Riley dumped a mound of the chocolate candies on Ms. Lang's desk like a pile of pirate doubloons, taking a red one and letting it linger on her tongue for a moment. She chewed slowly, working the little disk of chocolate around her mouth before swallowing. The taste was comforting. Crisp and then soft and a little too sweet. She grabbed another, a green one this time, and closed her eyes, savoring the little lump as it slowly melted. The trembling in her hands abated somewhat. She remembered that whenever she and Emily would split a package of M&M's, Em would always pick out all the yellow ones. She insisted they tasted better. Riley let her have them because they all tasted the same to her—though she would have given them to her regardless.

Now she instinctively avoided the yellow ones as she sat in Ms. Lang's chair, trying to assess the situation, approaching it the way her mother would, practically rather than panicked. She was still trapped, and she was scared, but was she in any *danger*? Riley glanced at the bloody paper towel taped to her hand, considered the bruise above her knee, the split nail on her toe. The only injuries she'd sustained had been self-administered. Darkness couldn't hurt you unless you weren't careful where you stepped. Laughter couldn't hurt you once you learned to tune it out. Cryptic messages. Flashes of memories. Slamming lockers. Terrifying, certainly, but none of it had caused her harm.

But it could . . .

It could. They could.

She could. Whoever *she* was.

It's only going to get worse. That's what Max said. But Riley wasn't sure she could trust anything Max said. For all she knew, he was the reason she was stuck here.

Riley paused, an M&M halfway to her mouth, stopped by another sound, like a flutter of bird's wings.

Or the ruffle of pages.

Riley took up her flashlight. "Max?"

The library responded with silence. She stood up, inching around the desk, taking slow, deliberate steps, careful not to stray too far from the door, like a toddler in the surf reluctant to let the waves crash above her knees. She let her flashlight skim the shelves, the walls, the floor, making a slow circle. There was nothing. No bisected frog. No writing on the walls. The books all held their positions, lined like battalions of soldiers along the shelves, showing off their spines.

All but one.

Riley's light skipped across it at first, then came back to find it lying on the worn carpet in the corner section marked *Special Collections.* That was the name Mrs. Grissolm gave to materials that couldn't be checked out because they were either too fragile or too precious to be trusted to teenage hands. A set of twenty-year-old encyclopedias that she held on to as relics of a different millennium. Copies of the school newspaper dating back three decades. Past editions of the school's literary magazine, *Musings*, which Riley got a poem into once; she could only remember the last two lines: *Your leaving is more of a beginning / than an end.* Cringy.

All of this was held on one bookcase, in the center of which sat the Northridge Middle School yearbooks, one from each graduating class, dating back to 1974. The encyclopedias and newspapers were never touched, but occasionally Riley would spot kids flipping through the yearbooks for a laugh. Pointing out hairstyles or how long certain teachers have been around.

One of those yearbooks had broken ranks with its sisters and now lay askance on the floor. The hard binding was green and white—Northridge's school colors—the cover sporting a silhouette of a student surrounded by music notes and footballs and drama masks, as if the yearbook staff had simply gathered whatever free school-related clip art they could google and slapped it on. Not that Riley had cared. She hadn't asked her parents to buy her one last year. She wasn't about to be that kid who had to fill the inside covers of her yearbook with generic messages from teachers and loosely acquainted classmates. There was only one person she would even want to sign it anyway, and by the end of last year, Riley was afraid of what that person would write.

Riley hovered over the yearbook now open on the carpet: 1988. Twenty years before she was even born. She brought her flashlight beam up to the empty crevasse where the book once stood, the shelf like a smile with a missing tooth.

Just put it back, Riley, she told herself. *Better yet, don't touch it at all.*

Except that it was clearly here for a reason. It couldn't have fallen from its tightly wedged spot. It's possible that another student had left it there earlier in the day, too lazy to put it back, except Riley had been helping in the library most of the afternoon after school and hadn't noticed it. Surely she would have encountered it while reshelving.

Which meant that someone, or something, *wanted* her to look at it.

Which is exactly why you shouldn't. But books held the answers to all of life's questions. Mrs. Grissolm had taught her that too. Maybe they held the answers to the afterlife's questions also.

Riley took one more circle of the room with her light and then crouched down on one knee, prepared to bolt for the door if the book itself started to flap and flutter its pages. She placed her hand on the cover, cool to the touch. She waited for it to spin wildly or burst into flames. It did no such thing.

With her bottom lip pinched between her teeth, she opened it.

As she suspected, the signing pages were blank. Mrs. Grissolm's collection was made entirely of spares, taken from the box of extras at the end of the year for posterity's sake. She turned to the first real page. A panoramic picture of the entire student body from 1988—three grades, hundreds of students, less than half of them smiling. Riley tried to imagine her mother and father growing up with the same feathery haircuts as these kids, dressed in their white-denim jackets and pastel polos. Hard to fathom, but it must have been so.

She flipped the pages one by one, slowly scanning, waiting for something to catch her eye. None of the names listed along the side of the photos stuck out to her. Lots of Shannons and Chads. Riley didn't know a single person named Chad, yet there were three of them listed on the same page. The only person she even recognized was Mr. Moorehead, one of the social studies teachers, a totally different person with a full head of hair, no wrinkles, and two fewer neck folds. She knew how much just one year of middle school could change a person; here was visual evidence of the toll forty years would take.

In between pages, Riley snatched looks behind her at the closed library doors, or to her right at the row of bulletproof windows, hoping for the glare of headlights in the parking lot. If someone were to drive by, she figured she could at least rush to the window and signal them with her flashlight. Three dots, three dashes, three dots. SOS. Her father taught her that. But the library door stayed closed and the parking lot remained empty.

The only sound was the whisper of her turning pages.

Riley flipped through the sixth graders with their shy smiles and delved into the seventh, the middle children of middle school, like her. She turned past the *A*'s and *B*'s to the next page and the next, wondering if she hadn't missed it already, whatever it was that she was meant to find. She knew there had to be something. She could almost *feel* it.

And there was.

Halfway through the seventh-grade class: one photo was missing.

No. Not missing. More like forcefully removed, revealing a thumbprint-sized hole in the page that showed clear through to the picture on the page behind it. Riley pressed her finger to the empty spot; the edges of the hole weren't clean from a scissor's cut or even the rough markings of a tear. Instead it looked as if someone had *scratched* out the picture over time, running their fingernail over it again and again, the steady friction removing layer after layer of the thick paper until nothing of the image remained.

Except there was still a name to go with the hole, printed off to the side in a block with the other students in that row so that Riley had to count. Fifth one from the left.

Heather Longmiller.

Riley whispered the name to herself. Barely audible at first, and then louder, as if expecting an answer, like a teacher taking attendance, waiting for the girl with the scratched-out face to call out, "Here!" But Heather Longmiller didn't answer. Riley placed her finger back over the imperfection in the page, feeling its tattered outline, wondering what this missing girl looked like.

Perhaps there was an easy way to find out.

Don't look, Riley. You don't want to know.

But she did. She had to. Because she had a feeling that she knew this girl. That she'd heard her voice.

Stop.

Give it back.

Please.

Riley took the yearbook for 1989 from its spot on the shelf and sat down with it in her lap. A glance at the door. Still shut. The parking lot. Still empty. Flashlight in hand, she opened the book and thumbed through the pages to the eighth graders, the short timers, the survivors. She found a now-familiar block of names and scrolled with her finger. *Michael Lang. Janice Lewin. Aaron Little. Kelly Lott. Cynthia Lowe.* Then she read through them again, just to be sure.

No Heather.

Riley flipped back to the seventh-grade section. Maybe she'd been held back. Bad grades. Too much missed school. But she wasn't there either.

Heather Longmiller had just disappeared.

And gone where?

Riley felt the handful of M&M's she'd eaten roll in her stomach, but the urge to see this girl, to find a picture of her, only intensified. *Seriously, it might be better if you don't know*, she thought. *Maybe better to just forget about it.* But she went back to the shelf anyway, grabbing the yearbook from two years before.

The 1987 yearbook was white and green like the others but sported the mascot on the front, the Northridge panther on the prowl. Riley flipped past the teachers to the sixth-grade class, running her finger down the list of names until she found what she was looking for.

Heather Longmiller, this time right where she belonged.

The girl looking up at Riley from the glossy page wasn't smiling. Nor was she pouting or frowning, like Riley was in her sixth-grade photo. This girl looked uninterested, as if she didn't even know she was having her picture taken, her chin turned slightly, eyes narrowed, looking out past the camera as if studying something on the horizon. Her straight dark hair split down the middle, falling past both shoulders, no poufy bangs, unlike most of the other girls on the page whose hair resembled tsunamis, filling the frame. This girl didn't strike Riley as being particularly beautiful or memorable. In fact, there was little to distinguish her at all, save for a set of thick, dark eyebrows that crested that pair of faraway eyes. If Riley hadn't been looking for her specifically, she might have glanced right over her.

Nothing to see here.

And yet, Riley recognized her. It had only been a moment, a flash, but Riley knew. This was the girl. The one who had been bullied in the gym. Perhaps—no, probably the same girl she'd heard whispered about in the hall.

Freak. Loser.

Riley flipped to the index, quickly scanning the list of names and their appearances. Most of them had three or four pages listed alongside them. Some had as many as ten.

Heather Longmiller had only two: the one Riley had just been on, and one other. Riley turned to the second, finding herself looking at a half-page photo of the Northridge choir, each of them wearing matching shirts with the school logo stitched on. And there, in the bottom row, standing clear on the end, was Heather. She wore the same curious expression, the look of someone outside of the moment, someone wishing they were anywhere else. Riley couldn't help but notice that while everyone else stood shoulder to shoulder, crammed in to accommodate the photo, the girl standing next to Heather made a point to keep some distance between them, so that even in this group picture, Heather seemed to stand a pace apart.

She was a singer, Riley thought to herself. Riley wondered if maybe that had been part of her start-of-the-year plan. One of the items on her sixth-grade to-do list. Join the choir? Check. It was more than Riley had done. She pressed her finger to the glossy page, tracing the oval of Heather's face. Here in her first year. Scratched out in her second. And in her third . . .

Just gone. Vanished.

But not forever.

Riley slammed the yearbook shut. She needed to find Max. She needed to find him and confront him, make him spill his guts. Ask him what had happened here.

Max. What had he said his last name was? T-something. Treader. Troder.

Trotter.

Trust me. Not the place I wanted to come back to.

With sweaty, shaking hands, Riley flipped back through the pages, finding the sixth-grade class again, thumbing past the *R*'s and *S*'s and to the *T*'s: Tarly. Teller. Trent.

Trotter.

Maxwell Trotter.

A spiky-haired boy smiled up at her with all his teeth. Chubby cheeked and broad shouldered. Dressed in a shirt and tie, the work of a mother who probably ordered the deluxe package with four dozen wallet-sized so she could hand school pictures out as Christmas gifts.

Maxwell Trotter who died and came back here, of all places.

Oh hell. He *knew* her. They were in the same class together all those years ago. And here they were again. Which meant there was more to it. Had to be. Things that Max wasn't telling her. Things she could only start to guess at.

You think you know. But you're wrong.

I'm not the one keeping you here.

"Heather," Riley whispered again.

Click.

Riley twisted around, the yearbook still open to Max's picture in her lap, startled by the sound of Ms. Lang's bottom drawer sliding shut. Her flashlight danced, searching the checkout area by the door.

"Max? Is that you?"

She set the yearbook down in the pile with the other two, stood up, and scanned the librarians' desks, sweeping left, then right, then up to the shelves behind them, the ones lined with stuffed animals.

Something wasn't right. Normally all of Mrs. Grissolm's literary stuffies sat up and looked out over the library like silent guardians, catching your eye as you went to check out your books. But now they were looking elsewhere. All of them, from Curious George to the Cat in the Hat, sat hunched with their heads hung, staring down at the floor behind the librarian's desk.

Riley swept her light over the shelf, taking a mental inventory of the menagerie that greeted her almost every day. There was one figure missing: the doll with the red hair and the button eyes.

Raggedy Ann. She normally sat between the monkey and the cat, but now she was gone.

Riley took a few tentative steps toward the desk. She'd seen enough bad horror movies to know that along with toothless hillbillies and nine-year-old girls who sang nursery rhymes, creepy dolls were a big red flag. And you didn't get much creepier than Raggedy-Freaking-Ann with her yarn-string hair and that horrifying jack-o'-lantern nose. Riley approached cautiously, keeping her beam aimed at the row of stuffed animals, waiting for George's head to spin or the Cat in the Hat to start hissing at her. The moment either of those happened, Riley was bolting for the hallway, spooky lockers or no. *Forget the library. This is freaking Elm Street*, she thought. Except Riley had never had a nightmare that she couldn't wake up from.

On the back shelf, the stuffed animals continued to stare at the floor, motionless. Riley slowly circled around the desk, keeping her distance, flashlight in hand, looking for the missing doll. She sucked in a sharp breath.

There she was. On the carpet beside Mrs. Grissolm's desk, twisted into an awkward shape, one arm trapped beneath her body, the other wrapped across her own neck. Her left leg was bent at an inhuman angle, her foot jutting up behind her head in the world's most painful yoga pose.

But it was the eyes that gave Riley pause. Those two button eyes dangled by a thread apiece, draping down the doll's cheeks to her shoulders like two black pendulums, hanging on either side of her blood-red nose. In their place, plumes of white stuffing sprouted, the cottony tendrils of the doll's brains leaking from her newly exposed sockets. The doll seemed to smirk knowingly at Riley with that stitched-on, half-moon smile.

As if it was about to whisper a secret only Riley could hear.

35

THERE ARE GHOST STORIES AND THERE ARE HORROR STORIES.
Riley's dad told her both.

Horror stories, he said, rely on the sudden scare, the shock of
the killer slipping out from behind the curtains while your back
is turned, the sickening sound of the slime monster slurching
out of the sink drain as you're brushing your teeth, the sudden
appearance of the masked stranger lying in wait underneath
your bed with knife in hand. Horror stories make you scream
and grab the arm of the person sitting next to you, leaving pink
crescents in their skin.

Not that Riley had ever done such a thing. Not that she
and Emily ever snuck down into her best friend's basement and
watched the *Scream* movies on a laptop with a blanket over their

heads, the volume turned so low they had to turn on subtitles, nervously giggling at the sex scenes and squirming when the blood began to gush.

Horror stories scare you in the moment. Ghost stories, on the other hand, scare you afterward. When you've had the chance to stop and think about them. When you've had some time to ask questions. It's a different kind of fear. The kind that follows you. The kind you can't seem to let go of.

There was one other difference, her dad said. Ghost stories are usually about making amends, discovering something that has been lost or forgotten and putting it back into place, like a set of keys stuffed into a wicker basket. Horror stories, on the other hand, are usually about revenge.

Had this been a Hollywood horror movie, Raggedy Ann would have leapt up, propelled by invisible strings tugged by some unseen marionette, chasing after Riley as she pushed through the library door. She would have looked down to find Curious George wrapped around her ankles, tripping her up so that the others could swarm her, holding her down with their furry paws while that creepy, red-faced caterpillar inched slowly up her chest, its segmented body arching, mouth wide, going for the throat.

But none of those things happened. And the longer Riley

stood there staring at the Raggedy Ann with her twisted limbs and dangling eyes, the less horrifying she seemed. Riley's heart still hammered, her skin was still rippled with goose bumps, but she could start to feel part of her fear give way to something else. Something like sadness, but not quite.

Riley crouched beside the stricken doll. It really was creepy—especially with that nose and the black button eyes. She sat the doll up and tried to fix the buttons back into place, but of course they wouldn't stay—not without some needle and thread. At least she could put the doll back where she belonged, arranging her limbs so that she looked more comfortable, even with her empty sockets.

Riley placed her back on the shelf, and she and Raggedy Ann regarded each other, assessing the damage: both in rough shape, but nothing that couldn't be fixed, she hoped. She rearranged the rest of Mrs. Grissolm's collection as well, putting everything back the way it should be, sure to drape one of George's arms across Ann's sunken shoulders. Then she went back to the special collection and the three yearbooks she'd left in a pile on the carpet. She shelved them each in turn, cleaning up her mess—'87, '88, '89.

Here and then gone, and in between . . .

Scratched out. Worn down. Erased from memory.

The doll with its dangling eyes. The voices at the gym. The whispers from the lockers. There was no denying that ghosts were real. Or that Maxwell Trotter was one of them.

But he wasn't the only one.

36

IT'S HARD LEAVING THE SPACES WHERE YOU FEEL SAFE. ESPECIALLY when there are so few of them.

At the start of the school year she hated leaving the house, her room, her bed, her bubble. Back when she had Emily, it wasn't so hard, but this year was different, and despite her parents' prophecies and platitudes, it hadn't gotten any better. If anything, Riley felt even more isolated than before. She'd been labeled a loner, which she could live with, but that didn't mean she didn't get lonely.

There were days she pretended to be sick, but it wasn't easy. Not with a nurse for a mother who knew the difference between a real cough and a fake one. You couldn't hold an oral thermometer to your lamp if your mom always insisted on using the instant digital kind that went in your ear, and the *Dad would let me stay home if he were here* argument had the exact opposite effect the one time Riley used it, her mother mockingly suggesting that Riley's father obviously must love her more, followed by instructions to call her if she really did start to feel bad. In truth, Riley thought, her mother should take it as a compliment that she didn't want to leave the house. Home wasn't exactly perfect, but it was still the one place she could just be herself, free of behind-the-back conversations and sideways looks.

Still, every weekday she managed to drag herself out of bed, slide into yesterday's jeans, pack the lunch that she may or may not end up eating by herself, and open the front door to go and meet the bus. And every day she took the deepest breath possible, as if she was preparing to hold it for the next eight hours.

She took one of those deep breaths now, twisting the door handle and stepping back into the dark hall, armed only with her flashlight and a whole new set of questions. Questions she thought Max might know the answer to. Answers that might help her get out of here.

But first she had to find him.

"Max? Max, where are you?"

She walked toward the end of the hall, noting with some small measure of relief that all the lockers were closed again. There were no lights on that she could see—only the swath that she cut through the darkness herself. She thought of her father out on the tracks. Of things that lurk just out of sight.

"Maxwell Trotter, I know you're out there." Riley's voice was husky, still raw from all the screaming in the supply closet—and all the shouting since. "Come on out. We need to talk."

You know . . . about the girl in the yearbook? The one you're clearly afraid of? Maybe even more afraid of than I am. Though she wasn't sure how that could be possible. He was a ghost after all.

Riley reached the end of the hall, half expecting a row of lights to flash on, illuminating a path for her to follow, but that didn't happen this time. She took a step back the way she came, thinking she could get her backpack before continuing to search for Max, when she heard a voice call out from the hallway behind her.

"Look who's still here."

Riley's head snapped around, the flashlight following. It wasn't Max's voice, but it was definitely one she recognized, one that normally would have curled her fingers into fists and caused expletives to escape her lips.

It was also one of the last voices she expected to hear.

"Grace?"

Riley aimed her flashlight at the other end of the hallway, but the light revealed only more rows of closed lockers and classroom doors. She took a step and called out again. "Grace, is that you?"

"Still here," Grace called out, her voice coming from around the far corner. The voice was different—not like Max's, which felt like it was inside her own head and outside it all at once. This one she actually heard, clear as a locker slam. It was Grace's voice, complete with Grace's not-so-subtle notes of condescension and disgust.

But it's not her, Riley told herself. *It can't be her. It's this place playing tricks on you again.* Yet it sounded so real. And Grace Turner was definitely not a ghost; she had been very much alive when she shoved Riley into the supply closet. Not unless something unfortunate (because it *would* be unfortunate, Riley told herself) had happened to her in the last few hours.

Riley moved cautiously toward the adjoining hall, where all the performing arts classes were held. "Grace? Are you down there?"

"Still here," the voice called back from that direction.

Riley swallowed hard. The flashlight was slippery in her hand. She started down the hall.

Seriously, Riley? Haven't you learned anything? You know it's not her. You need to go find Max. Tell him what you know. Ask him what he knows. Or better yet, go back to the front doors and pound on them until your palms turn purple. Try the phones again. Try the windows. Find a freaking spoon and start digging your way out. Just don't follow that voice.

Except it was clearly Grace speaking, and she could *hear* it—it wasn't just inside her head. It was *real.* Riley moved a few paces down the hall.

"Here," said Grace.

Riley stopped, aiming her flashlight in the direction of the voice, lighting up the door beside her, the side entrance to the auditorium, one of two that led directly backstage. The last time she'd been through here, she'd been carrying her clarinet (the oboe's only slightly less annoying cousin, Riley thought), dressed in a black skirt and white blouse that her mother found at Goodwill because she knew her daughter would only wear it when she was forced to. Riley hadn't been looking forward to the concert. Even after a year of band, the clarinet still sounded like a mouse being squeezed to death in her hands. But then so did the rest of the band, so at least she didn't have to worry about standing out; her squeaks just blended with the wails of all the other tortured mice. And it's not as if the choir that performed after them was filled with future Beyoncés either; half of them just lip-synced the lyrics. Nothing good ever came from standing out. At least not in her experience.

She opened the door and stepped inside, ignoring her better instincts but incapable of ignoring the musty smell. She arced her light up along the rafters, down the crimson curtains, past the ropes and pulleys, and along the once-shiny wood floor now blemished with gouges and stains. The backstage area was crowded with chairs and music stands scattered haphazardly, huge wooden sets pushed off to the side, gathering dust. Riley spied the facade of the castle from *Shrek* and the trees that served as the home to the Lost Boys in last year's production of *Peter Pan*. Boxes of props were strewn about—foam swords and a plastic hook and tin cans full of glitter for Tinker Bell. Think happy thoughts.

Shove it up your wishhole, Tink, Riley thought to herself.

"Grace? Are you in there?"

Of course she's not in here. Not for real.

Yet Grace's voice responded, coming from somewhere in the room, perhaps from behind the thick velvet curtain. "Do you know what happened?"

Did she know what happened? Where? Here? In this room? In this school? She had images, flashes—enough to realize that there was a history here. There was writing on the bathroom stall door, there were rumors in the halls, but she didn't completely understand. She didn't know the whole story.

"Do you know?" the voice called again.

"I don't. I don't know," Riley whispered, shaking her head.

She crossed the threshold, taking quick breaths. The curtains were closed, obscuring the vaulted room full of empty seats where her mother and father had sat only a month ago, clapping politely to the intermediate band's butchering of "Greensleeves." It always felt strange being backstage, seeing the clutter and the chaos, knowing that on the other side of the curtain, everything was always so orderly, so carefully choreographed, so artificially perfect. A lot of things were like that, Riley thought. Bright and blemish free on the outside, messy and chaotic and broken where you couldn't see.

Riley tiptoed through the maze of music stands, trying to pinpoint the origin of the voice that still called to her.

"I want you . . . ," the voice began.

Riley shined her light into the corners, past the ladders and the workbench smelling of sawdust, cardboard boxes full of unusable pieces of wood and empty spray paint cans. The discards. The castoffs. Dumped here and forgotten.

". . . to think about . . ."

Broken props and matted wigs. A busted spotlight. A piano missing a key. One of the white ones.

". . . what you did."

Riley spun in a slow circle with the flashlight gripped in both hands. The voice sounded so much like Grace's. What if she *was* here, hiding from Riley, teasing her, still torturing her for what she'd done? Could she have been the one locking the doors and windows, cutting the power? Was that even possible?

She really needed to stop asking that question.

Riley let the flashlight fall to her side. She looked up, at the ceiling, too dark to discern, calling up to the rafters. "Listen, I said I was sorry, all right?" Though, admittedly, she hadn't meant it. Either time. She'd only been hoping that Grace would back off, that the Elles would let go of her. She'd been hoping that Emily would remember all the promises they made to each other the year before—promises made while huddled under blankets, in that giggly-yet-deadly-serious space between lights out and drifting off. Promises about best-friends-forever, which turned out to be best-friends-about-six-months. Riley blinked away a tear of frustration—*don't cry, Riley, don't let them see*—and shouted up to the rafters again, "What do you want from me?"

This time her call was answered with a squeal, the turn of an old rusty hinge. Riley twisted, holding her flashlight like a lightsaber, its bright eye resting on something long and thin against the back wall.

A mirror. But not like the wide, flat ones hanging in the bathrooms. This was one of the old swivel kind, oval, like a giant sideways eye, set into a dark wood frame with an ornately scrolled top. Riley couldn't remember seeing it before. Maybe it was another prop—perhaps from some long-ago production of *Beauty and the Beast* or *The King and I*. Or maybe it was for the actors about to take the stage to make sure their makeup hadn't smeared, that their glued-on mustaches weren't lopsided. It looked almost like an antique, but Riley couldn't imagine anything of real value being left to slowly rot or rust in the dark corners of her middle school auditorium. She took a step closer and stared at her reflection.

She looked like hell. Her eyes were still swollen, her hair a stringy, sweaty mess despite the chills she got. There was a spot of blood on her sleeve, presumably from the cut on her hand, and another on her jeans, no doubt from the same. She didn't look at all like the girl who reluctantly left the house this morning.

In fact, the longer she looked the stranger she appeared. Her eyelashes seemed longer than she was used to, and her sea-green eyes seemed to have taken on a sickly yellow tint in the glow of the flashlight. Riley inched forward. The shape of her nose seemed a little off to her as well—a little flatter, a little duller, as if pressed gently to a window. And was her hair darker than usual, or was that just a trick of the shadows? The whole image was off somehow.

Riley squinted into the mirror as the features of her face shifted, seeming to vibrate and blur along the edges, obscuring the fine lines, turning one face into two. Until the girl staring back at her wasn't really her anymore. Or not *only* her. There was a face behind hers, coming to the surface, replacing her own.

The girl in the mirror stared back at Riley, hair parted straight down the middle, eyes glazed and distant, looking just like her picture.

"Heather?" Riley whispered.

As if on cue, there was another squeal and the curtains behind Riley started to open, the heavy red velvet sweeping along the floor, the pulleys complaining as the ropes wound through with a hiss, tugged by an invisible hand, revealing the other side. She turned away from the mirror with the face that wasn't quite hers to look out over the empty auditorium, letting her light jump from empty seat to empty seat. No audience. Nobody.

Just Riley, all by herself on the stage.

The curtains fully open, she got that feeling again, the dizzying sensation, the needle of pain just behind her eyes. Then, suddenly, she wasn't alone anymore.

Riley saw it before she heard it this time, the vision forcing its way into her head like it had back at the gym: the auditorium suddenly full of students. They were slapping and jostling each other in their seats, all their faces shadowed by the darkness so that only their motions stood out. A room full of bodies. But she could still hear them, the whispers and snickers they traded, amounting to a kind of indistinct roar. And then . . .

A cough. A cleared throat. The sounds coming from the

very place where Riley stood. But not from her. She was holding another breath.

The roar diminished, the shadows in the auditorium stilled. Another voice echoed in Riley's head, adult and unfamiliar. *Next up, a vocal performance by Heather Longmiller. Seventh grade. Accompanied by Max Trotter on guitar.*

Riley spun in a circle, taking in the whole stage, expecting some glimpse of the girl from the yearbook, the face in the mirror, but there was none. No sign of the dead frog either. Nothing. Just her.

A stark silence fell across the auditorium, weighted with quiet dread. Riley stood there, waiting. Five seconds. Ten. Riley continued to stare out into the crowd, paralyzed. *"Max?"* she whispered. Then, even softer, *"Heather?"*

Riley jumped, startled by another cough erupting from somewhere out in the faceless crowd. Indistinct murmurs. The shadows squirmed in their seats. They pointed up at the stage, aiming their fingers straight at Riley. She could just make them out, leaning over to each other, trading whispers, filling the silence with a barely audible buzz.

And then a voice drifted in. Hesitant at first, faltering, but hauntingly familiar.

There was no accompaniment. No guitar as promised. Just

the voice singing a cappella. Tremulous. Timid. Tender.

Ooh, baby, do you know what that's worth? Ooh, Heaven is a place on Earth.

Riley recognized the song—or at least the tune. Something she'd heard on some retro playlist somewhere, or maybe in an old movie. The girl's voice shook, the notes trembling, yet with each measure the lone voice grew louder, more confident, attempting to fill the giant void of the auditorium. Riley circled the stage with her flashlight, still looking for the source of the singing, but found only the mirror again, the same image—at once her and not her, looking lost and terrified.

The voice faltered. A missed note. The shadows shook, the tremble of barely suppressed laughter. The whispers started up again. Riley felt her cheeks start to burn, that angry swell, the quickening heart. She wanted to shout at them to shut up, but when she opened her mouth, no sound came out. Only the girl's melancholy voice, surrounding her, still shaky but somehow pushing on, determined to cut through the static, determined to see it through. She sang about love and spinning stars and coming home. About being lost at sea. About being found.

And underneath it all, Riley recognized the sadness in the girl's voice. The secret desperation. The sense of longing. The desire to be seen and heard.

The shadows twittered and twitched. Riley's skin itched. The girl's voice filled the stage.

And then, finally, mercifully, it was over. After a moment of quiet, there was a scattering of applause from the faceless crowd, but even that could barely be heard over the indistinct murmuring that followed. Until the shadows themselves disappeared, taking their whispers with them.

Riley blinked once, twice. The vision, so crisp and so real a moment ago, already dissipating like a lifting fog. The auditorium sat before her, empty. It was just her now, her personal spotlight shining down at her feet, leaving the rest of her in the dark. She felt something catch in the back of her throat and struggled to choke it down, the last broken notes of that song she hardly knew the words to lingering.

She turned back to the mirror, to the face she recognized, the yellow-green eyes looking back at her, hurt and confused.

"What happened to you?" she whispered.

Riley reached out to touch the mirror, to touch the girl's face, to make some kind of connection. She said her name as one finger pressed gently to the glass.

Heather.

With a startling crack the mirror shattered at her touch, splintering into a thousand pieces. Riley screamed—a sudden, terrifying screech imitated by the broken face that watched her. She felt her feet mysteriously pulled out from under her, a moment of pure weightlessness, a total loss of control. Her limbs flailed. She sensed herself falling, thrown backward by an unseen force.

Riley's head snapped back, striking the hardwood floor, taking away the last bit of light.

37

RILEY KNEW WHAT IT FELT LIKE TO HURT DEEP DOWN.

She also knew what it felt like to hurt someone else. She'd hurt a few people in her life. Maybe more than a few. Maybe more than she even knew.

Some really were accidents, like Caroline Silton's run-over fingers. Some were premeditated—like the embarrassment Daniel Delano must have felt shoveling that turd out of his backpack. But most were somewhere in between—in that weird space between instinct and intent, where the whole world seems to speed up to match your racing pulse. The actions are deliberate—you *want* the other person to feel what you feel— but you don't think about how long that hurt will last.

Riley found herself in that space all too often, wanting to

lash out, knowing she shouldn't. Of course she had a temper, and she struggled sometimes to control her impulses, but she'd never hurt anyone so badly that it came back to haunt her.

Except for once.

His name was Jordan Walker. And in her defense, she'd warned him.

It was indoor recess; the dark gray clouds outside had filled to bursting, unleashing a fury that waterfalled down the windows, forcing the kids of Mrs. Landry's fourth-grade class to entertain themselves in the room. For some that meant Mastermind or Uno. For others it meant Minecraft. A couple of girls—not Missy and Sharonda, obviously—had broken out a rubber-band bracelet-making set and invited Riley to join them, but she declined.

In hindsight she should have said yes; then none of it would have ever happened. Instead she grabbed her graphing notebook from her backpack and opened to her latest endeavor.

Riley wasn't hugely into art. She could draw a decent train (just the engine) and a mutant unicorn-dog-cow sort of thing. She didn't make her own comics like half the kids in class. But she did make the best mazes.

She couldn't remember exactly when she'd started drawing them. End of third grade? Over the summer? They started out simple, maybe two or three dead ends, but quickly increased in complexity, filling up an entire page. Pipe mazes and arrow mazes. Mazes with doors requiring keys that forced you to double back. Mazes with lava or misshapen dragons (unicorn-dog-cow-dragons) that you had to circumvent. She drew mazes on the backs of place mats when her parents took her out to dinner. She drew them in the margins of her worksheets at school. She even drew one in marker that was the full length of her forearm, though it smeared during gym class, making it impossible to solve. If she made a particularly complicated maze, she would sell it to a classmate for the cookie in their packed lunch, proving it a lucrative talent, at least.

She never felt the need to run through her mazes herself. She was the creator. She already knew the way out. She enjoyed the technical aspects of drawing them, though—working through the branches and dead ends, deciding how long to make a detour before slamming the door shut. She liked that feeling of control. No matter how winding or convoluted her mazes got, no matter how many branches or walls or wrong turns she put in them, it was always in her power to decide the outcome. Not like real life. Real life, she decided, was a maze created by other people, and sometimes it felt like they'd forgotten to put in an exit at all.

That's what she turned to on that Wednesday afternoon instead of making bracelets: a tightly packed over-and-under labyrinth that took up a two-page spread in her notebook. She'd been working on it for three days, but the end was in sight. If she spent all of recess on it, she could finish. Riley went to sharpen her pencil—the lines for the maze were thin and precision was important—then went back to her table, hunkering over her notebook, tongue poking out of the corner of her mouth as it always did when she drew.

"Another maze?"

Riley glanced up to see Jordan Walker staring at her. His table space was empty. Jordan was one of those kids who didn't know how to spend free time with no screen attached, and he'd had his computer privileges taken away earlier in the day for watching YouTube instead of doing his math. So now the only thing he could think to do was bother her.

Riley ignored him.

"Can I try it?" he asked, ignoring her ignoring him.

"It's not finished yet," she replied. There was no one else sitting at their table. The others had been sucked into the card game over on the carpet. Jordan apparently didn't like card games. He didn't like being quiet and leaving other people alone, either.

"Can I try it when you're done, then?"

"Probably not."

Riley's parents had taught her to be honest, and honestly, Jordan Walker was one of the last kids in the class she'd give one of her mazes to. Not unless he paid her. Three days' worth of work, a two-page spread—this maze was worth at least a few bucks.

Jordan leaned across the table. His breath smelled like hot dogs. "Don't mess up," he said.

Riley shot him a threatening look over her pencil top. "I won't."

Jordan shrugged and leaned back in his chair. Riley considered telling him to go find something else to do. Draw a maze of his own or find someone to build a domino run with or crack open a freaking book, but for the moment he seemed occupied picking at the edge of the tape that held down their table number. She went back to her drawing, tongue between her teeth.

She saw his hand reach out and lifted her pencil just in time as he gave her notebook a little jiggle. He grinned across the table at her as if he thought he was being clever.

Riley scowled and pointed her pencil at his nose. "Don't you *dare* do that again."

Jordan's face turned red momentarily, but his annoying smile remained.

When she thought about it later, she wondered if she'd said something else, if she could have avoided what came next. Maybe if she'd said, "Please stop," making a request instead of giving him an ultimatum. Or if she'd raised her hand and told Mrs. Landry, or just picked up her notebook and moved to a different table. Even if she'd told him that he could buy the maze from her when she was finished, that might have been enough.

But she hadn't done any of those things. She'd said the first thing that came into her head, because that's what she usually did.

She should have seen it coming. Jordan was one of those kids who would drink ketchup on a dare. He once licked the bottom of a muddy shoe because some other kid promised him a Pokémon card. So it shouldn't have surprised her when, ten seconds later, his hand darted out again, faster this time, palm slapping down on the page opposite the one she was working on, jerking it sideways, causing Riley's pencil tip to stray, scratching an errant black line that cut clear across the center of her maze, scarring it.

She shouldn't have been surprised, but she was.

And so was Jordan—to find Riley's pencil suddenly sticking out of his hand like a flagpole.

Sharp lines require a sharp tip.

Riley marveled momentarily at how easily it had sunk in. She would have thought the lead would snap off against the skin, causing the rest of the pencil to glance off or maybe break in half. But she had gotten lucky—or unlucky—catching the soft web of tissue between Jordan's thumb and forefinger, the perfect spot for slipping past bones, letting the pencil drive in past the edge of its shaved nose.

Jordan Walker stared at his hand in shock. Riley stared at it, too, horrified. Not at the sight of it—there was almost no blood—but at the realization that she'd put it there. It had happened so fast, the sudden fire in her cheeks, the surge of adrenaline, fingers instantly reconfiguring themselves into a fist, holding the pencil like a knife, plunging it downward into the soft flesh. Just like that. Three more seconds passed with both of them ogling the pencil poking absurdly out of Jordan's hand. Then, like the awkward laugh that comes too long after the joke is over, he screamed.

"I'm sorry I'm sorry I'm so so sorry." The apologies spilled over each other as Riley pulled her own hands close to her chest, rising up out of her chair, taking a step backward. "Oh god."

"Look what you did!"

Jordan held his impaled hand by the wrist with his other one, the pencil starting to lean a little. By now they had the attention of everyone in the class, including Mrs. Landry, who let out a "Jesus H. Christ!"

A panicked Riley—wanting to help, wanting to disappear, wanting to reverse time, wanting to draw an exit in the floor beneath her like one of her mazes—did the only thing she could think of: she reached across the table and yanked the pencil free. It slipped out just as easily as it had slid in, its tip now coated dark red. It had gone almost all the way through. Jordan screamed again. The wound, now free to bleed, burbling up a tiny stream that trickled down the length of his thumb. He looked like he might faint.

"Someone get some tissues! Now!" Mrs. Landry said, snapping her fingers as she fished for her protective gloves. "Someone else run down and get the nurse!"

Jordan had gone white. He couldn't take his eyes off the tiny blood-spitting volcano in his hand. "She stabbed me! You stabbed me!"

There was no denying it. Riley was still holding the gory weapon in her hand.

Mrs. Landry was by his side now, a wad of tissues pressed tight to the hole Riley had made. Riley could hear Sajan Patel's Nikes clopping down the hall. She could feel the cold sweat on the back of her neck. The rest of the class was silent, circling around, gawking and taking in Jordan's shouts and Mrs. Landry's assurances that he was not about to die.

Riley couldn't look any of them in the eye. She laid the bloody pencil down softly next to her notebook and kept her eyes on the one line on her maze that didn't belong. The one scratched clear across the middle, ruining everything.

38

"*RILEY? CAN YOU HEAR ME?*"

Riley's eyes fluttered open. Her hand, the one with the two-inch cut that would probably leave a scar, swung reflexively, defensively, lashing out, though this time it missed the frog sitting three feet away. The dead knew to keep their distance. Or maybe they learned from experience.

"*It's okay. She's gone.*"

Riley stared up at the ceiling. She was alive. Hurting, but alive. Either that or her personal version of the afterlife had metal catwalks and aluminum ductwork and smelled like sawdust and sweat. Her flashlight was still shining on one side of her. Max sat hunched on the other, swaddled in his duct tape bandage.

"*At least for now,*" he added.

Riley took a breath, closed her eyes, tried to remember how she'd ended up unconscious on the floor. Her brain was hazy at first, but then slowly it came back to her, why she'd come into this room to begin with. The voice. The song. The shadows in the crowd. She tried to pull herself up to a sitting position, but a sucker punch of pain caused her eyes to cross, convincing her not to move too fast. The back of her head throbbed. She must have hit it when she fainted—because that had to be the explanation, that she somehow lost her balance and went down? She reached behind and gave it a tentative rub. She could already feel a knot starting to rise.

"What happened?" she asked.

"I don't know. But if I had to guess, I'd say you did something to make her mad."

Her.

Heather.

She remembered it all now. The face in the mirror. The look in her eyes. Riley reaching out. The glass shattering, splintering outward from where she touched it, the cracks radiating like an aftershock. The scream that followed was Riley's, but not only hers. There was a moment when she felt like she was floating, flying. It was a strange, dizzying sensation, like the feeling you get when you launch yourself from a swing at the height of your

264

arc. A feeling of absolute freedom and absolute terror. A total loss of control.

And then there was darkness.

Riley swept the wood floor for her flashlight, pointing it at the standing mirror, now in a hundred fragments, shards and slivers like shark's teeth, revealing the blackness underneath the silvery glint. She tried to concentrate through the pounding in her head. There were all the hows, of course—how had the mirror shattered at Riley's touch, how had she lost her balance and blacked out, how could she see the things that she saw, hear the things that she heard—but Riley had pretty much given up wondering how.

It was the *why* that haunted her.

"Are you okay? Did she hurt you?" Max asked.

She.

Riley conjured the black-and-white picture of the girl in the yearbook and stuck it side by side in her head with the picture of the beaming, neck-tied boy on the next page. She angled her flashlight's beam at the frog.

"Heather, you mean. Did Heather hurt me." She doubted frogs could wince, but she definitely saw Max's vessel twitch, his little white throat quiver. Just hearing the girl's name was enough to get a reaction. "You knew her."

It wasn't a question. The face in the mirror—it was a face Maxwell Trotter had seen a hundred times before in a previous life . . . so to speak. *Heather Longmiller, seventh grade. Accompanied by Max Trotter on guitar.*

"I saw your picture in the yearbook. You were in the same class," Riley pressed.

"We were just friends," Max answered, his voice suddenly cold. *"And then we weren't."*

There one year. Gone the next. And in between? So much could happen in those in-betweens, Riley knew. In the span of one year, your grades could slip. You could start to pull away from your parents, who sometimes forget to ask you about your day. Your best friend could blow you off, push you away, leaving you to spend the summer by yourself, wishing you were somewhere else, some*one* else. But whatever Riley herself had been through in the last year, it seemed Heather had it worse.

Riley sat up straighter and settled her throbbing head in her hands. She looked sideways, out across the auditorium. She could still picture all those blank faces, staring at her. Pointing at her.

No. Not at me.

"I heard her sing. I'm not sure how, but I heard her. Right here on this stage. She was singing this song . . . all by herself." Riley made only a small attempt to hide the accusation. *You were supposed to be up there with her.*

Max seemed to gloss over it. *"Yeah. She sang constantly. She would even hum to herself in class while the teacher was talking. Didn't even realize she was doing it. Some people would tease her about it."*

"Some people," Riley pressed.

"Other people." The echo of his voice in her head sounded defensive.

It's always other people. The kids in the gym. The laughter in the cafeteria. The whispers in the auditorium. It almost seemed like the whole school was set against her.

"She was an easy target," Max continued. *"Sometimes she made herself a target."*

Riley shook her head. How do you *make* yourself a target? Riley pictured the girl from the yearbook photo standing up on that stage, vulnerable and alone, desperate to finish her song— all by herself, if she had to. Was that what he meant? Because she didn't run and hide? Press herself into a corner? Or was there something more?

"It wasn't me," Max added quickly. *"I'm not the one to blame for everything that happened."*

Riley glanced at him and then looked back at the shattered mirror, her own face fragmented, distorted by the broken glass— hers and not hers.

"And what *did* happen?"

Do you know what you did?

"You have to tell me, Max," Riley insisted.

Max's voice came to her, softer now, less defensive. Almost defeated.

"I'll tell you," he said. *"But I think you already know."*

39

SOME THINGS ARE EASILY FORGOTTEN—ERASED BY DISINTEREST OR simply eroded by time—but others stick with you. They go on your permanent record. Not the one they supposedly keep locked away at school but the kind of running total of your life that somehow follows you like your own shadow—the stories that accumulate, the labels and nicknames, the under-the-breath conversations.

Did you hear what happened?

Did you hear what she did?

After the Jordan Walker incident, things had to change. Riley had to change. Or at least she had to try. There are consequences for your actions, she was told. You don't stab your classmate with a pencil and expect to transition straight to circle time.

After Jordan's mother arrived to take him to the ER; after a lecture from the principal on how violence and aggression were never the answer; after her own mother had come to pick her up, looking confused and crestfallen, mumbling apologies on her daughter's behalf while casting barbed looks at Riley, who sat sort of folded in on herself in the corner, her nose already pressed to the closest wall she could find; after the one-day suspension was served and the apology letter written and delivered, along with a check to cover the expenses for X-rays and stitches; after all that, Riley's father came home.

She hadn't seen him in four days, but he didn't hug her like usual. And he didn't call her his little monster. Not this time.

"So, you want to tell me what happened?"

Honestly, no, she thought. She'd already told the story a half dozen times. To the teacher. To the principal. To her mother, who couldn't believe her ears the first two times and asked to hear it a third. But she knew she didn't have a choice. Her father listened carefully from his spot on the edge of the bed. She decided to skip the gory details, even though he never did.

When she finished, the first thing he did was apologize for her ruined maze. "That sucks. It was a good one?"

"Two pages," she said.

"Lots of dead ends."

"All dead ends. I didn't get a chance to make the exit."

Her father nodded. "I'm sorry that happened. But your reaction was a little extreme, don't you think? Stabbing him like that?"

Riley shrugged. *Reaction* was the right word. And extreme, at least, wasn't the same thing as wrong. Extreme she could cop to. "I wasn't thinking," she said. "I was just mad."

She knew he, of all people, would understand. Her father was no stranger to anger; the refrigerator door could attest to that. Of course, the fridge didn't bleed and whine and threaten to sue you.

"I get it," he said. "But you know that's still no excuse for what you did. You hurt that boy pretty bad. You're lucky you didn't do more serious damage."

She could have severed a nerve. She could have punctured a blood vessel. She could have made it so that Jordan Walker could never hold a pencil with that hand again. That's what her mother the nurse said.

Riley looked down at the folds in her comforter, afraid to look her father in the eye. "I'm sorry," she said for what felt like the hundredth time. "I just . . . I had to do *something*."

Conner Flynn sighed and hooked one arm around her, pulling her close. She could smell his piney aftershave mixed with his sour sweat. His arm felt massive resting on her slender shoulders, the weight uncomfortable, but she didn't slough it off.

"Listen. People are going to push you. That's just how it goes. And when they do, you have to be strong. You can't let them knock you off track. But you have to be strong *here*." He pointed to her chest, to her rapidly thrumming heart. "You can still stand up tall without pushing back. You know what I'm saying?"

Riley nodded. She understood.

But she didn't agree. Because sometimes somebody pushes you so hard it's impossible to keep your feet underneath you. Sometimes they push you so hard you are teetering on the edge, and the only way to make enough space to save yourself *is* to push right back.

The next week, at the school's recommendation, Riley's parents took her to see a therapist.

Dr. Rickets's office was bland, intentionally inoffensive, the walls painted a vanilla beige and adorned with pictures of the therapist's family, including one of her posing with a daughter at high school commencement—proof that she had successfully raised a kid. A glass jar of butterscotch candies sat invitingly on the corner of her desk next to her nameplate: Annie Rickets, LMHP. Riley wasn't sure what LMHP stood for, but it sounded prestigious, which is to say pompous.

The session started with introductions, Riley squeezing between her parents on the couch, pressing her hands between her thighs, her lips shut tight, taking everything in and not letting anything out. Then came thirty minutes of one-on-one time, which Dr. Rickets insisted wasn't an interrogation, because Riley didn't have to answer the questions if she didn't feel like it. Except the uncomfortable pause after each one was too much, so she answered them anyway, hoping it would speed things along. She'd eaten three butterscotches already.

"Do you know why you're here?" Annie Rickets, LMHP, asked.

Yes. Because I stabbed some jerk with my pencil. Sorry. Some boy.

"How are you feeling right now? Are you angry? Upset? Worried?"

Nervous. Ready to go home. And hungry. Can I have another butterscotch?

"How did you feel when that boy ruined your maze?"

Pissed off. Sorry. Ticked off.

"It's okay to feel pissed off sometimes. And how did you feel afterward, when you realized what you'd done?"

Guilty. And worried.

"Worried about the boy?"

A little. Also that I'd get in trouble.

"With your parents?"

With everybody.

"Do you feel angry a lot of the time?"

Only when somebody does something to make me feel that way.

"And how often does that happen?"

Just about every day.

The questions kept coming. Do you get along with the other kids at school? Do you have any problems making or keeping friends? Do you get along with your parents? Are you happy at home? What calms you down when you're upset? If you could change any one thing about your life, what would it be?

Riley answered them all honestly. All but one.

"Did you mean to hurt that boy, Riley?"

Such a funny choice of words. Did she *mean* to? Riley knew she couldn't say yes, even if it was partly true, so she shrugged.

Annie Rickets, LMHP, made a note on her iPad.

When the not-interrogation was over and Riley was handed some pamphlets to look over in her free time, the therapist brought her parents back into the room.

"Riley is a smart, sensitive girl, full of emotions, like most kids her age. And all of those emotions are perfectly normal; it's just a matter of finding an effective and productive way of expressing them. I don't think an incident like this one is likely to repeat itself. She knows what she did was wrong and she knows she needs to try and keep her anger in check, so we discussed some exercises and activities she can do to help keep things in balance—calming breaths, counting to ten. As her parents, it's important for you to be supportive and communicative, but also to set high standards, because you have a lovely and intelligent daughter who can certainly live up to them."

Great, Riley thought. *Thanks for raising the bar, Annie Rickets.*

The therapist then said she'd like to see Riley again in two to three weeks, and maybe once or twice a month thereafter. "Just my recommendation."

Riley went to two more sessions and ate eleven more butterscotches, not counting the five she snuck into her pocket on that first day. Then, because money was a little tight and insurance didn't cover any of Annie Rickets's hundred-and-fifty-dollar-an-hour fee, she stopped.

It was mostly Riley's decision. School was back to tolerable by that point. Jordan Walker had switched to another class. And while some of the kids purposely ignored her or gave her funny looks, she kept her head down and ignored them back. She got used to sitting by herself at lunch.

After that first week she'd also learned not to use the pencil sharpener anymore so she wouldn't have to hear the "uh-ohs" some of the kids whispered under their breath. Instead she made do with whatever pencil she had at hand, no matter how blunt it was. It was fine. Most of their work was done on computers, and Riley had stopped making mazes anyways. What was the point, after all?

She already knew how they were all going to end.

40

HE DIDN'T TELL HER THE WHOLE STORY.

He didn't need to. She'd seen the writing on the bathroom stall door. She'd heard the girls giggling as they scribbled across the bra. She'd covered her ears against the insults as they chased her down the hall.

What she didn't know—what Max still needed to tell her—was how it all ended.

She needed to know how Heather Longmiller ended up here.

Because maybe, just maybe, that would tell her why *she* was still here.

"Some kids never really fit in," he said. *"She had trouble making friends."*

Lots of people have trouble making friends, Riley thought to herself. *That doesn't turn you into a ghost.*

At least, she hoped not.

"It wasn't just that," Max continued. *"She had other problems. Problems most people didn't know about."*

He wouldn't even say her name. "But you knew."

Max didn't answer immediately. The pause was answer enough. He knew. He knew because they had been friends.

Until they weren't.

"She had trouble at home," Max said finally. *"Her father drank some, her mom was hard on her, and her parents fought all the time. She couldn't stand it there. But then she came here and it wasn't much better."*

No safe spaces. Riley thought about the mantra she whispered to herself every day when she walked through the front doors that now trapped her here: just survive. She wondered if Heather whispered something like that every time she walked through these very same doors. "So then what?"

"I guess she had enough. The kids here, they just kept pushing. And nothing got any better at home. So one day, she just snapped."

Snapped. The long black mark tearing across the page. The animal crackers scattered in the mulch. The tip of the pencil sinking in. The sharp sting of a hand across a cheek.

Do you know what you did?

Riley glanced at the broken mirror, remembered the feeling

of weightlessness, the loss of control. "Tell me."

"It was the last week of school. Everybody had already gone home, but she stuck around. Waited for the teachers to leave. I guess nobody noticed she wasn't on the bus. Nobody cared that she hadn't come home."

Microwave dinners. A silent house couched in darkness. A young girl all alone.

"Once the place was empty and all the doors were locked, she snuck into the gym, grabbed one of the baseball bats from the supply closet, then she just went crazy. Ballistic. She smashed everything she saw. Windows. Desks. She went into the bathrooms and broke all the mirrors. Smashed the trophy case outside of the gym. She put dents in the lockers, tore up the cafeteria. It was a rampage."

She had to do *something*.

"When she'd finished, she took a thing of red paint from the art room and left a message for all the students in the vestibule, written right across the floor."

Riley didn't need Max to tell her what Heather wrote. "Nothing to see here."

Max's head bobbed. *"The administration disagreed. The school was trashed. She was suspended for the last three days, but most of us knew she was never coming back."*

The slamming of lockers. The whispers in the hall. *Good riddance.*

Riley conjured Heather's face from the yearbook, straight hair split down the middle, thin lips pressed into the slightest frown. And that distance in her eyes—somewhere else. Or just wishing she was.

"That summer her family moved out of state and I didn't hear anything about her again . . . until the accident."

Riley squinted at the frog, half hidden in shadow. "Accident."

"I don't know everything," Max admitted. *"Her father was driving. It was a head-on collision. She wasn't wearing her seat belt."*

A sharp breath. Another flash of pain.

"At least that's what I was told."

Riley could picture it. The shattered glass. The screech of tires. The body lifted, floating. Head snapping backward. And then . . .

Gone. Just gone.

Riley rubbed the back of her neck, just below the rising knot, the radiating ache. All she could think was that they were the same age. *Had been* the same age.

"Her name was all over the halls those first few days. So young. And with everything that had happened, how she'd left, it was all anyone could talk about." Max paused again. *"But then . . . I don't know . . . over time, the whole thing just kind of . . . faded."*

"You mean everyone just forgot about her," Riley prodded.

"Like I said, she didn't have a whole lot of friends."

Riley stared hard at Max. "She had you."

"And I already told you we weren't friends anymore."

Riley conjured up the chubby-cheeked boy from the year-book. There was something else he wasn't telling her, something that maybe he was afraid to tell her. She looked back out over the empty seats of the auditorium, picturing Heather standing onstage all by herself. Where was her accompaniment? Where was Max while Heather was up here, exposed and all alone? She turned back to the ghost still crouched some distance away. He could obviously see the look she was giving him, even in the anemic light. *"It's not what you think,"* he began.

What *did* she think? This girl who had been singled out, teased and tormented until she had to move away. And this boy—her friend once, at least until he wasn't—grown up, moved on, and then somehow pulled back here, his spirit held hostage by the girl he'd forgotten. Trapping him here. Trapping both of them here.

"Why didn't you just tell me all this from the start?"

"When? While you were kicking me across the room? Or while you were trying to stomp on me in the hall? Or when you were blaming me for everything that's happening?"

Maybe he had a point. She hadn't really given him much of a chance. Of course, in her defense, he was a ghost inhabiting the body of a disemboweled frog. And she was having a day.

"*Besides,*" Max continued, "*I didn't think you would believe me. I knew you would have to see for yourself . . . just what she's capable of.*"

Riley rubbed the back of her head again. He was right. She'd seen and heard and felt more than enough.

Max pressed on. "*But now you get it, don't you? It's all her. What's happening to you? To me? It's all her. And there's nothing I can do about it. Her spirit is stronger than mine. Every time she gets close, I feel this, this terrible . . . emptiness. It's not like pain. It's worse than pain. All-consuming. It's torture. She's punishing me, Riley, and I don't deserve it. I'm a good person. I was a good person. But wherever I'm supposed to go, whatever I'm supposed to do, I can't. Because she won't let me. I'm stuck here . . . just like you.*"

But not just like me, Riley thought. Because eventually somebody was going to come and find her. She wasn't a ghost; Heather's spirit couldn't keep her here forever. Not like Max.

Unless of course . . .

Max seemed to read her thoughts again. "*She wants you, Riley. I don't know why, but she does. And she'll find a way to keep you here, I'm sure of it . . . unless you find a way to stop her.*"

"*Stop* her?" Riley protested. "How am I supposed to *stop* her?"

"*If I knew, I wouldn't still be here.*"

Riley thought back to all her father's stories. How do you get rid of a ghost? You chop the heads off zombies. Stab vampires in the heart with a sharp stick. Put a silver bullet in a werewolf's skull. But ghosts? The only way she knew to vanquish a ghost was to find out what it wanted, what kept it anchored to this world. Find the tie that bound it here and then cut it loose.

Of course most of her father's stories ended with the ghost still unsatisfied, continuing to haunt this world long after those who knew it had moved on. The steps still creaked and doors still rattled in their jambs. Faces of the lost still appeared in frosted windows. The train continued along its interminable course. The ghosts in his stories almost never got what they wanted. In life or in death.

But if they could . . .

Riley stood up, a double punch of dizziness and nausea nearly sending her right back to the floor, but she managed to stay upright, feet planted beneath her. She set her jaw and took a breath.

"Wait. Where are you going?"

She glanced down at Max, hunched by her boot, apparently no longer afraid of being smashed. "To find her," Riley said. "And then I'm going to do whatever I have to to get out of here."

Because there was no way *anyone* was keeping her here forever.

41

THERE WERE DAYS SHE WONDERED WHAT IT WOULD BE LIKE, WHAT it would *feel* like. The end. And after that.

Not that she *wanted* it to happen, not that she wished for it, even in her most self-pitying moments. But still, the thought came to her, as she imagined it did to most people. In lonely walks home and hours spent suctioned to her phone, idly clicking through the shouting and the static, in the empty hours she could never seem to account for. At her desk, daydreaming through the steady diet of droning lectures and dull videos that threatened to be the death of her outright. In the hallways at school, catching snippets of conversations that had nothing at all to do with her—conversations that underlined how few people even cared she existed. That's when her mind gravitated toward thoughts of death.

They always came with questions. Would it hurt? What if there wasn't anything on the other side? What if nothing you did in this world made a bit of difference after? Sometimes she wondered where the ghost train would take her when it came, if it took her anywhere. If there was even anywhere to go.

There were no ready answers. Or at least none that she put much stock in. The Flynns weren't particularly religious. They never went to church. They bowed their heads and shut their eyes if someone else gave a prayer or blessing and had taught Riley to do the same out of respect for everyone else's beliefs. They never discussed reincarnation. Heaven and hell were settings for books and movies, *Hercules* or *The Good Place*. They were no more real to her than Narnia or Wakanda. That didn't mean that they didn't exist—only that she'd never received a postcard proving it.

If anything Riley imagined death as stillness. As darkness and silence. Like being deep under the ocean where no light could reach. Something peaceful and quiet and cold.

She'd felt something like it once, she thought. Just this past summer. That night at the lake. When she'd snuck out of the house her parents had rented for the week, leaving a note on her bed on the off chance they caught her in the act, tiptoeing across the hardwood floors and slipping through the patio door, which slid open with a murmur. Finding her way by moonlight along the dirt path that led down to the water, her towel draped across her already tanned shoulders. She knew exactly where she was going. She'd been planning to do this for six months, after all.

She just hadn't planned to do it alone.

They'd made a list long before, she and Emily, sitting side by side on Riley's bed, the window crusted with snow, a bag of barbecue chips between them. A list of all the things they'd do on the trip, scrawled upon a piece of pink stationery. The challenge to see who could eat the most ice cream over seven days. The competition to see who could get a secret stalker photo of the hottest boy. The journal they were going to take turns keeping—Riley already had one they could use, a rainbow-riding narwhal on the front. The episodes of *The Office* that they would rewatch in the car on the way there. There were plans to take watercolors and try their hands at painting nature scenes. There were less confident plans to try and cajole Riley's father into letting them try a sip of beer. Riley was finally going to learn how to do a back handspring. Emily was going to teach her. Nails would be painted and then repainted. Guacamole would be liberally consumed.

One thing they definitely decided on was sneaking out of the house late at night and going for a midnight swim. The lake they were renting on was modest in size—maybe a dozen other houses surrounding it, nothing like the bracing and brackish waters of Lake Michigan, though still plenty chilly, her father said. Riley fully expected to lose all feeling in her feet. Still, it would be worth it for the story they shared.

But those were December dreams. By the start of summer it was obvious that Emily wasn't coming with them anymore. Excuses were made—volleyball camp followed by a visit with Emily's grandmother—but those were solely for Riley's parents' benefit. Riley knew the real reason.

Emily wasn't coming because Emily didn't *want* to come.

Her parents didn't press too hard. No doubt they suspected something was up when their daughter's best friend had stopped coming over on the weekends. Her mother asked Riley if she wanted to invite someone else.

Yeah, right. Who? was what she thought.

"No, it's okay" was what she said.

And so Riley found herself alone on that Thursday night—or, more accurately, Friday morning—sneaking out of the rental house by herself, determined to make good on at least one of winter's promises, with or without Emily Sauders by her side.

The sharp rocks along the path bit into Riley's bare feet, but she didn't care. The trail that wound down to the lake was short, a three-minute tromp that passed through a swath of birch and sugar maple trees whose leaves held still that night, keeping her from having to jump at their rustling, though the shadows their branches made in the full moon still gave Riley a shiver. Her father had lots of stories that took place in the woods at night. They all ended badly.

Riley shivered again when she got to the lake and skimmed her toe across the surface of the water. She'd been swimming just that afternoon, but then, the sun had been out. Now, with the temperature dipping into the fifties, the water just felt frigid, bordering on glacial. She thought about turning back. It had been more of a dare after all, Emily raising an eyebrow at her, telling her no way, certain that Riley would chicken out.

What? You don't think I'll do it?

I think you will sneak out of the house, but you won't get in the water.

And you will?

I will if you will.

That was the promise. Sworn over a chip. Sealed by hooked pinkies smudged with barbecue powder.

Through the winter and even into spring Riley had clung to that hope, that Emily would maybe keep their promise. Even when it became obvious what was happening, when the strain of their friendship became too much to ignore, Riley thought of the summer and the house on the lake and the plans they had made, hoping that a week together—just the two of them hanging out, engaged in easy conversation again, laughing and holding hands—would be enough to put things back to normal. It had to be enough.

I will if you will.

Then came the note that broke Riley's heart, and all the hope she'd been holding there.

Fine. Whatever, she told herself. *Her loss.* Though she didn't really believe it.

Riley looked out across the lake. It was well after midnight. A few lights shined from decks and porches across the water, but no one else was out there. No boats. No bodies. No movement at all. She was truly alone.

"You can do this," she told herself in a hushed voice. "It won't kill you."

Unless she got hypothermia. Unless she swam out too far, got tired, and drowned. Unless some giant fish swam up beside her, brushing against her leg and giving her a heart attack. Then, yes, it just might.

Riley peeled off her sweatshirt and joggers, revealing the bathing suit she'd secretly worn to bed, the same two-piece she'd picked out the month before—the day her mother tried to embarrass her to death in the Kohl's. She actually thought she looked pretty good in it, not that there were any cute boys to see her now. She huddled her clothes into a heap and stood right at the water's edge, skin already prickling. She hesitated. The water looked pitch-black. Impenetrable.

"Be brave."

She took her first step, just up past her ankles. A thousand icicles stuck her like pencil lead, yet she took another step, and then another, her feet instantly numb. Her breath quickened.

This was stupid. She should turn around. Run back to the rental. Curl up back in her bed under the pile of warm blankets she'd stolen from the living room. What did it matter anyway? It's not like anyone would know whether she did it or not. Know, or care.

Except her. She would know, and somehow that was enough. Riley clenched her teeth to stop them from chattering as she went waist-deep and then plunged even further, bringing the freezing water clear up to her chin. She thought her heart just might stop. She could feel the cold in her bones and kicked out with her feet just to make sure her legs still worked, though she couldn't see them beneath the surface. This was insane. She was insane.

She'd heard that before. Crazy Riley Flynn. The trees watched silently, making no judgment one way or the other.

She swam out several feet, far enough that the bottom dropped out and she could no longer touch. It was far enough. She felt her heart hammering away, her legs churning beneath her. Above her, the winking sliver of a crescent moon. Beneath her, darkness.

Riley let herself sink.

Eyes shut, lips tight, slowly letting the air out through her nose, dropping till her feet touched the muddy bottom, digging in with her toes. Anchoring herself there in the deep.

For five seconds. Ten.

This, she thought. *This is what it's like. Not the actual dying, but after.*

Fifteen. Twenty.

Emily should have been here. They should have done this together. It wasn't the same without her. Nothing was the same anymore. Hard to imagine it was going to get any better.

Twenty-five. Thirty.

It was so quiet down here. So quiet and so, so cold.

Thirty-five. Forty.

See. I told you I would do it. I kept my promise.

A full minute passed before Riley's lungs started to burn and her instincts kicked in. She pushed off, darting up through the inky water and breaking through the surface, sucking in a greedy, glorious breath. Riley wiped her eyes and swam back to where she could easily touch. The water was still chilling but her teeth had stopped chattering at least. She was finally starting to get used to it.

She stretched out her numb limbs and lay back on the smooth black glass of the lake, blinking up at the mess of stars scattered across a matching black sky and thinking about everything she'd done.

And everything she still wanted to do.

42

THE HALLWAY WAS COLD. COLD AND SEEMINGLY SOMEHOW EVEN darker than before. Riley's fingers felt stiff wrapped around her flashlight. Her legs still wobbled; her head still spun. But none of that stopped her. She wouldn't let it. The moment she got into the hall, she called out Heather's name.

Screamed it, actually.

It was one of Riley's prescribed coping strategies. When she felt frustrated or angry or upset, she was told to remove herself to somewhere private and let it all out. Don't muffle it with a shirtsleeve or a pillow. No silencers. Shake the windows. Scare the dog. You can even curse if you feel the need, Annie Rickets said, as long as your parents don't mind—or at least aren't home to hear you.

Riley guessed that Heather's spirit could hear her no matter how loud she was, but that didn't stop her. She *wanted* to scream.

"What do you want from me? Why are you keeping me here?"

She started down the hall, staying in the center, flashlight tight in both hands. She wondered which voice would answer her this time. Grace's again? Or maybe it would be Jordan Walker. Or Daniel Delano. Or any of a dozen teachers or principals Riley had disappointed over the years. Maybe all of them, all at once, telling her the same thing:

I want you to think about what you did.

Except this one wasn't on her. Riley had done nothing to Heather Longmiller. The girl was dead long before Riley was even born.

"I know what happened. I know what you went through," Riley called out. "And it sucks, all right? But I didn't do it. So why won't you just let me go home?"

Home. To a sink full of coffee-stained mugs and a counter littered with bills and toast crumbs. To a couch hiding caches of half-popped kernels beneath its cushions from so many movie nights with her mother. To the wood table she'd permanently stained with marker when she was little. To the twin bed where so many ghost stories had been told, most of them more sad than scary. It didn't matter so much anymore that nobody would be there when she got there. She knew they would come home eventually.

If only the ghost would let her go.

"What do you want?" Riley cried again, her throat swollen from the effort. She stared down the dark hallway, waiting for a response. Ten seconds. Twenty. Thirty. Finally her shoulders sagged, her anger spent. Her head still pounded. Her hand throbbed. She felt total exhaustion wash over her. Her knees buckled and she dropped to the floor.

"Please just let me go," she whispered.

The bulb in her flashlight suddenly blinked out, allowing the darkness to envelop her completely.

She wondered if this was it. Quiet and cold. Dark and still. She'd felt this way before.

The light blinked back on again. Just a brief flash. Then back off before blipping right back on again. Three short bursts. Then three longer flashes. And three short blinks again.

SOS.

Riley struggled back to her feet. The flashlight blazed back on again and stayed on this time, the beam pointing ahead toward the turn that led to D-hall. She twisted around to see if there was some other sign of Heather's presence and the light blinked back off, but as soon as she aimed it back at D-hall it flashed again. Riley's finger was nowhere near the button. The battery wasn't fritzing out.

The ghost of Northridge Middle School was talking to her. Heather Longmiller was showing her the way.

Riley looked back at the auditorium and called Max's name. No answer. She thought about what he'd said. How it was torture for him. The agony and emptiness he felt whenever she came near. How he wouldn't even say her name, as if he was afraid it might conjure her beside him.

Fine. She wouldn't wait for him. Her path was laid out before her, a funnel of light shining straight ahead. She thought of her father's story, the one about the tunnel through the mountain and the passengers who never made it to the other side because they got stuck in the dark. That wouldn't be her. Her father never stopped the train to wait for the sun to rise. He pushed through because he always had somewhere he needed to be.

So did she.

"Be brave, Riley," she whispered, and took a step toward the light.

43

SHE WAS WAITING FOR HER WHEN RILEY FINALLY RETURNED. NO telling how long. Could have been a minute. Could have been an hour.

Sitting on the front porch with the light on, dressed in her nightgown, an afghan borrowed from the couch wrapped around her legs, a cup of coffee in her hands. It had to be almost two in the morning.

Riley paused on the trail, clothes tucked under her arm, towel hanging from her shoulder like a cape. The dirt clung to the soles of her wet feet. She thought of the note left on her bed—*Gone swimming. Be back soon. Go back to bed.* The last command half said in jest, the thirteen-year-old girl giving orders

297

to her own parents, though really she was only urging them not to worry. Obviously her mother had been up, had found the note, and now Riley was caught.

She wished it had been her father. If he'd been the one to see the note, he probably would have come to the lake looking for her, but then he probably would have jumped right in, pajamas and all. Her mother, on the other hand, sat on the porch preparing the lecture Riley was about to receive.

May as well get it over with.

Riley made her way up to the house and sat in the white wicker chair next to her mother. She folded her still-wet hands in her lap.

"How'd you even know I was gone?"

"I check on you sometimes," her mother said. "And you're not as stealthy as you think. How was your swim?"

Riley analyzed the question, the facial expression, the tone of voice. No trace of sarcasm or disapproval. She took a moment to consider her answer. "Peaceful."

Amanda Flynn nodded and took a sip of her coffee. "Yeah. I really like it out here. It almost feels like time has stopped. Like there's this little pocket where the normal rules just don't apply."

Riley nodded. That was how she felt too. Like she'd escaped into some otherworldly dimension, if only for a moment.

Floating in that lake, looking up at the fingernail moon, Riley had felt weightless for the first time in forever.

"Though that still doesn't mean you should be sneaking out of the rental house at one in the morning."

Here it comes, Riley thought. She quickly ran through the list of words her mother would use to describe her this time. *Irresponsible. Reckless. Childish. Foolish.* She'd heard them all before. She considered apologizing, except she wasn't sure she could sell it. She wasn't sorry. Maybe a little for making her mother worry, but not enough to regret it. Not enough to want to take it back.

What her mother said, though, was "I get it."

Riley stole a quick glance. Her mother was smiling.

"It may be hard to believe, but I was thirteen once."

"A long, long time ago," Riley said.

"Hey, don't push it. Point is, you aren't the first girl in the world to sneak out of the house and do something scary and exciting and maybe just a little bit stupid. And you're certainly not the first girl in the world to feel the way you do."

"Feel what way?"

"Like nobody understands what you're going through," her mother said. She took another swig, the cup held tight in both hands. Her eyes were fixed on the dirt path leading off into the dark woods that circled the lake. "Was it scary?"

"A little," Riley admitted. "But I think only because I was alone." She paused, debating how much she should say. "We were supposed to do it together."

"You and Emily?"

Riley nodded.

"You two having problems?"

She nodded again. That was one way to put it.

"You want to talk about it?"

That one was harder to answer. She did, and she didn't. She worried that if she opened up now, too much of herself would spill out and she would lose what little bit of happiness she'd found tonight, that the floating feeling would go away and it would be too hard to get back.

"Not really," she said.

"Okay. Well. If you do . . ."

They sat in silence for a moment more, tucked inside that pocket, listening to the cricket song. Riley rubbed her hands along her arms.

"Was it cold?"

"It was *freezing*," Riley admitted.

Her mother set her cup on the table between them and unwound the blanket from around her legs, swaddling Riley in it instead. It was probably just in her head, but Riley instantly felt warmer.

Her mother smiled. "Next time, come and get me. We'll go together."

Riley nodded. It was a promise.

She leaned over the side of her chair and let her mother pull her in.

44

THE LIGHT PULLED AND RILEY FOLLOWED IT.

Despite the shivering, she could still feel sweat trickling between her shoulders. The pain in the back of her skull had dulled somewhat but now seemed to spread throughout her body. She felt dizzy and disoriented from hitting her head on the stage, the sound of her steps echoing long after she'd taken them. The cut on her hand had inexplicably opened again—she could feel the fresh blood oozing beneath the bandage.

She still wasn't sure what had happened back in the auditorium, if the ghost of the girl who haunted these halls had meant to hurt her or if it had only been Riley fainting and tripping over her own feet.

An accident.

Heather Longmiller had died when she was only Riley's age. But her ghost didn't haunt the road where her life was taken or the house where she grew up. It was here. Northridge Middle School. It had returned to this place specifically. It was here because it wanted something.

The pictures of Paris and Barcelona greeted Riley as she turned into D-hall: the armpit of the school. Quieter and less crowded during passing periods because nobody stashed their stuff here; these lockers hadn't been used in thirty or forty years. She moved cautiously; every third or fourth step she'd swing the flashlight right or left, and with every excess movement the beam shut off until she pulled it back to center, keeping her on course. The message was clear: to turn around and go back—to the auditorium, to the library, to the front entrance—would mean staying in the dark.

"Be brave," Riley whispered again, talking to herself just so she could hear a voice, any voice. *But don't be stupid*, she added inside her head.

Halfway down the hall, the flashlight blinked off again, stranding her in the darkness. Riley wondered if she'd taken a wrong turn or gone too far. Maybe the whole thing was a trick to get her away from Max, to get her alone. Maybe Heather really did intend to hurt her somehow. She stopped and panned slowly, right to left. When the beam came back on, its eye illuminated the row of lockers beside her, focused on a black-and-silver plate with the number 1237 stamped into it. The locker had a scratch down its middle, cutting through the yellow paint to reveal the silvery steel underneath. She had never noticed it before, the scratch, despite walking through this hallway every day.

Riley looked back the way she came and called out Max's name, wondering if maybe he'd followed her, but his voice wasn't in her head. She held her breath and placed her bandaged hand against the cold metal, right above its jagged scar.

Immediately the hallway erupted in whispers, just like the ones she'd heard before, multiple voices overlapping with one another so it was impossible to tell what direction they were coming from. Riley instinctively shut her eyes and put her hands over her ears, but it was no use: the voices were inside her head, speaking only in fragments.

"Did you hear . . ."   " . . . what happened . . ."

        " . . . an accident . . ."

                        " . . . so sad . . ."
        " . . . she was so weird . . ."

                " . . . kind of pathetic . . ."   "She left last year . . ."

"... trashed the school ..."   "... I barely remember ..."

"Some kids ..."

"Not me ..."   "... used to tease her ..."

"... she had no friends ..."   "... call her names ..."

"... except for one ..."   "... then she moved away ..."

"That girl ..."   "... and we never saw her again ..."

"... the crazy one ..."   "... totally flipped out ..."

"... she got kicked out ..."   "... how could I forget?"

"... put a hole in the wall ..."   "... kind of a freak ..."

"... put a hole in his hand ..."   "... I know that girl ..."

"I want you ..."

"What's her name again ..."   "... to think ..."

"... I just can't remember ..."   "... about what ..."

"... that poor, poor girl ..."   "... you've done."

Click.

Riley dropped her hands and opened her eyes. The voices were gone, and locker 1237 was open, just a crack.

Switching the flashlight to her bandaged hand, Riley inched the locker door open further, its old, unused hinges groaning in protest. She tensed, ready to slam it shut again if something jumped at her, but there was no bogeyman lurking inside. No piles of bones or grinning skulls. There was nothing, in fact. No discarded jackets or magnet-backed mirrors. No half-peeled stickers of some old pop star or discarded candy wrappers. The locker was empty. Riley stood on her tiptoes and brushed her hand along the top shelf, just to be sure, coming away with only dust.

Nothing to see here. And yet this was where the light had led her.

Just as she was about to shut the door, the flashlight bulb started to glow brighter, the light exploding with new intensity. The metal handle grew warm, then hot, causing Riley to drop it, shaking out her fingers. The flashlight clattered to the floor, spinning until its beam was fixed back on the open locker, the light fading back to normal.

Riley bent down to take up the flashlight again. That's when she saw it. In the circle of light, crammed into the underside of the bottom shelf, wedged into the curled metal lip that hid the screws holding the shelf in place: a packet of folded pages, tucked toward the back so that anyone looking straight on would easily miss them. You'd have to know they were there. Or someone would have to show you.

Riley glanced down the hall one more time, then she crouched down and tugged the papers free, careful not to tear them. They were obviously notes, like the kind kids sometimes still passed when they were afraid to take their phones out in class, except those were usually no more than four or five sentences long. These looked more like letters, written on blue-lined paper and carefully folded into neat squares. There were five pages in all. The top one was composed in messy cursive, much like the sloppy signature Riley had learned to forge.

Riley unfolded the packet, careful to keep all the pages in order, and focused her light. She bit down on her lip, already anticipating, with a kind of stomach-souring dread, what she would find written there.

The first letter began *Dear Max.*

45

THE FIRST TIME SHE READ IT, IT PISSED HER OFF. ONLY LATER DID she realize how much it hurt. How deeply it cut.

The note handed to her by Tyler Coles, given to him by Taylor Rogers, given to *her* by Emily Sauders. Riley's best friend.

No. Not best. It hadn't been *best* for a while. Ever since Emily started volleyball, meeting that group of shiny new girls Riley didn't want to hear about but did anyway. That was followed by further trampling on the unwritten codes of friendship that the two of them had been drafting since the day they met: picking Sophia Shara as her lab partner, sitting in a different spot at lunch, responding to Riley's questions with increasingly short sentences. Over spring break they had hardly seen each other, even though both of them had stayed in town, every one of Riley's invitations to hang out parried with some excuse. *Sorry, running errands with my mom. Dinner with family friends. Headache—think I'll just sleep all afternoon.* Riley had been tempted to stalk her, to bike the four miles to Emily's house and hide in her bushes, peering through her window to see if she was ever telling the truth, but she resisted. That's not what best friends do.

Not best. But still good. At least okay.

Until the day Riley unfolded the note Tyler handed to her to find Emily's pristine print marching across the page.

The preamble was friendly, or at least polite, a velvet glove stretched over a twenty-pound sledgehammer. *You are nice*, it said, which Riley knew wasn't always true. *And funny. And cool. And you've been a good friend.* The last part was mostly true, she hoped. But then the glove came off. There was no paragraph break. No chance for Riley to catch her breath.

But I feel like we've been drifting apart.

She meant she'd been drifting away.

And maybe that's a good thing.

In no way was it a good thing. How could it be a good thing?

From there it just kept coming.

I feel like we have different interests.

I still think we can talk and hang out sometimes.

I think you should try to make some new friends.

309

And then:

Thanks for understanding.

Riley read the note three times, each pass causing her to fidget more and more in her seat. She tried to make eye contact with Emily, but her former best friend had her own eyes squared on Mrs. Zeitner, who was reminding the class how superlatives worked. *Sad. Sadder. Saddest. Big. Bigger. Biggest.*

Riley's cheeks flared. Her fingers clenched. She wanted to hit something. To stand up and kick over her desk. To find something fragile and smash it into a thousand pieces.

She wanted to scream.

Crappy. Crappier. Crappiest.

She'd been dumped. Replaced by the girls on the volleyball squad. By the boys Emily sometimes flirted with even though she was terrible at it. Riley wasn't enough for her anymore—that's what the letter said. Sometimes something comes along that's better than what you've got, or at least it seems that way. As this new thing rises to the top, it inevitably pushes everything else down a rung.

Best. Better. Good.

And then whatever's below good. Whatever's sitting there at the bottom.

Fine, Riley thought. If that's what she wanted. She crumpled the note and stuffed the wad into her backpack. She avoided

Emily for the rest of the day. It wasn't hard; Emily clearly wanted to be avoided.

That night Riley sat at her desk in her room and uncrumpled the note, reading it one last time. She promised herself she wouldn't cry—and she held to that promise, tearing the note into a hundred little pieces instead, enough so that she could no longer make out any of the words. Then she took the pieces to her window and dumped the confetti over the edge, watching a few scraps get caught in the rosebushes below—already in full bloom at the prospect of summer—while the rest drifted across the lawn like snowflakes.

Going. Going. Gone.

46

THESE LETTERS TOLD THE REST OF THE STORY. EVERYTHING THAT Max didn't. Maybe not the hows, but at least the why.

It wasn't a horror story, though there were parts that made Riley shiver. There were other parts that made her heart ache. But this wasn't just about the bullying at school or the troubles at home. This was a story about a girl who grew detached from the world. A girl who seldom smiled and saw no reason to fake it. A girl who stood a pace apart in the choir and sang mostly to herself. A girl who struggled to make a connection with those around her.

Except for one—the boy who she'd known since elementary school. The boy she grew up with. Who waited for her by her locker and sat with her at lunch. Who walked home with her from the park after baseball practice and gave her her first awkward kiss underneath the bleachers by the tennis courts—though the letters didn't say it was awkward. Not in the least.

The boy's name was Maxwell, but everybody called him Max.

The girl's name was Heather, but people called her other things.

Some people.

She told herself she didn't care what they thought or what they said. It didn't matter. Because she had him, and he was enough. Sometimes it only takes one person to see you for who you really are.

The notes all started *Dear Max*. They were all signed *Love, Heather*.

In between there were promises and proclamations. That she would always be there for him if he needed her. He was the only one she could talk to. He was the only one who understood everything she was going through. There were mentions of others—parents, teachers, students—but they were always on the outside, at best absent or oblivious, and at worst . . . Riley had already seen them at their worst. It was the two of them against the world. Heather and Max.

Right up until it wasn't.

The handwriting on that last sheet of paper was much neater than the rest, the cursive unhurried, no cross-outs or do-overs, as if it had been recopied to ensure there was no mistake. The note was so much shorter than the others, though it started just the same.

> *Dear Max,*
>
> *I know you told me to stop writing, but I promise this will be the last time. I wanted to say I'm sorry. I know I made things hard for you. I didn't mean to hurt you or embarrass you. I care about you—more than I think you realize—and don't want to see you unhappy. So if it's really what you want, I promise I won't bother you anymore.*
>
> *Love,*
>
> *Heather*

Riley read this last letter twice, the others already piled on the floor by her feet. It was as if she was reading it for the third time that the voice in her head interrupted her.

"You found them."

Riley arced her light to see the small dark blob hunched at the end of the hall. She hadn't heard him coming. He didn't seem interested in getting too close.

"They're yours."

"They're not mine," Max insisted.

"They're addressed to you."

"That was a long time ago. I gave them back to her. I . . . I didn't think I'd ever see them again." He sounded curious. And wary.

Riley gathered the rest of the pages by her feet, holding them out in a tight fist. Pages full of memories, of time spent together, of secrets shared. Held hands and broken hearts. "I thought you said you were just friends."

"We were just friends," Max insisted. *"And then we weren't."*

He made it sound so simple, but Riley knew it was never that easy. There was no such thing as a clean break. There was always something left behind. Hundreds of little pieces. "You pushed her away."

Max's voice crept back into her head, suddenly defensive again. *"No. It's not like that. You don't understand. I tried."*

"You abandoned her."

"I was there for her when nobody else would be. But I couldn't be the only one. You don't know what it was like. What she *was like. She was always there. I couldn't breathe. It was just . . . too much."*

I know I made things hard for you.

Riley shook her head. "She needed you."

"She needed help," Max countered.

"So why didn't you help her?"

The voice practically exploded in Riley's skull this time.

"Why me? What about her parents? What about all those kids who called her names? The ones who teased her in the locker room? Who moved their bags so she couldn't sit next to them on the bus?"

The laughter in the cafeteria. The whispers in the halls.

"I'm not the only one who ever hurt her," Max said.

No, Riley thought. Just the only one she really cared about.

In all her father's stories, the ghosts always came back to haunt the living, driven by memory and longing, attached to the world by sorrow or regret. But what if a spirit could haunt another spirit, holding it prisoner?

What if the dead could haunt the dead?

"It's not fair," Max continued. *"Why should I have to pay for what everyone else did?"*

Riley looked down at the pages in her hand. The written account of Heather Longmiller's last year at Northridge Middle School. The last year of her life. The only evidence of what she'd been through, offered up to the one person she was sure would understand.

She promised not to bother him anymore. There at the end.

And yet here they both were.

"You should burn them."

Riley blinked at him. "What?"

"Those letters. There's something about them. Can't you sense it? Just seeing them, being this close to them. I can feel them drawing

me in. Pulling on me. Holding me back."

He was right: Riley *could* sense something about them. Maybe not in the same way Max could, but she understood that there was a power in the story they told. Besides, Heather was the one who led her here. Riley was meant to find these letters. There must be a reason.

"You have to burn them," Max insisted. *"Get rid of those memories. Of everything that happened here. That must be what she wants. To take away the pain."*

What do ghosts have to be afraid of?

"And what will happen if I do?" Riley asked.

Max didn't hesitate. *"Then maybe we can both go home."*

317

47

A GHOST CAN TAKE MANY FORMS.

Laughter in a room. Writing on the wall. A slamming door. A flower that never loses its petals. A whistle that comes to you as you're falling asleep.

Some ghosts talk to you directly, taking on visages frightening or familiar. Others find different ways to make their presence known. The flicker of a bedroom light. A howl of wind like a plea for help. Your own name whispered in the dark.

Sometimes the spirit's will is manifested in a particular object, something familiar. A fireplace. A wicker basket. A pair of glasses. A packet of notes.

Though the objects themselves are mundane, the memories they carry give them power. They are anchors, tethering the spirit to the world of the living. Burn them, smash them, destroy them, and you negate that power. You break the bond.

You set them free.

"Hopefully," Max added.

"You aren't sure?" Riley asked. But Max only knew how he felt when he saw those pages again. Their mere presence tormented him. Max was stuck here, he said, because of things that happened too long ago, things that should finally be laid to rest. *"Those letters are the key to unlock the door."*

Riley was *more* than ready to unlock the door.

Which was why she found herself standing in Mr. Bardem's room, the place where this all started—for her at least—sweeping the walls with her flashlight, pausing momentarily on the supply closet door, still slightly ajar. Not like she left it. She thought of all the half-dissected frogs still sealed up in their plastic bags, imagined them all getting free, hopping after her with their bellies split and their entrails dragging behind them, and choked down another upsurge of Ms. Lang's M&M's.

"It's okay," Max said. *"You're not alone. We can do this together."*

Riley looked at him sideways, wondering how many times he'd told Heather the same thing or something like it. She wondered what made him stop saying those things. Maybe, like Emily, he just moved on—found new friends. Or maybe standing up for Heather Longmiller, being the only one, just got to be too hard and he couldn't take it anymore.

"The sooner the better," Max prodded.

The Bunsen burner sat on the lab counter at the front of the room, right beside Mr. Bardem's desk. She'd seen him use it before, at the start of the year. There was only the one—middle schoolers couldn't be trusted with methane or fire, let alone the combination of the two—but Riley had paid attention when Mr. Bardem explained the safety precautions anyway, connecting the rubber tubing to the gas valve and then to the intake on the burner, checking to make sure everything was sealed tight. *Wouldn't want to accidentally blow up the school,* he'd said, earning him groans of disappointment from the class. The flint striker—a rusty-looking device that seemed like something from the Civil War—creating just enough of a spark to ignite the tiny stream of gas emitting from the burner's mouth, blooming with a bright blue flame.

The top gas valve was there in plain sight, but there was a secondary safety valve in the locked cabinet underneath the marble counter. Riley knew exactly where the spare keys were kept.

"Lift me up," Max insisted.

She put her hands to the floor and let the frog climb into them. If he was cold, she didn't feel it; there was no warmth in her hands either. She thought back to the lake and the way her feet had gone numb. There was something to be said for not feeling anything.

"Holding me with your bare hands? I guess you're not afraid anymore."

Riley snorted. If only that were true.

She set the frog gently on the table by the sink with its collection of eyewashes and soaps, then set down her flashlight as well, propped so that she could better see what she was doing. Riley pulled the stack of folded letters from her pocket, just a few pieces of notebook paper. Maybe there was nothing special about them at all and she just wanted to believe that this would work—that these pages, these words, were the only thing giving Heather her power over her, over the school, over Max.

I don't know, Horatio.

If it meant her getting out of here, it was worth a shot.

She set the packet of letters on the table before bending down to unlock the cabinet, finding the gas valve clearly labeled in Bardem's writing. She twisted it twice around and then opened the one on top as well, checking first to make sure the tubing to the burner was secure. She grabbed the flint striker from the tub with the beakers and glass stirrers.

"We should hurry," Max said, the echo of his voice in her head taking on an edge.

Riley stopped and listened. For what, she didn't know. More

laughter? More sobbing? The turning of knobs, the scrape of chairs, the creak of a door? But she heard nothing. No sign of the spirit who had written these letters so many years ago. Only the pages themselves and the memories they held. Memories of a girl who couldn't seem to let go.

"Just do it. Burn them."

Mr. Bardem had said that a Bunsen burner reaches temperatures of 1,500 degrees Celsius. Enough to cremate a body, he added. Enough to burn through skin and bone. Ashes to ashes.

Riley held the top of the striker above the burner's mouth. She tried four times to light it, then she adjusted the valve on the burner itself. On the fifth strike the spark caught with a quiet *woosh*, producing a burning blue teardrop flame no bigger than her fingernail, barely enough to provide a second sliver of light in the deepening darkness of the room.

Riley took up the pages and unfolded them again. Her eye caught the signature at the bottom.

Love, Heather.

That's how she ended them, even the last one.

Even when she was letting him go, there was still that hope. That connection. That need.

Riley hesitated.

She wants you for something.

That's what Max himself had said. The yearbooks, the

lockers, the gym, the shattered mirror—everything had led Riley to this. But why? Why not lead her straight to the letters to begin with? Why would Heather put her through all of this, making her relive the experiences that had haunted her, feel the pain and embarrassment she felt? What was the point of it all?

Max sensed her hesitation. *"What are you waiting for? We have to do this. It's the only way."*

The only way, Riley repeated in her head.

The pages were only inches from the fire. Max was right: if she destroyed them, there would be no more record of what Heather Longmiller had gone through that year, the year her picture vanished from the yearbook, the year she was teased and tormented, slipping deeper and deeper into isolation and sadness. Was that how you set someone free? By erasing their memory? By forgetting what's been done to them?

Was that really what Heather wanted?

Was that why she was here?

Riley took a step back, away from the flame.

Max's vessel hunched in the yellow halo of the flashlight, eyeing her. His voice erupted in her head. *"What are you waiting for? Just burn them already. Don't you want to go home?"*

Yes, of course. More than anything. Even though her mother was probably still at work, changing bandages and bedpans, and her father was out on the rails, squinting ahead into the stretch of black fog that his headlights couldn't reach, she wanted to be there when they came home. She wanted to be with them. To talk to them. Tell them she was sorry for acting out, for getting into trouble sometimes. But also to tell them how hard it was. That you couldn't always just float above it all or put it all behind you. She hoped they would listen. She thought they would. After all, everyone needs someone to hear them. Or else how do you even know that you matter?

How do you know that you even exist?

Riley set the pages gently back on the counter, far from the flame. She shook her head. "I don't . . . I don't think this is right."

The frog took a small jump toward her. *"Please, Riley,"* Max pleaded. *"I need you to do this. For me. For us. I can't be stuck here forever. I told you, it's torture. You read the letters. You know it wasn't my fault. Don't you see? I don't deserve this."*

She did see. And it wasn't fair. Max Trotter wasn't the one who bullied her in the locker room or mocked her in the cafeteria. His laughter wasn't part of the chorus that haunted Heather Longmiller while she was here.

He was only guilty of letting her go.

"Do it," Max pressed, his pleas changing to commands, his desperation shifting to anger. *"Then we can both move on."*

Forgive and forget. But you could do one without doing the other. Riley hadn't even heard Heather's name until today. This girl who had gone to the same school as her, this girl who had died so young. This girl who felt trapped, alone, rejected. Who just needed *someone*.

Riley stepped away from the burner and frowned at Max. "I'm sorry. I can't. There has to be another way."

"There is no other way! I thought you, of all people, would understand. That you would help me."

Riley froze. "What do you mean, I would *understand?*"

"Forget it," Max replied. *"It makes no difference anymore. You're just like her."* The frog blinked once slowly, its throat bulging as if letting out a sigh. Then it suddenly collapsed on the table, its body deflated, legs splaying out beneath it, the spirit that possessed it abandoning it, leaving only an empty shell.

But not gone. Max was still with her. His voice rang sharp and clear in Riley's head.

"If you won't do it, then I will."

48

GHOSTS HAVE THE POWER TO MANIPULATE THE PHYSICAL WORLD;
Riley had learned that firsthand.

And some ghosts are more powerful than others.

Max knew what he was doing.

Riley felt a tickle like a breath on the back of her neck before
a current of air picked up the stack of letters she'd set on the
counter, scattering them. The pages shot upward and then fell
back down like maple leaves. All except for one, which hovered
for a moment above the blue tip of the burner, suspended there
as if held by an unseen hand. She recognized it just before it
caught—it was the last letter. The one that said *I'm sorry*.

The blue tip turned bright orange as the old paper caught
fire, the flame quickly curling the edge of the note. Riley

screamed and reached for it, bringing her hand too close and singeing her thumb but managing to snatch the page, slapping at it with her forearms, smothering the flames against the stone counter, the charred edges leaving gray flakes on her shirtsleeves.

The shouting in her head came from everywhere at once, like the laughter in the cafeteria, like the shouts in the gym and the whispers in the hall. But all the same voice this time. All Max's voice.

"I don't deserve this! Let me go!"

Another rush of air in the otherwise stifling room and the letters lifted again, save for the half-burned one still clutched tight in Riley's hand. Another letter brushed its corner against the Bunsen burner's fiery tongue just long enough to ignite, only this time the page continued to drift, the flame spreading as it floated to the other side of the counter. Riley reached for it with her free hand but missed. Cursing, she circled around the counter, scrambling toward the burning page and leaving ashes on the floor, but as she stepped toward it to put out the flame, one of the stools at the adjacent lab table toppled in front of her, catching her across her shins, causing her to stumble and fall, smashing onto the cement floor.

"I won't let you stop me!" Max cried.

Riley grunted, ignoring the jolting pain in her forearms and knees, crawling over the stool to the burning page, slapping at it with her bandaged hand. The raw white blister already bubbling up on her thumb made her blink away tears as she scrabbled to her feet.

"You can't save her, Riley. Neither of us can. What's done is done."

He was right. She knew she didn't have that power. But there was one thing she *could* do: she could show Heather Longmiller that she wouldn't be forgotten. She could show her that she wasn't alone.

Leaning across the table, Riley reached out with her burned hand and grasped the gas valve on the counter, twisting as hard as she could, but the knob wouldn't budge. The same force that had shut the windows and the doors seemed to be working against her now. "Stop it, Max," she growled.

She twisted as hard as she could, but the burner continued to spit its steady flame. The pages fluttered back up into the air again. Riley snatched for them in the dark, clawing for them, hovering just out of reach. In her head, Max continued to rage.

"You're just like her," he repeated. *"I should have never let you out. I should have never—"*

Suddenly Max's voice was cut off as the door to Mr. Bardem's room slammed shut, the exact same moment Riley's flashlight blinked out. Her spine stiffened. The temperature dropped perceptibly, so much so that Riley could see the mist of her own breath in the meager glow of the burner's flickering flame. She felt a tremor in the floor that vibrated through her whole body. The stools began to rattle on top of their tables, the windows shaking in their frames.

Max screamed—it was truly a tortured, mournful sound—and Riley felt herself stumbling backward, pushed by some unseen hand into the table behind her, her own hand slipping off the valve. Then, just as suddenly, everything around her grew quiet and still.

But Riley knew. She could feel the shift. The sudden pull. She could sense it in her gut and even deeper—down in her bones.

The ghost of Northridge Middle School was right beside her.

49

SHE WAS HERE.

Not in a flash or fragment of a painful memory. Not in shouts swirling around a gym or a declaration written backward in a bathroom mirror. Not in a slamming locker door or a shard of shattered glass. Her spirit was here, a nearly physical presence, hovering close. Riley could sense her, like the thickness in the air on a humid day, a thing that surrounds you, *permeates* you, so much so that it felt as if the quick, frantic breaths Riley took were somehow tinged with the girl's essence, taking her in, absorbing her.

Heather didn't speak. She didn't weave words inside Riley's skull the way Max did. But she showed Riley something. Just a flash. A vision, much like the ones Riley had glimpsed before.

She saw a girl locked in a dark supply closet all alone, screaming and pounding on the door, twisting the knob, cursing and crying, desperate to get out. The girl pounds and kicks, she pleads and shouts, she cusses and spits. She feels angry. She feels betrayed. She feels lost and alone. There is so much confusion, so much doubt. Part of her thinks she deserves it, being shut out, left behind, that she has somehow brought it all on herself. Part of her feels like the whole world is set against her. She wishes she was somewhere else. Wishes she was someone else.

Mostly, though, she is afraid. Afraid of being stuck in this place forever. Afraid that no one will ever try to find her. She is afraid of the dark because she doesn't know what waits for her there. She is afraid of what will happen next because she doesn't know how long she can hold her breath each day. So she slaps and kicks and curses. She rages and lashes out, with the hope that someone will notice.

And then, at last, there is a flicker of light. The girl opens her eyes wide.

I know, she says. *I see.*

And the door opens.

Riley blinked, the vision gone, the contours of Mr. Bardem's room revealing themselves again. Across the desk, the valve feeding the burner began to turn, twisted by an unseen hand, the blue flame growing smaller and smaller until it disappeared completely. Riley stood there, paralyzed, watching the light vanish, and for a moment there was nothing. The heaviness in the air was gone, leaving only darkness and silence.

Then, out of that darkness, she hears two voices, both of them familiar—one inside her head and one outside it.

The first says, *"Thank you."*

The second calls her name.

50

SHE COULDN'T TELL IF THE VOICE WAS REAL OR NOT, NOT UNTIL SHE saw her. And even then she had her doubts. Emily Sauders had been Riley's friend once. Good. Better. Best. Until they weren't.

Now the same girl who had helped drag Riley into the supply closet—or at least stood by and watched—stood in Mr. Bardem's doorway.

"Riley?"

The flip of a switch and Riley was suddenly blinded, squinting through the flood of light at the other girl, one hand holding Riley's backpack, the other pressed to her mouth.

"Oh my god, did you *just* get out of there?"

Riley glanced at the supply closet, still cracked open. She tried to picture the scene from Emily's eyes: the girl she and her friends had locked away, standing in the dark, hand bandaged with napkins and duct tape, blood spotting her clothes, shoes stinking of vomit, loose papers scattered at her feet, and a dead frog splayed out on the table behind her.

But no sign of ghosts. No rattling windows. No writing on the walls. Riley and Emily were the only two souls in the room. At least as far as she could tell.

It took a moment for Riley to process, to get her bearings. Emily had just said something to her. *Did you just get out?*

It was a yes-or-no question. But some answers only lead to more questions, and more and more, until you get to the ones you don't have answers for. The ones that can't be dreamt of. So Riley just nodded, afraid to speak, uncertain of what she might say.

Emily's eyes went wide. "Oh . . . oh god. Oh crap, Riley. I'm so sorry. I didn't know. I thought . . . I mean, I tried calling your house as soon as I got home. And when you didn't answer . . ."

She didn't have a chance to finish because her mother, the school secretary, suddenly appeared behind her, still dressed in the uniform she wore for her night job as a waitress, her mouth set in a circle of surprise at finding Riley Flynn right where her daughter confessed to having left her.

"Riley?" Mrs. Sauders said in disbelief, then sharply turned to Emily, her tongue a whip. "Holy hell, Emily Sauders! What on earth were you thinking? You seriously locked Riley in a supply closet and *left* her there?"

Left behind. But not—as it turned out—forgotten.

"I can't believe you," Mrs. Sauders continued. "I *work* here, for chrissake! You could get *expelled* for doing something like this, you know that?"

Riley saw tears glazing her former friend's eyes as her mother chastised her, Emily barely managing to keep her head up, her whole body starting to wither under Mrs. Sauders's pointed stare. Riley coughed and both heads turned.

"It's all right, Mrs. Sauders," she said hoarsely, doing her best to steady her voice. "I'm okay. I just want to go home."

Emily's mother's expression softened, the anger in her face melting into a weak smile. "Oh. Right. Absolutely, dear. Of course. Let's go. We'll give you a ride." She waved at the room with its opened closet and tipped stool. "We'll just get this all cleaned up in the morning."

Mrs. Sauders turned back to her daughter and started whispering, the two of them locking eyes, giving Riley enough time to gather the sheets of paper scattered along the desk and floor, some of them flaking ash from their burnt edges. She hastily refolded them and stuffed them in her back pocket before grabbing the flashlight, clicking the button to make sure it still worked. It went off and on at her touch, just like it was supposed to.

The dead frog she left on the table. The vessel was broken, its spirit gone. Neither Emily nor her mother said a word about it. Maybe they didn't even notice. Nothing to see there.

Yet as Riley made her way to the door, she thought she heard something. A soft humming, haunting and melodic and heart-breaking, the notes of a song she'd heard before, sung without accompaniment. *Do you hear that?* she almost asked. But she could tell by their expressions that they didn't. They stood in the hallway, waiting for her, ready to take her home where she belonged.

Of course they didn't hear it, Riley thought. Why would they?

The song wasn't meant for them.

51

LIGHT GREETED HER EVERYWHERE SHE WENT, AND SHE SOAKED it up.

All across the school the electricity seemed to be working just fine again. The clocks ticking. Bulbs burning. Heaters humming. As if the building itself had been brought back to life. Riley imagined she could feel the air getting warmer with every step. They walked single file, Mrs. Sauders leading the way, her daughter, head hung, chin in chest, right on her heels. Riley brought up the rear, a few paces off, but close enough that she could clearly make out the color of the hairband that kept Emily's ponytail in place—gray. Close enough that, with a few quick strides, Riley could reach out and take Emily's hand if she wanted to. But she didn't. Not yet.

They walked without a word, Mrs. Sauders's stern footfalls the preamble to a speech that she was probably composing in her head, Emily shuffling her steps, Riley taking glances behind her with every other breath, waiting for something to happen. A flicker. A rattle. A whisper. At one point, out of the corner of her eye, she thought maybe she saw something move—just a twitch—and she whispered Max's name. Both Emily and her mother turned around.

"What's that, dear?" Mrs. Sauders said.

Riley shook her head. "Sorry. Nothing," she said. "Trick of the light."

Mrs. Sauders frowned—she really hadn't *stopped* frowning—but she let it go.

As they entered the main hall headed for the front doors, Riley saw the sign hanging on the wall: *Welcome. Beinvenue. Nayak. Yokoso. Salaam.* Her heart quickened. There, underneath the banner, sat the sculpture, its copper branches that had sliced open her hand bent back into place, its heavy stone pedestal perfectly squared up with its wooden stand. Riley's eyes darted to the fire alarm, nestled snugly back into place as well, ready for the next prankster to give it a pull. Everything was right back where it belonged. It was as if Riley had never been there. As if she'd never tried to bust her way out.

She thought of the basketball sitting beneath the hoop in

the gym. Of the black button eyes she'd left dangling from the sockets of Mrs. Grissolm's doll. Of the smashed mirror staring through the open curtains of the stage. Had *all* of those things been fixed as well? Everything back to normal? She wondered about the puddle of vomit she'd left by the gymnasium door. She wasn't about to go and look.

Ghosts have power. They can move stuff around. Fool with the lights. Hijack the phones. Open and close doors. They can trap you, torment you, torture you.

But they can also help you find the things you've lost, leaving them in the basket by the sink. They can help you fix what's been broken.

"Riley? You okay?"

Riley blinked and looked over at Emily waiting for her by the front door, holding it open for her as if leaving the school was the easiest thing in the world. The fresh air tickled the hairs on Riley's arms. She filled her lungs with it, holding it as long as she could. The sky was studded with stars. She could make out the chirp of crickets over the electric hum of the lampposts. She thought of her mother sitting on the porch, waiting for her. She would see her soon.

But as she walked through the door, Riley paused. She couldn't help but notice the mark: the small nick in the glass from where she'd tried to break through. Such a tiny thing.

Barely a chip. Probably nobody else would ever notice it. They wouldn't realize it was there, and even if they did, they couldn't be expected to care what had caused it.

But she would know. She would remember. And that—she hoped—was enough.

Sitting in the Sauders' car, pulling out of the parking lot, Riley felt a tear forming. Just one. She let it slink halfway down her cheek, tracing a path like a pencil tip through a maze, before wiping it away.

52

RILEY'S FATHER TOLD HORROR STORIES AND HE TOLD GHOST stories. Sometimes they overlapped, but not always. The ghost stories—the *real* ghost stories—were always more sad than frightening. They haunted you in ways you didn't always expect.

Like the story of the husband who always left a freshly cut rose on his wife's windowsill every year on her birthday, even though he'd been dead for the last twelve of them.

Or the boy who froze to death in Stalingrad in 1944 but still tracked in snow every now and then, leaving size-four boot tracks leading to and from his old, abandoned house.

Of the family of four who could be seen sitting on the docks at night, clothes sopping, waiting for their ship to arrive so they could finally get their luggage, which sat, along with said ship, at the bottom of the sea.

Of the mother who still sang whispery, lulling lullabies to her son at night, even though he was pushing forty and had two sons of his own who she'd never gotten to meet.

But he never told her the one about the girl who died so young, her seat belt unlatched, her whole body thrown against the windshield with enough force to snap her neck. Or what she'd been thinking of the moment before impact, before the light turned and the car swerved, before the glass shattered and her spirit was wrenched away.

But Riley knew.

They were thoughts of the boy who used to hold her sweaty hand when nobody was looking. Who talked to her past midnight on the phone and hid behind the bushes and waited for her as she snuck out of the house. The boy she thought she loved and was sure had loved her back—if only for a little while. If that boy was thinking of her, even now, now that she was gone. Or if he'd forgotten about her already. How she'd been the one to let *him* go, there at the end.

And how, if she had it to do over again, she might have tried to hold on a little tighter.

53

FINALLY, SHE WAS HOME.

Mrs. Sauders had asked—in a way that sounded more like insisting—if she wanted Riley to call her parents, to let them know where she was and to try to explain what had happened. Another apology was called for, she said, a more formal one. The look Mrs. Sauders gave Emily told Riley that lots more apologies were on the way.

Explanations would be harder to come by, however, and Riley wasn't interested in offering any. For all Emily and her mother knew, it had taken Riley almost three hours to figure out how to pick the lock and get out of the closet. They'd arrived just after she'd made her escape.

That was one story. The easiest one. The one they'd already

assumed was the truth. She could have corrected them, but then they might not have taken her home. They might have rushed her to the hospital, or insisted on staying with her until her mother picked her up, thinking that she was hallucinating, in shock, or just full-out crazy. Riley wasn't even sure what she was going to tell her parents. She had already decided that any other version, any version closer to the truth, would be heard by them first, if at all.

So she kept quiet during the ride and thanked Mrs. Sauders for driving her, promising she would call her mother the moment she walked in the door. She also promised to tell her parents what Mrs. Sauders's "thoughtless and irresponsible bully of a daughter" and her equally thoughtless bully friends did, because rest assured, Emily would be marching down to Principal Warton's office first thing in the morning to confess her crimes.

To all of this Emily offered not one word of protest. In fact, she hadn't said anything since getting in the car, but from Riley's vantage behind the driver's seat, she could see Emily barely holding back tears of her own.

The Flynns' driveway was empty when they pulled up, the lights in the house all off, and Riley could tell by her frown that Emily's mother was fighting every parental instinct leaving her here. She offered a reassuring smile. "I'll be fine. Really. Thank you."

Riley opened the door and slid out, her legs jellied, her head still pulsing. Without asking or being told to, Emily got out of the car with her. "I'll walk you up," she said.

They were silent as they made their way to the porch. Emily waited for Riley to fish her key out of her backpack and unlock the door before she spoke again. "Listen, Riley . . . ," she started, eyes on her toes, hands shoved into the front pocket of her Northridge sweatshirt. "I can't even imagine what that must have felt like back there. Being stuck in there like that."

No. You probably can't, Riley thought. "Forget it," she said, twisting the knob, just wanting to get inside, to be someplace safe again, but Emily angled herself between Riley and the door, looking up now with glassy eyes.

"Just hear me out," she said. "I suck, all right? I know it. And I feel terrible. I should have stopped them. But . . . I don't know . . . I guess I was scared of what they would say. What they would think of me. It was stupid, and I hate myself for it. And I know you'll probably *never* forgive me for this . . . or for anything, really. And honestly, I don't blame you."

Riley thought about the letters nestled in her back pocket, their edges burnt, but most of the words—and the memories they contained—intact. Some things were worth saving. Besides, Emily had come back for her. Maybe that was enough.

"I wouldn't say *never*."

Emily sniffled and swiped at her eyes. Then she nodded and gave Riley a quick hug that felt a little forced, but not completely unfamiliar, the kind of thing you could learn to settle back into over time. "So you'll be okay?"

Riley considered it. It was too big a question. Would she be okay? Probably. Yes. Not tonight. Or tomorrow. But eventually. Maybe. Once her head stopped throbbing and the cut on her hand had healed. Once she'd had some time to come to grips with it all. But she saw the look Emily was giving her, full of guilt, but also genuine concern. The look one friend might give another.

Riley offered up a tight-lipped smile.

"I will if you will."

It wasn't a promise. But it was close enough.

54

THE FIRST THING RILEY ALWAYS DID WHEN SHE CAME HOME WAS turn on the lights. The second was flip on the TV. The channel didn't matter; she just needed the noise.

This time she didn't bother with the television, though. She wanted it quiet. She wanted to be able to hear the creak of footfalls on the wood floor. She wanted to know if there were whispers in the house. She stopped to listen.

No voices. No laughter. No sobs. Just the buzz of the refrigerator and the sound of Mrs. Sauders's wheels crunching out of the gravel drive. Riley looked at the clock on the stove: 9:14. She'd been trapped in her school for only a few hours, but it felt like so much longer. She would say that it felt like an eternity, except she knew better; she was still in no position to say what forever felt like.

Riley dropped her backpack by the door, her flashlight tucked into the front pocket where a dead frog had once hitched a ride, and then peered through the blinds to make sure the car was gone. Despite Riley's attempts to soften the impact, to insist that she was fine, she had no doubt Mrs. Sauders would still lecture Emily the whole ride home. She wouldn't be allowed to forget this one for a while. Deep in her heart, Riley hoped it wasn't too long; nobody should have to pay for their mistakes indefinitely. Not when they've owned up to them, at least.

She locked the door, slipped off her boots, and slowly made her way to the bathroom to properly clean up her hand, turning on every light as she went. The quiet was manageable, but the darkness was something else. She spotted the home phone hanging on the wall and knew her next step would be to go back to check the messages, to see if her mother had called, and if so, to call her back and assure her that she was safe, maybe even ask her to come home early so that Riley wouldn't be in the house all alone.

Riley gripped both sides of the bathroom sink and stared into the mirror. She recognized the girl looking back at her this time: the split ends, the narrow, distrustful eyes, the jutting chin. But it wasn't the same girl that had slunk out of the house that morning. This was some other version, one that had been lurking beneath the skin and blood and bones. She felt in the back pocket of her jeans for the packet of pages partially burnt. It was probably just her imagination, but they still felt warm.

A ghost is only as strong as the memories that keep her here. But Max was wrong about what Heather Longmiller wanted. Some ghosts aren't looking to be let go. They are looking for something to hold on to.

Or someone. In a moment of darkness, in a moment of desperation, Riley had made a promise: that she would hold on as long as she could. Hopefully that meant at least one other soul was forgiven tonight. Riley thought about the last thing Max said to her as the flame went out, when he realized what she'd done. He didn't stick around for her to say *you're welcome*.

Riley hadn't done it for him, though.

In the bathroom mirror, the girl refused to smile, though the distance in her eyes was gone. Riley reached up with her bandaged hand and touched her cheek. The glass was cool against her fingertips, but it didn't break. Not this time.

"I see," she whispered.

She stood that way for a while, until the sound of tires pulling into the driveway stole her attention. It was still too early for her mother to be home. Perhaps it was Emily, come back for another apology, or maybe Mrs. Sauders decided she just couldn't leave Riley alone after all. Riley made her way to the front hall, arms crossed, heart pounding, listening for footsteps coming up the sidewalk.

What she heard instead was a whistle. Two long notes. Like the signal of the train pulling into its final stop.

She recognized this whistle. She knew what it meant.

Riley held her breath, undid the locks, and opened the door.

SIXTEEN
MONTHS
LATER . . .

THEY HAD HER SURROUNDED. THERE WAS NO ESCAPE.

She was surprised at how tiny they were. Granted, some were spurting, a few almost as tall as her, even with three years between them; but most of them still had a long way to go. Maybe over the summer they would squeeze out another inch or two and surprise their friends, but most of them were going to feel like they were walking among giants, at least at the start.

Tiny or not, it was fun to see their faces the moment they walked through the door and took in the sheer size of the place.

Their eyes blown wide with terror and awe as they stared at the enormous hallway bustling with bigger kids.

"Welcome to the next three years of your life," she told them.

She remembered how she'd felt walking into this same school for the first time, seeing the sign on the wall. Despite its polylingual invitation, she'd felt anything but welcome. That's why she made sure to keep smiling now, even though she wasn't normally a smiley person—to help put the squirming ones at ease.

Her paddling of noobs looked especially nervous as she herded them together in the gym. Three boys, five girls, one pair potentially boyfriend/girlfriend, judging by the way their hands kept finding each other. That's what dating was in the fifth grade: awkward looks and sweaty, fumbling hands. *Just wait*, she thought.

She introduced herself, told them her name and her interests, how she was on the girls' soccer team (JV, because she wasn't that good) and president of the book club ("We meet in the library every Thursday before school. Ms. Lang usually brings doughnuts"). She told them how she had recently had her own school orientation—at the even bigger high school down the road—and how she'd survived that and so they would survive this.

Then she led them along the prescribed route, pointing out the offices and the auditorium—"There's a talent show at the end of the year"—the art room complete with its very own kiln, and the science lab "where they will probably try to make you cut up dead animals, but you can always refuse." She told them that if they were vegetarian, they would probably want to pack their lunch. In hushed tones she gave them a description of the principal's motivational posters, though, in all honesty, it had been a while since she'd seen them. They might have changed.

Afterward, she led them to the cafeteria and pushed stale cookies on them, amazed at how much sugar eleven-year-olds could put away. One beanpole of a boy named Miles ate four. It was supernatural.

"All right. We've got fifteen minutes before the final presentation. Does anyone have questions?"

Miles, aka Cookie Monster, was the first to raise his crumby hand.

"Yeah. Is it true that a teacher got caught vaping in class last year?"

Of course that would be the first thing someone asked about. "It wasn't during class. It was during his free period. But yes, he did, and he no longer works here." *We all make mistakes,* she thought. *And eventually, one way or another, most of us pay for them.* "Anyone else?"

Several more hands shot up, the kids tossing out questions about homework requirements and after-school clubs and if she had any idea what the fall musical was going to be this year.

They wanted to know who the mean teachers were. She was tempted to tell them that when it came to meanness, the teachers weren't the ones they had to watch out for, but she didn't want to scare them. Finally a shy-looking girl whose tag read Letitia raised her hand.

"Is it true that this school is haunted?"

Riley paused, taken by surprise, just for a moment. But she quickly recovered, smiling. "Where did you hear that?"

Letitia crossed her arms. "My friend Anna is a sixth grader here, and she says there've been strange things, like people hearing things and stuff getting moved around with no explanation. You know, mostly after school's out, when most everybody's gone? She says it's been going on for a while but nobody has any proof."

Riley used one hand to scratch absently at the jagged white scar on the other. "Well, what do you think?" she asked.

"I think it's all just a bunch of older kids making up stories to try to scare the younger ones."

Riley smiled. Yes. That's how it always starts. Stories. Rumors. Whispers in the hallway.

"You want to know the truth?"

They all nodded.

She took a deep breath, carefully considering what she was about to say. "Okay. The truth is, you've got bigger things to worry about than ghosts. Trust me on this one. You've got pop quizzes and cheer tryouts and two hours of cross-country practice four days a week. You've got vocabulary tests and group projects." She started ticking off her fingers. "Art portfolios. Band concerts. Dances. Zits. Dress codes. Bad hair days. *Worse* hair days. Forgot-your-deodorant days. Not to mention friends and parents and all *their* drama, plus, you know, *life* . . . as a *teenager*, which you are all going to be whether you like it or not. I mean honestly, who even has time to worry about ghosts?"

Seven fresh faces stared up at her, taking all that in, but Letitia was undeterred. "So wait, does that mean the school is haunted or not?"

Riley shrugged. There was no fooling this kid. She went with her second answer.

"I don't know, Horatio. Maybe not. Maybe so."

Letitia gave her a funny look. Somebody else said, "Who's Horatio?"

Riley let her eyebrow stay arched for a moment, then she clapped her hands together. "All right. I think it's time to head to the gym, so grab one last cookie for the road if you want and . . ." Riley saw ghost girl's hand go up again. "Yes?"

"Yeah, sorry. One more question." Letitia looked around at her classmates as if debating whether or not to ask it, worried about what they might say, what they might think. But she didn't let it stop her. "Does it get any better? I mean, I know it's middle school and all, but it can't be *all* bad, right?"

Riley thought about everything she'd been through the last three years. Some things she'd made peace with. Some she still regretted. One or two even kept her up at night. But she was still here. Still standing. Riley glanced across the cafeteria and spotted her good friend with her own group of Panthers-in-waiting. Emily caught her eye and waved.

She realized she was hesitating. She turned back to the group and gave the inquisitive girl a warm smile.

"No. It's not all bad," she said. "And it does get better."

Letitia smiled back, relieved. That was all she needed. Just one person to tell her it would be all right. When Riley stood up, the girl tucked in right behind her like a shadow, matching her step for step. As she walked, Riley started to whistle softly to herself.

The girl, recognizing the melody, began to hum along.

ACKNOWLEDGMENTS

Thank you to everyone who made this book possible. To Adams Literary for getting behind every new genre I decide to dabble in, be it fairies, aliens, superheroes, or ghosts. To everyone at Walden and HarperCollins for their tireless efforts and creative support. More specifically, my thanks to David DeWitt and Amy Ryan for the book's design and to Ileana Soon for that haunting cover; to Kathryn Silsand for sharpening my prose; and to Donna Bray, Vaishali Nayak, Emma Meyer, and Lena Reilly for helping me to share this story with the world. An elbow bump to Jordan Brown, my editor for a decade now—thanks for always pushing me to dig a little deeper. And as always, all of my love to my friends and family, especially the big three. Couldn't do this without you.

There is a lyric from the musical *Dear Evan Hansen* that I mulled over as I wrote this book. It goes, "But if you can somehow keep them thinking of me / And make me more than an abandoned memory / Well, that means we matter too." I think Riley is right: forgiveness is essential to healing and growth, but forgetting can be counterproductive. If anything, the power of memory makes us more compassionate, more understanding, more empathetic. It helps us to acknowledge the missteps of others and to learn and grow from our own mistakes. The ghosts of the past can help us to grapple with the sins of the present and, in turn, envision a better future.

I, for one, can't wait.